Soul of the Wildcat

Soul of the Wildcat

Devyn Quinn

APHRODISIA

KENSINGTON PUBLISHING CORP.

http://www.kensingtonbooks.com

APHRODISIA BOOKS are published by

Kensington Publishing Corp.
119 West 40th Street
New York, NY 10018

ISBN-13: 978-0-7582-3121-5
ISBN-10: 0-7582-3121-0

First Trade Paperback Printing: December 2009

10 9 8 7 6 5 4 3 2 1

Acknowledgments

This book is dedicated to the two people who made it possible:

To my incredible agent, Roberta Brown, who continues to hold my hand when I am in meltdown mode. Without her support I would not be where I am today.

Thanks also goes to Peter Senftleben, my incredible new editor. The man truly has the patience of a saint, and for that I am grateful.

1

Binoculars pressed to her eyes, Dakoda Jenkins watched the cougar pace the confines of its cage. Sinew and muscle strained as the cat fought against captivity. Blood-chilling screeches poured over dangerously bared fangs.

Her breath caught at the raw beauty and power exuded by the large, tawny, long-tailed feline. By the size of it, the sleek cat was a male. The sound of the cougar's roars rippled across her ears. A hot flush prickled her skin as her heart sped up, filling her mouth with a sultry tang. A slow trickle of heat pooled inside her core. Something about the cougar's enraged power drew her in, exposing and then scraping her nerves raw.

Heart missing a beat, Dakoda shifted her focus toward two men working around the cougar. Awe turned to anger. There were times when her job sucked.

Today was one of those times.

Dressed identically in faded jeans, flannel shirts, leather jackets, and military-style hiking boots, they were in the process of loading the cougar's pen onto a travois fashioned between two packhorses. It didn't take an expert to recognize both men were clearly accustomed to surviving in the harsh mountainous terrain.

Swallowing thickly, Dakoda lowered her binoculars before glancing toward her partner. Watching the lustrous cat fight so valiantly for its freedom was painful to watch. The strain of keeping still, of not rushing to defend the cougar, made her teeth ache. "Is that really what I think it is?" she whispered in a hushed, low tone.

Lowering his own specs, Ranger Gregory Zerbe nodded. "What you are seeing is the real thing, the *Puma concolor couguar.*" He took a longer look, barely suppressing the low whistle slipping past his lips. "Magnificent. It's a perfect specimen in every way."

Dakoda carefully slid her binoculars back into their protective case. She didn't want to look again. The sight made her sick. "Then it is true. The Eastern cougar is making a comeback in these mountains." A little thrill went through her at the thought. This was much more than she'd ever bargained for when she'd signed on as a ranger cadet working in North Carolina's South Mountains State Park.

A recent graduate of the program, this was her first assignment as a full-fledged state park ranger. She'd worked hard to be assigned to resource and protection management, primarily what veterans like Gregory Zerbe called the P-patrol. P stood for *poachers:* those idiotic assholes who preyed on the land's natural resources with the intent to destroy.

Zerbe made another affirmative motion with his head. "Reports of the cougars' presence have been coming in since the Wildlife Resources Commission sent in a team to verify the cougar's reemergence from extinction about two years ago. Thanks to their findings, even more land outside the state park's holdings is now earmarked by the government to be preserved."

Back and legs cramped from squatting behind the heavy foliage shielding them from the cougar thieves, Dakoda mentally willed herself to overcome the discomfort and remain rooted in place. One false move would blow everything. If those animal-snatching bastards managed to take off on horseback, there would be no way to follow them on foot.

"That must make the local natives happy," she commented in an attempt to take her mind off her discomfort. The territory directly abutting the state park belonged to the *Tlvdatsi*, a tribe of the Cherokee Nation. Though she'd never personally encountered any of the Indians on her patrols, she was aware the natives guarded their land and its boundaries very closely. Fiercely proud and protective of their heritage, they were not inclined to let strangers onto their property. The reservation was closed to outsiders, but even those safeguards didn't stop those determined to commit illegal acts such as trespassing.

Crouched beside her, Zerbe scratched his own scruffy face. With his deeply tanned skin, heavy brow, and handlebar moustache, he looked like a classic pioneer, one of the settlers who might have come through the area looking for gold in the 1840s. If not for his ranger uniform, most would likely mistake her tall, lanky partner for one of the poachers. "The cougar is sacred to their clan, and you can bet Uncle Sam is doing all he can to make sure their totems and traditions are preserved. There won't be any vacation resorts moving into the area anytime soon."

Shifting to ease the aches in her legs, Dakoda settled down on her knees. She sighed inwardly with relief. Despite the sharp rocks digging into her knees, the cramps in her legs were easing up. The humidity, though, was another matter. Sweat plastered her heavy uniform to her skin and gnats buzzed all around, sticking to her damp skin.

"An environmental act still won't stop men like those," she

grumbled, bushing a stray lock of hair off her forehead. Though she wore her long hair tucked up under her ranger's cap, a few stray pieces had snuck down, clinging to her sweaty skin. Thirst scratched at her parched mouth, but she ignored it. Her khaki uniform clung in all the wrong ways. Perspiring heavily, she was a nasty, stinking mess.

Following the scumbags through the forest without being detected had been a chore of perseverance and sheer determination. Evergreens, pines, and oaks soared up across the rugged terrain, so thick in some places the sun was entirely blocked out. Remote and damn near inaccessible, the landscape branching off the Appalachians and carved out of the Blue Ridge by erosion was still pristine, almost untouched by the invasion of modern civilization.

Through the last two months, rangers on patrol had worked hard to catch up with the canny outlaws. When the trails became impenetrable by machine, they'd had to abandon their ATVs and strike out on foot. Horses could take the rough terrain, but wheels had no chance in these parts.

It was pure luck they'd stumbled onto the poachers at work. The poachers were obviously very pleased with the day's bounty.

"Not anytime soon," Zerbe half spat, half growled. He pointed down the ridge, toward the left. Their high vantage point allowed them to see everything going on without being easily detected. "The bigger one, that's William Barnett." His finger jerked right. "That tall one is his brother, Waylon. We've actually had him in custody, damn it. The fucker made bail and hightailed it back into hiding. Everyone calls him Skeeter."

Dakoda cocked a brow. "Skeeter?"

Zerbe's jaw tightened. "Because he's crazier than a mosquito carrying malaria. He's been known to take shots at anything that moves, including people, if you get my drift."

Dakoda got the drift. The men they hunted were wanted criminals, ruthlessly pillaging the land of its natural resources.

Her thoughts raced. *Putting the cuffs on these two outlaws will be a pleasure.*

"They both sound like charming fellows," she replied under her breath.

Zerbe rolled his eyes to indicate his own disgust. "Both of them were born and raised in these mountains. They've got a permanent settlement, but only God knows where. Between the state park holdings, the Cherokee reservation, and the acres of private property, there's no telling where it's located. In these parts, mountain folk burrow in deeper than ticks in skin. They know coming onto state and reservation lands is illegal, but they don't give a tinker's damn. To them, the land owes them a living and they're going to take it."

Zerbe's words were suddenly interrupted when a loud roar split the air again.

Dakoda peered down into the ravine. She didn't need the binoculars to see that the cougar inside the cage had renewed its fight. Lunging against the bars, the big cat pressed its claws against the narrow wire, attempting to slash at the men.

A wall of red fury passed in front of her eyes. The cougar was fighting for its freedom with every last ounce of its strength. It clearly didn't want to be taken alive. "What are they going to do with it?"

Reaching for his shotgun, Zerbe didn't blink an eye when he answered. "They sell them on the black market. There's a huge demand for wild game, dead or alive. Bears, foxes, deer . . . But this—" He made a motion with his head toward the edge of the ridge. "This is the most valuable because this species has been listed as endangered since 1973." Using the greatest of skill, he quietly jacked a round into the chamber. "And now that we know they're back and being hunted by assholes like those two, it's our job to put a stop to it." He stood, holding his weapon. Loaded and ready to use. "Those sons of bitches aren't making off with any live cougars if I can help it."

Cranking to her feet, Dakoda felt a fresh rush of adrenaline hit her bloodstream. Suddenly she didn't feel hot, sweaty, or utterly exhausted.

Gregory Zerbe shot her a look. "Keep your hand by your gun, but don't draw unless necessary," he advised. "I want your hands free to handle these." He flicked a pair of handcuffs off his belt. "Once we've secured the prisoners, we'll get back to the ATVs and radio in for a chopper to come and pick us up."

Dakoda took the cuffs, hooking them to her utility belt. Though choppers were usually reserved for search-and-rescue operations, they were equally useful when extracting captured fugitives. She mentally imagined how the two men would look behind bars. Given their track records, both would be spending a long, long time in prison.

"What about the cougar?" she asked, concerned about its safety.

Zerbe didn't hesitate. "Because it's one of the first live cougars we've actually laid eyes on since reports began coming in, I imagine it'll be held for tagging and then released for tracking. If there's one, there are more."

Dakoda's mind sped further with the thought. *More* meant females, and possibly cubs. Though males were accustomed to roaming the land, the momma cats weren't as inclined to travel when raising their young. The idea of these men trapping vulnerable young cubs was more than she could stand.

Unsnapping the latch holding her service revolver in its holster, she grinned. "This time the big cats are going to win."

Falling into position behind her partner, Dakoda took each step carefully. Her thick-soled boots made nary a sound, her steps muffled by the decaying foliage covering the hard ground. Despite Greg's warning not to draw her weapon, her hand rested loosely on the grip.

Anticipation revved up her instincts and her movements

were on autopilot. Blood thrummed in her veins as the rangers eased down the ridge, moving cautiously behind the poachers and their horses.

True to its nature, the cougar kept fighting hard. Spooked by its unearthly yowling, the horses champed at their bits and nervously stomped the ground. Dragging the travois out from under the edge of the cage made it impossible for the men to properly load and secure the flimsy thing. By the look of it, the cage was only meant to be a temporary means to hold the vicious animal. If the lock broke, they'd all probably be running like the ground was on fire.

The men didn't notice they were being stalked until Gregory Zerbe stepped out of the brush. Dakoda followed closely behind him.

Rifle leveling on the two, Zerbe smiled. "Howdy, boys."

Hearing a foreign voice, the two men immediately whirled. One made a grab for his sidearm. The other sensibly fought to keep the horses from bolting, keeping tight hold on the reins. Lose those horses now and they'd all be afoot.

Body stiffening, Zerbe's steely gray eyes went as hard and dark as a thundercloud. "I wouldn't do that if I was you, boys," he warned. "This shotgun is loaded, locked, and ready to talk business."

The larger man, earlier identified as Willie Barnett, slowly let his hand fall away from his gun.

"Well, I'll be goddamned," he said in the drawl so familiar to the region. "If it ain't Ranger Do-Right." Sucking on the wad of tobacco stuffed into his lower lip, he spat a brown stream of goo. "It's been a long time since we've seen a lawman around here." He rocked back on his heels. "I hear one of your rangers had a little accident."

Gregory Zerbe released an agitated breath, but refused to be baited. "If you boys think I forgot you crippled my partner with one of those damn traps of yours, you're wrong."

Dakoda's gaze moved to the horses, loaded with saddles and packs. The traps in question hung like grisly ornaments, and were definitely not the type that were safe or the slightest bit humane. These kind were nasty—and illegal to use. Two rows of sharp spikes closed together like fangs.

An icy chill shimmied down her spine. She knew Gregory Zerbe's last partner had also been a rookie. She also knew Dennis Macomb was presently sitting behind a desk because he'd lost his foot, courtesy of the vicious trap he'd accidentally encountered. That one wrong step had cost the young man a promising career in the field.

Anger and disgust twisted Dakoda's stomach into tight knots. The traps were custom designed with the intent to maim, to immediately cripple anything caught in the wide-open jaws. Once triggered, those sharp spikes were guaranteed to penetrate flesh and bone, then hold on tight.

Fighting to swallow her disgust, Dakoda sucked in a calming breath. The fact anyone would use the wicked things to snare helpless wildlife was more than an outrage. It was evil. Pure evil. The more the victim fought, the more damage the trap inflicted.

Willie Barnett's shit-eating grin widened. "Looks like you got yourself a new partner there, Ranger Do-Right." He smacked his lips. "At least this one is easy on the eyes."

Speaking for the first time, Skeeter Barnett nodded in agreement. "That's one nice-lookin' woman." He snorted a giggle. "I could take a piece o' that, easy."

Dakoda scowled and tried to look menacing. Her gaze skimmed the scrawny outlaw. A battered felt hat covered a stream of stringy hair that probably hadn't seen a washing since the day he was born. His deeply scarred skin was caked with at least ten layers of sweat mixed with the dirt of hard trail riding. Downwind from him, she could smell the stench of human neglect.

Dream on, lice boy, she thought, breathing through her mouth. There was no way in hell she was taking her hand off the grip of her gun. Her other hand hovered near the cuffs.

"Shut up!" Refusing to be baited, Gregory Zerbe took a step closer to the outlaws, making damn sure any shot he took would be a fatal one. "As much as I'd like to pull the trigger and put you vermin out of your misery, the law won't let me."

Hearing his words, both men cackled. Agitated by the sound of their laughter, the angry cougar lunged violently against the cage. As it threw its head back, its dangerous jaws gaped open, releasing a long, loud roar. The shriek it unleashed was deafening.

Dakoda's heart rate bumped up several notches. For some reason she had the feeling the great cat was trying to speak to them, warn them. Bashing its huge body against the bars, it unleashed an earsplitting yowl.

Dakoda held her ground, refusing to be intimidated. *Something isn't right . . .* she thought wildly. *Come on, Greg. Let's cuff them and get going.*

She didn't have the chance to say what was on her mind. By the set of their stance, it was clear the Barnett brothers weren't going down without a fight.

"The law?" Bug eyes bulging, his features twisting into a scowl, Willie Barnett scoffed, spitting more slimy tobacco juice toward his captors. "What makes you think the law exists in these here mountains?" Without waiting for an answer, he poked a defiant finger into his own chest, and replied, "The only law out here is the law we make. You hear me, ranger man? Out here, we are the ones who make the rules."

Gregory Zerbe was losing patience. "You and what goddamned army?" he snapped.

A lazy voice drawled from directly behind Dakoda: "How about this goddamned army?"

They had company. *Unexpected* company.

Fear rocketing through her veins, Dakoda reached for her gun. She whirled. Straight into the sights of a double-barreled shotgun. A double-barreled shotgun pointed straight at her gut.

The man holding the gun smiled. "Be still, little girl," he advised in a low, even voice.

Her heart skidding to an immediate halt, Dakoda froze, not daring to move a single muscle. *Oh shit.* Though her fingers were wound tightly around the grip of her weapon, and she'd even had it half drawn, she somehow managed to suppress the instinct to pull it out and take her best shot. Given that the man holding the shotgun stood barely a foot away, it was clear she'd lose.

Oh, yeah. She'd lose. *No doubt there.* And losing meant dying. That was something she wasn't ready to do.

The stranger grinned at Gregory Zerbe. "Looks like we got ourselves a little standoff. You got mine and I got yours."

"I can see that, Rusty." Clearly familiar with the newcomer, Zerbe held his own weapon rock steady. "But there's no reason anyone has to get hurt."

"We'll see . . . ," Rusty warned vaguely.

Without really wanting to, Dakoda eyed her captor. Unlike the other outlaws, he had a strangely pale complexion. He was tall and thin, and his long red hair was tied back at the nape of his neck.

Nobody moved, except to breathe. Strangely, the cougar had also gone quiet. Almost as if the animal understood the danger of the situation.

The redheaded stranger made a gesture with the barrel of his weapon. "Now you be a smart little girl and get your hand off that gun."

"Just take it slow, Dakoda," Zerbe advised.

"Okay." Forcing herself to stay calm, Dakoda withdrew her hand. "We all want out of here." *Alive,* her mind filled in.

A thin smile parted the newcomer's lips. "Maybe. Maybe not." A strange glint behind his pale blue gaze said he didn't care if neither of them walked away.

"I think it would be best if we just made a trade and let things be today," Zerbe suggested. "You boys go your way and we'll go ours."

Dakoda silently agreed. Out here, in the middle of nowhere, they had no backup. They were on their own, with only their own wits to survive on. A false step could be a fatal one. The notion of her career ending in these lonely mountains wasn't pleasant. Killing two rangers and hiding the bodies would be damn easy. *The remains would probably never be found.*

Such a grisly thought was hard to ignore. She shouldn't be thinking that way but couldn't help it. That's just the way her mind worked.

Willie Barnett broke in. "I agree with Ranger Do-Right, Rusty. We don't want no trouble here today." Surprising, considering who was speaking.

More antsy than the others, Waylon Barnett didn't agree. "We got the drop on them, goddamn it," he argued.

Dakoda's pulse skipped a beat at the innuendo behind his statement. Full of deadly threat. Three outlaws easily outnumbered two rangers. The odds were not good or fair. But nothing about life was fair. You just took the hand life dealt you and did the best you could.

Right now the anticipation of getting out alive was a very slim one. There were no promises or guarantees anyone would walk away.

Rusty nodded and grinned. "That's pretty much true, Ranger Do-Right. My little queen here is awfully pretty. I'm sure you'd hate to see her guts splattered."

Keeping her hands in place, Dakoda tried not to wince. Guts splattering didn't sound pleasant at all. Were that to happen, she'd probably be dead before she hit the ground.

Somehow Gregory Zerbe remained rock steady. "I'm reasonable enough not to want anyone killed today," he said slowly.

Shooting the uniforms a glare, Waylon Barnett jabbed a finger at the rangers. "Let 'em go today and they'll just come back tomorrow." He speared his brother with a glance. "Both of us got warrants, and you're just gonna let them walk away?"

"I'm willing to settle this peaceably," Zerbe interrupted.

The scarred outlaw ignored him. Tension rolled off him like a foul odor. Though he didn't look as if he possessed many brain cells, the few he did have were obviously working together. And the idea they were forming had already occurred to Dakoda. No doubt Gregory Zerbe had also followed the track.

"That's stupid, man," he bellowed. "I don't know about you boys, but ain't no way in hell I'm gonna be sittin' in one of their jails."

Ice drizzling through her veins, Dakoda shut her eyes, sure she'd be hearing the blast of gunfire any second.

Fortunately, a saner head prevailed. Sucking up a mouthful of tobacco juice, Willie Barnett spat a thick brown wad toward Zerbe. "Oh, hell. Let 'em go, Skeeter." He grinned though a mouthful of stained teeth. "They ain't very good trackers if they didn't even figure out Rusty was guardin' our tails."

Of course they'd had no damn idea there was a third man. It was a mistake not to be made a second time. That is, if they ever got a second chance.

Though he kept his weapon level, Rusty slowly stepped back. "You heard the man," he said, motioning for Dakoda to rejoin her partner.

Dakoda hurried over toward Zerbe. As she did so, the cougar stood up on its hind legs, placing its great paws against the bars. She couldn't be sure, but Dakoda was fairly certain she saw something akin to envy in its amber gaze.

She'd be walking away.

The cougar would have to be left behind.

Her throat tightened. Cutting the men loose meant losing the cougar.

Damn it all to hell.

His own weapon in place, Zerbe followed her lead as she edged toward the direction from which they'd arrived. "I'll be back, you bastards," he muttered under his breath. "Count on it." Walking away wasn't something Zerbe easily accepted.

Dakoda winced. *Now* wasn't the time to antagonize these men. "Let's go, Greg," she urged quietly. "There will be another day."

"Just get gone," Rusty urged. "The faster, the better."

Just as it seemed everything was under control, the event took a turn for the worse.

Waylon Barnett clearly wasn't agreeing with the plan. Rushing up to his cousin, he grabbed the shotgun. Something brutal and cruel twisted his features as he lifted the gun and aimed.

"No, Skeet! Don't!" Willie Barnett lunged at his brother. He might have been a poacher, but he wasn't a murderer.

That didn't hold true for Waylon Barnett. Glaring at them with vicious intent, he pushed past his brother and leveled the shotgun squarely at the two rangers.

Realizing the danger, Gregory Zerbe suddenly gave Dakoda a body-jarring shove, sending her flying toward the ground.

Dakoda stumbled, landing flat on her side. A soft rush of air broke from her lungs when she hit the hard ground. *What the hell is he doing?*

Reacting instinctively, she rolled aside, struggling to climb to her feet. Her heart pounded fiercely. Her lungs burned with the need to drag in a breath of air, but she couldn't seem to make herself breathe.

Her gaze swung toward the man who was determined they wouldn't be going anywhere anytime soon. Her eyes widened, adrenaline seared her veins. *Surely he isn't—* She braced herself against the inevitable. Her stomach performed a slow roll of anxiety. A series of horrible images slithered into her mind. Worry morphed into sheer, unrelenting panic.

A single loud crack split the air.

BLAM!

The shotgun roared, blasting liquid fire directly at her partner.

Time unexpectedly turned into a surreal slow-motion blur as the unstoppable assault of double-ought buckshot shredded Gregory Zerbe's guts even as the force knocked him backward. His body hit the ground hard, falling in a lifeless heap. Blood pooled around his mutilated corpse, forming a gruesome halo.

Dakoda's mouth dropped open. The odor of fresh gunpowder clotted her throat, as choking as the fear bubbling up from her belly. Shock radiated through her. Tears burned behind her eyes. It was all she could do not to scream. If she started, she was afraid she'd never stop.

Fighting to keep her wits, she scrabbled on hands and knees to the fallen man's side. Hands cupping his cheeks, she searched his face. His fathomless gaze collided with hers when she looked into his eyes. A single look was all she needed to know he was dead.

Dakoda made a noise in a voice she didn't recognize as her own, a keening wail burbling up from her throat. "Greg—no!" She paused a moment, panting, trying to pull her thoughts together, but fear sent her brain cells scattering like ashes in a high wind. How the hell had this happened? Why had it happened?

She had no answer.

All she knew for sure was that Gregory Zerbe was dead.

Murdered in cold blood right before her very eyes.

Bitter acid welled up from Dakoda's gut. She forced herself to swallow, determined not to vomit. Her body felt paralyzed. Numb. Nothing in her training had adequately prepared her for this. She forced herself to reach for calm before hysteria started to take root.

A man's hand suddenly closed around her arm, pulling her to her knees. Fingers like steel bands dug into her skin. Her gun was snagged from its holster, effectively disarming her.

Dakoda instinctively reared back. She cried out in shock, jerking away from the numbing clasp, but it still held tight. Her gaze zeroed in on the man Gregory Zerbe had identified only as Rusty.

A chill invaded Dakoda's bowels, tightening like fingers determined to tear her insides apart. Terror temporarily blanked her mind, a whiteout of pure, unadulterated fear. For a second or two she couldn't breathe. The cold continued to tear at her heart, ripping away piece after tiny piece.

The tall redhead jerked her arm again, attempting to drag her to her feet. "Nothin' you can do to help him now," he said coldly.

Dakoda's fear darkened and curled, a fresh rush of rage eating through her inertia like battery acid. She gathered the last reserves of her energy in a concentrated burst. "Rot in hell, you murdering bastards!" Her voice was sharp edged, nearly frantic.

Rusty's face revealed no regret whatsoever. He released a short laugh. "Goddamn, I can't believe you killed him, Skeet," he drawled, giving the dead man a prod with one scuffed boot.

A snarl immediately rolled past Dakoda's lips. "Leave him alone!" The command escaped before she had time to consider the consequences. At this point, she didn't care. She already knew she wouldn't be going anywhere. No way they'd let her walk away now.

Skeeter looked unrepentant. "He needed killin'," he spat, glowering darkly at the downed ranger.

"Now what the hell are we going to do with her?" Willie Barnett demanded.

Waylon's deluded gaze cut toward the caged cougar. "Didn't we promise those Asians we'd bring them two pets for their zoo?"

A nod. "Yeah."

Waylon Barnett snorted a giggle. "Then this is our lucky day, boys." Delighted with his brainstorm, he grinned like a shit-eating hound. "Looks like we've just made our sale."

A cold, damp sweat rose on Dakoda's skin. She trembled before she could stop the reaction. Whatever the outlaw was raving about, she was sure it wouldn't be pleasant.

2

Dakoda had assumed Waylon Barnett was joking when he'd proposed caging her with the cougar.

He hadn't been joking.

Assume makes an ass out of me.

Crouched in a corner of the pen, Dakoda warily eyed the huge animal lounging barely five feet away. To her relief, the big cat remained still. Eyes half closed as it dozed, the cougar lay on its side. Stretched out, the cougar was almost as large and heavy as a grown man.

Dakoda swallowed thickly. "Good kitty. You stay there and I'll stay right here."

Barely daring to turn her head, she peered through a crack in the thick log slabs. The compound the outlaws called home stretched out around her. In the cul-de-sac of an obscure valley, a series of overhanging cliffs provided natural shelter for the small settlement that had taken root. Most everything was constructed from logs: cabins, sheds, and a small corral for keeping the horses penned.

Still, not every item smacked of pioneer living.

The outlaws had more than a passing acquaintance with the outside world. A series of beat-up F-150 pickups and a couple of ATVs were an indication trails passable by more than foot or hoof existed.

"Slick operation," she muttered.

More than anything there were cages. Lots of cages. All shapes, all sizes. All clearly meant to keep animals penned and controlled.

Including the two-legged ones.

Gregory Zerbe was right, of course. These people had lived in the mountains all their lives. And they'd burrowed in permanently. There was no way to measure how far they'd traveled since her capture. Just as she had no idea where this place might be on a map.

Memory of her late partner brought a hitch to Dakoda's throat, a thickening that presaged blurred vision and lots of tears. She hated the idea he'd lay cold and alone in an unmarked grave. He deserved better.

So did she.

Dakoda swallowed hard, desperately struggling not to remember his grisly death. She'd deliberately tried to blank Greg's murder from her mind, refusing to let her memory push rewind, then play. It was no use. Every moment was irrevocably etched inside her skull.

She cast another wary glance toward the cougar, listless save for an occasional flick of its tail. Its amber eyes were narrow, not directly focused on her, but aware of her presence nevertheless. A low rumble emanated from its throat.

A warning.

You keep your place and I'll keep mine.

Dakoda gulped. *My very last breath might be arriving sooner, rather than later.* Her thought was a grim one, and not very pleasant to contemplate.

Reaching up, Dakoda fingered the thick metal band around

her neck. After the indignity of wearing her own handcuffs, she'd hoped to be rid of her shackles. Not so. Like the cougar, she'd been fitted with a collar. Since her capture the animal had been unnaturally docile, as though the sight of seeing another taken and chained had temporarily robbed it of the will to be defiant.

Had she not known better, Dakoda would have sworn the beast was showing an intelligent response to their mutual plight of captivity.

Their coop looked more like a cell a human being would be confined in. The floor was plain dirt, packed hard and swept clean. A bunk was built into one wall. A crude table and chairs occupied another corner. A chamber pot and basin for water shoved under the bunk served as personal facilities. Altogether the space probably measured twelve by twelve feet, if that much. Between the cougar and herself, there wasn't much free room to move.

The rock and the hard place.

These two forces threatened to grind her to dust. Bitterness took root, but she wouldn't let it beat her down. Life had handed her more than one raw deal, and she'd managed to survive. Fresh determination kicked in. She'd hold on to the memories, hoping to someday use them to punish the men who'd killed Greg in cold blood. She wouldn't give up until her very last breath.

Cradling her arms around her knees, Dakoda gave the cougar another wary glance. "Looks like it's just you and me, kitty." The rumble of an empty stomach reminded her just how near danger lurked. That cougar was probably just as hungry.

She winced. It vaguely occurred to her the outlaws had locked her up with the cougar as a method of torture. The big cats were carnivores and could easily take down a grown man.

The way it looked, she probably wouldn't live through the night. The sun was beginning to arc into the west, on its way toward setting. The temperature would soon begin to drop, drastically. Days in the mountains might be warm, but nights bordered on uncomfortably cool.

Tightening her grip on her legs, Dakoda propped her chin on her knees. She knew a search-and-rescue team would be sent out once she and Gregory failed to turn up, but the chance of rescue was probably slim to none. The outlaws knew how to survive, how to hide, in these mountains; they'd been doing it for generations uncounted.

There would be more than one anxious person awaiting news. Gregory Zerbe had a wife and kids at home, people who would want to know what had happened to him.

Dakoda frowned. She had . . . nobody. Not one person on the face of this earth cared if she lived or died.

Somehow she'd gotten through a childhood that could be described as pure hell. Her mother was a druggie, an itinerant wanderer who'd dragged her daughter throughout the state. With little education and few morals, they survived by hook or by crook. Time after time, Dakoda found herself waiting out long months with one caregiver or another as Jenna Lee served time in jail for petty larceny. Her father was unknown, one of the many rabbits running through her mother's briar patch.

Most of Dakoda's sitters were men, most of whom hooked up with her mother to party. Some would stay a few days, some a few months. The rare ones hung on a few years, maybe because they felt sorry for her. As she'd gotten older, their care and concern had turned carnal. By the time she turned four-teen, Dakoda wasn't a virgin anymore. She was also beginning to experiment with drugs and alcohol.

By all expectations, Dakoda was pretty much assured of walking straight down her mother's well-worn path. No one expected anything out of a juvenile delinquent, nothing more than trash from the wrong side of the tracks.

Salvation arrived in the form of her mother's last hookup, a man named Ashton Jenkins. Unlike the rest of the men who'd passed in and out of their lives, Ash was a good man, a responsible man. A cop, he'd spent his life enforcing the law, not breaking it. For once good luck had been on Jenna Lee's side when she'd gotten picked up for shoplifting.

Dakoda had to smile when she remembered Ash Jenkins. Though he was a big brawny man who took no shit, he was surprisingly gentle with women. Ash really loved Jenna Lee and tried to do right by her and by her teenaged daughter. For the first time in their lives, they had a home. Stability. A responsible man who brought in a paycheck instead of a six-pack and a crack pipe.

It didn't last.

Jenna Lee wasn't the kind of woman who could easily settle down into domestic tranquility. She craved her parties, the booze and drugs that made her small, dead-end life just a little less boring. Less than a year after marrying Ash, her mother packed up and moved out in the middle of the night. Disappearing yet again with another man.

Normally, that meant the man would pack up and leave, too.

Not Ash Jenkins. Instead of cutting and running, he'd stayed on, applying to the court to become Dakoda's legal father so he could finish raising her. Her days of running wild and running with the wrong crowd were over. Despite the fact she'd hated every minute of it, Ash Jenkins had taken her ass and whipped it into shape. By time she graduated from high school, Dakoda was a straight-A student.

Though he'd seen her into college, Ash Jenkins hadn't lived to see her graduate. A punk with a gun shot him down during a convenience-store robbery gone bad.

To honor his memory, Dakoda had chosen law enforcement as her own career. She already knew she wouldn't be staying in the city, though. Born and raised in North Carolina, she'd always lived in the shadows of the mountains. Something in their tranquility beckoned to her spirit. They represented a stability she'd rarely known throughout her life. Simply, they reminded her of her stepfather.

Though Ash Jenkins's killer was never caught, Dakoda knew exactly who'd killed Gregory Zerbe. The first time, the crime had gone unpunished. If she had her way, it wouldn't happen a second time.

All she had to do was figure out how to get out of this place alive. Given that her roommate was a wild-ass cougar, that possibility was a very slim one, indeed.

Tired of sitting in her cramped position on the hard ground, Dakoda eyed the cougar for any sign of aggression. The cell was darker now, everything around her turning murky and indistinct as night stretched over the mountains.

The big cat didn't move.

Taking a deep breath, she stretched out one leg, then the other. The ache in her knees eased a little. No telling how long she'd been sitting, letting her mind roam. At the moment, remembering the past was slightly more pleasant than contemplating her future.

Sensing her movements, the cougar's amber eyes snapped open. Its ears flicked and its gaze brightened, wary and alert.

Realizing her movements had disturbed the animal, Dakoda flashed a wavering smile. "Nice kitty," she soothed. "You just lay right there and be still." She fought against the instinct to curl back up into a little ball, make herself as small as humanly possible. As a ranger cadet, she'd taken classes on wild animal encounters. Staying calm was the first key. Not agitating the animal was the second. Most wild animals normally avoided human contact, becoming aggressive only when they sensed danger.

Dakoda's empty stomach rumbled again. She swallowed thickly, though her mouth was too dry to offer much liquid. Hunger was another factor that drove a wild animal to attack.

Just as soon as the cougar got a little rest, it was going to get

antsy. A twinge deep in her bladder warned that her own discomfort would soon be increasing tenfold.

Inching around the cougar to use the chamber pot wasn't
the most appealing notion she'd entertained lately. The idea of
her pants around her ankles and her bare ass hanging out damn
near sent her into a spasm. That cougar would probably love to
take a nice bite out of her tender rear.

Dakoda might have laughed if the situation hadn't been so
damn serious. The cell wasn't going to be big enough for both
of them much longer.

A sudden commotion of voices and movement outside the
cell caught her attention. Heavy steps were punctuated by a series of guffaws. The grating of a lock and fall of a heavy chain
allowed the cell door to open.

The cougar immediately leapt to its feet. It coiled into a defensive crouch; a low growl emanated from its throat.

Dakoda quickly pulled her legs back up toward her chest.
"Oh shit . . ." she muttered. Now wasn't the time to piss that
big cat off.

A flash of light hit Dakoda in the eyes. Shielding her face
with a hand, she watched two of the outlaws step inside. The
one she recognized as Willie Barnett carried a battery-powered
lantern. He also carried a small cooler, the kind used for storing
food and drinks.

Dakoda welcomed the light; nobody wanted to be trapped
in the dark with a cougar. She eyed the cooler. *Food, I hope.*

The redheaded man who'd ambushed them followed a close
step behind. Rifle in hand, he pointed it at the cougar. "Keep
your place," he warned. "Or I'll blow you to kingdom come."

Dakoda froze. "Okay," she said slowly, voice wavering
more than a little.

Willie Barnett laughed. "Not you, little girl. Rusty's talking
to Jesse there, reminding that mangy Indian to mind his manners."

Dakoda's gaze swiveled to the cougar. *Mangy Indian?* She didn't get it. Whatever the meaning was, it flew right over her head.

Though the cougar couldn't possibly understand human words, it must have recognized and comprehended the danger the men represented. Backing up a little, it settled down on its haunches. Its eyes narrowed into slits, and a low growl emanated from its throat. Bowed, but not yet broken.

Willie Barnett walked over to the table. Setting down the lantern and cooler, he tugged out a chair. "Come here."

Dakoda assumed he was speaking to her. She shook her head. "I think I'll stay right here." No reason to trust these men. They hadn't shown anything but their bad sides.

The man called Rusty made a motion with his rifle. "The cougar won't bother you." He thumbed back the hammer on his rifle. "Guaranteed. Ol' Jesse may be cursing himself for wanderin' off his own land, but he ain't entirely stupid. He knows them claws and teeth ain't no match for my friends Smith and Wesson."

Must be the moonshine, Dakoda decided. The men must have gotten hold of a bad batch of rotgut. Talking to the cougar like it was human—like it understood—was the work of a seriously deranged mind.

Opening the cooler, Willie Barnett made a motion with his hand. "Get on over here and eat."

Dakoda considered refusing. The smell of the food the men had carried in was beginning to permeate the small cell, filling the air with the enticing aroma of meat cooked over an open flame. Mouth watering, her neglected appetite gave a ferocious kick. Her stomach didn't intend to be denied much longer.

Easing to her feet, Dakoda slowly made her way to the table. She took the chair Barnett had pulled out for her, lowering herself into place. Another whiff of cooked meat hit her nostrils.

Barnett began to empty the cooler. "It ain't the best, but it's edible," he grumbled, ripping open a foil-covered packet heaped with meat.

Dakoda surveyed the bounty. Ribs, still on the bone. A plastic bag of something that looked like trail mix lay beside a six-pack of plastic bottles filled with water. There was no cutlery, no napkins. Certainly no fancy dessert.

Her senses wavered, reminding her she hadn't eaten since noon. That was a long time ago. The life she'd had before encountering the outlaws hardly seemed real now.

She picked at a piece of meat that appeared to be more charred than edible. *When you're hungry it's a feast,* she reminded herself. That didn't mean she wanted to eat. Still, she realized the value of keeping strong, of staying aware. Lifting a piece to her mouth, she chewed slowly. Slathered with a tangy sauce and peppered, it tasted better than it looked.

"Eat up," Barnett said gruffly. "We've got buyers coming in the next couple of days, and we don't want you looking scrawny."

Dakoda swallowed the bite. The tough meat scratched her throat, nearly gagging her. She coughed out the single word, "Buyers?"

A smile tugged at one corner of Rusty's mouth. His gaze traveled the length of her body, lingering on her breasts. "You an' Jesse here are bein' sold. Got a good price for the both of you."

Dakoda's stomach twisted. The remnants of her hunger vanished. "Sold as what?" she asked slowly, though there was really no need to ask. It didn't take rocket science to put two and two together.

Willie Barnett flashed an evil grin. "You'll both be performin' for your new owners . . ." Reaching out, he stroked her long hair away from the back of her neck, baring her nape. "Damn shame we have to sell both of you. You sure are pretty. I wouldn't mind a little entertainin' myself."

Dakoda's skin prickled under his nasty touch. A spike of disgust stole her breath. A knot of foreboding settled beneath her rib cage as a shiver rippled down her spine.

She wiped her mouth with the back of her sleeve, fighting the sudden rise of nausea. "I'd fuck that cougar before I'd fuck you," she snapped without thinking. She hated it when a man put his hands on her uninvited. Having suffered through multiple molestations as a young adult, she'd had more than enough of men pawing on her. Nobody touched her without her permission.

Nobody quickly became somebody. And that somebody had bad intentions on his mind—and the strength to back it up.

Barnett's smile vanished. Jerking her out of the chair, he slammed her back against the wall. Her skull cracked the hard wall, sending a smattering of purple stars shooting in front of her eyes.

"Maybe I'll just have a little piece of you right now," he threatened, pinning her with his weight. A blast of foul odor hit her square in the face. His teeth were stained with tobacco, and his breath was as putrid as week-old road kill.

Dakoda struggled, writhing against him in an attempt to break free of his crushing physique. Taller and stronger, the mountain man wielded a brute's strength with ease. Capturing her wrists, he easily pinned her arms above her head. His knee expertly moved between her legs, forcing them apart. His free hand worked the front of her uniform open.

Realizing his intent, Dakoda felt a numbing wave of sickness reel through her mind. Nausea rose in her stomach and spread through every part of her body. Fear turned her blood to icy water.

"Don't," she grated.

Even as she groaned in violent protest and squirmed beneath him, the outlaw pressed in on her. "Ready to be fucked right, honey?" Willie growled as his hand cupped her left breast and squeezed. He ground his hips against hers. The hard ridge of his erection left no doubt he intended to take her right there, standing against the wall.

The trembling started deep inside her. She tried to control it, but that wasn't happening. All she could think about was Greg, how he'd shoved her out of harm's way mere seconds before the outlaw pulled the trigger. In saving her life, he'd unwittingly condemned her to something far worse.

Dakoda steeled herself for the assault to come. She'd figured rape would be on their minds, and she was right. It was inevitable, not a matter of if, but when.

She closed her eyes, mentally distancing her mind from her body as he rolled her nipple between thumb and forefinger.

It would be easier that way.

I don't have to remember this . . .

A shattering roar split through her senses. Lunging forward, the big cat swiped one enormous paw across the outlaw's back. Clothing and skin were ripped to shreds.

Willie Barnett screamed. Pushing away from Dakoda, he whirled, aiming a vicious kick at the cougar. "Get off me, Jesse!" A stream of foul curses spilled from his mouth.

Unwilling to back off, the cougar bared its fangs. Ears pinned back against its massive skull, it crouched, preparing to spring into action.

Turning his rifle around, Rusty swung the butt of the weapon toward the cougar's head. The stock connected soundly with the big cat's skull, landing with a gut-turning smack. "Get back!" he shouted at the big cat. "Get back or I'll kill you now."

The cougar reeled, dropping to the ground. The blow had opened a deep gash. Blood leaked from the gaping wound. A half-growl, half-moan emanated from its open mouth.

Legs losing strength, Dakoda sagged to the floor. Heart sinking, her breath whistled in and out of her lungs as she watched Willie Barnett approach the downed cougar. Enraged by her screams, the animal had gone on the attack, doing what came naturally.

Furious that he'd been injured, Barnett was on the warpath. "That was a stupid thing to do, Jesse," he said, his voice chill with anger. Drawing back his foot, he delivered a kick to the animal's ribs with one booted foot.

Finding new strength, the cougar immediately leapt back to its feet. Amber eyes flamed, alight with hellish fury. Mouth opening, nostrils flaring, the big cat snarled threateningly. Sharp fangs snapped at the outlaw's leg.

Barnett stumbled back, cursing. The cougar bared its teeth savagely. Lethal intent gleamed in its slitted gaze.

If it got the chance, it would do its best to kill him.

3

The cougar was pissed. No doubt about it. Its defensive stance radiated threat and menace.

A prickling sensation ran up Dakoda's spine as she watched the cougar watch her. Reflected in the light of the lantern, its amber eyes snapped with an unnatural chatoyancy, as if an electrical charge had been wired to its tail and the energy turned on full power.

This time the cougar wasn't putting up with any shit from human beings. Pacing the small cell from side to side, a series of low growls slipped from its mouth. Sides heaving, it panted heavily, nostrils flaring with every breath it took.

Careful to make no sudden moves, Dakoda eyed the beast. Thank goodness she still had the lantern and the light it provided. Had the men left her in the dark again, she was sure she'd have fallen to pieces right then and there. At least she could see. As long as she could see, she could judge the situation and decide her next best move. Being shredded and devoured just wasn't her idea of a good way to die.

Not that being hit full force in the gut with double-ought

buckshot was preferable. At least Gregory Zerbe had died quickly and didn't suffer. Cougars smothered their prey, grabbing their victims by the neck and crushing their necks. One or two minutes of pure terror would be followed by the realization the reaper wasn't only knocking on the door, he was grinding down full throttle.

Be an iceberg, she advised herself, *and chill.* The idea of dying alone shook her to the very center of her being. Somewhere in the back of her mind she'd hoped to meet the right man, settle down, and, someday, raise a family. A real family. Nothing like the one she'd known as a child.

Snuffling a growl, the cougar kept pacing.

Dakoda's thoughts of a future of any sort slowly drizzled away. "It's just you and me, big boy," she said, attempting to keep her voice level and soothing. "The bad men who hurt us are gone." Once the big cat got back on its feet, the outlaws had beat a hasty retreat. True to their natures, they were cowards in every way.

The cougar ignored her.

Typical male.

Dakoda considered her options. She really didn't want to spend the night standing in a corner. For one, she was tired. For two, she was hungry. For three, she really needed to pee. Her bladder was beginning to nag. If she didn't get a chance for relief soon, she'd burst. The idea of wetting her pants was as unappealing. If worse came to worst—and she suspected it would—she would soon be making her corner her pit-stop. The bunk and the precious chamber pot were on the cougar's side of the cell.

Her side had the table.

Dakoda's gaze settled on the aluminum foil heaped with meat. *And I have the food.* Inspiration arrived, manna from heaven. Hope glimmered. Perhaps she could mollify the fuming cougar with a peace offering.

Inching over to the table, Dakoda reached out. Snatching a piece of meat from the pile, she held it out in front of her. "Here, kitty," she said softly.

Attention shifting toward the new distraction, the cougar ceased its relentless pacing. Blood still seeped from the narrow wound the outlaw's rifle had inflicted, but it wasn't enough of a flow to cause much concern. The cougar's broad pink nose flexed, scenting the morsel.

Dakoda held the meat out, as far away from her body as physically possible. Sacrificing a limb wasn't at the top of her list of things to do. "I know you're hungry, big fella," she continued, trying to establish some sort of verbal rapport. Animals were intelligent creatures, well able to think and function in their quest for survival. The poachers certainly seemed to think so. They'd spoken as if the big cat were fully capable of understanding and responding accordingly.

Neither one of us were very smart, came the dissenting thought. *We both got caught.*

She dangled the meat. "Come here, boy. Come and get it."

Menace fading a bit from its predatory gaze, the cougar paced forward, lifting its head higher as it approached. Massive jaws opened.

Dakoda tossed the meat into the yawning void. "Here you go."

The cougar devoured the morsel with a single gulp, grinding meat and bone together with gigantic teeth. It swallowed. A sound emanated from its mouth, a sigh of relief. The cougar was just as hungry and tired as she was.

Dakoda tossed another bite. "Good kitty," she soothed. "Nice kitty. You just eat this meat and forget about eating me, okay?" Keeping her movements slow, she continued until nothing remained of dinner except the trail mix and bottles of water.

The cougar looked at her, cocking its head in question.

Dakoda showed empty hands. "No more," she said, shaking her head in an exaggerated manner. "All gone." She felt a little silly talking to the animal, but that was better than the alternative—being killed by the cougar.

As though it understood, the cougar dropped to the floor. Now that its stomach was full, the feline set to another equally important task. Grooming. A pink tongue whizzed across its fur.

Relieved the cat was occupied, Dakoda snagged the trail mix and a bottle of water. Inching around the cat, she headed toward the bunk. Since the cat wasn't looking her way, she felt a bit more comfortable taking care of vital business.

Retrieving the lidded chamber pot, Dakoda set it by the bunk. It wasn't anything she wanted to use, but she had no choice. People had gotten along just fine before modern plumbing was invented. Nevertheless, embarrassment reddened her cheeks as she undid her pants, then squatted. *Men are so lucky. They can pee standing up.*

Consideration of the cougar taking a nice chunk out of her skinny butt hurried her along. Release was immediate and welcome.

Sliding the used chamber pot back under the bunk, Dakoda sat down on the bunk. Covered with a few ragged blankets, it offered a welcome respite from the cold, bare ground. If she had to split the cell with the cougar, at least she had the better half. Still she was acutely conscious of the threat not so far away. A single bound was all it would take for the big cat to overtake her.

Glad to be off the floor, she drew her legs up. Less temptation. Those ivory-white teeth could snap off a foot in no time flat. Since the cougar might still be hungry, her best bet was not to tempt it. It hadn't attacked her yet, a definite plus in her book. She'd consider herself lucky if she saw the sun rise tomorrow.

But the passage of time held no promise. None. Willie Barnett had claimed he was selling her off. Like she wasn't a human being, but a piece of property to be haggled over, bartered for. Her gaze fell on the cougar. *Like an animal.*

Dakoda regarded her own skimpy meal, nothing close to the double-bacon cheeseburger and fries she'd like to sink her teeth into. Dieting had never been a concern. She'd always been tall and thin, on the scrawny side. Her build was boyish; washboard breasts, stomach, and the barest hint of an ass. "Two raisins on a surfboard" was how one lover had characterized her figure.

The asshole who'd made the unkind remark was now an ex-lover. Since her split with Thad almost a year ago, she'd sworn off men for a bit. As a teen, she'd followed her mother's lead, looking for love in all the wrong places, mistaking promiscuity for affection time and time again. Though the physical side found some gratification, the emotional side hadn't.

Dakoda had to admit she loved the feel of a man's body pressed next to hers. Muscular. Powerful. A man who was fit, who kept himself in shape, was a turn-on. Chest like a rock wall, six-pack abs, a tight round ass. The musky scent of hot male skin . . .

Need jolted through her, sending a shock all the way to her toes. She had denied herself for so long, just thinking about a man's physique could get her revved up.

Taking a ragged breath, Dakoda fanned herself with a hand. Amazing the subjects the mind could wander onto when stressed. Sex was the last thing she should be thinking about. If the cougar hadn't attacked, she would be a rape victim about now.

Her gaze traveled back to the big cat. It was easy to remember the first time she'd laid eyes on the splendid beast—and the powerful reaction she'd felt deep inside. Stretched end to end, it was at least six feet long, maybe more. Its chest was bulky, thick with muscle. Long legs stretched out endlessly. And the paws, the paws were huge.

She smiled. "If you were a man," she murmured, "you'd be outstanding." Despite her remark, she craved more than sex. She craved an emotional connection, a meeting of the minds.

And if wishes were horses, then beggars would ride.

No such luck. Otherwise she'd have called upon a few and wished herself far away from this place.

Her smile faded. As always, her mind journeyed to places it had no business visiting. Must be how incarcerated souls passed the time without losing their sanity. Wishing, and wondering about the path not taken.

Dakoda's stomach churned, reminding her she needed to eat. She picked up the bag of trail mix, tearing it open. The aroma of nuts and dried fruit tickled her senses. She scooped up a handful. Popping the bite into her mouth, she chewed the crunchy mass into a pulp before swallowing. *Delicious.*

She cracked open the bottle of water, gulping down the tepid liquid inside. More handfuls of trail mix followed. A few minutes later the bag was empty. Satisfied her throat hadn't been cut, her stomach stopped growling.

But the pressure building at the back of her mind hadn't eased.

Dakoda reached behind her head, gingerly fingering the lump growing there. The wall was inflexible and she'd taken a hell of a wallop. "Just what I needed," she muttered. A concussion. Headache and fatigue were definite symptoms. Even with some food in her stomach, she still had both.

Finished with its grooming, the cougar rose. Its lean frame flexed and stretched with familiar movements. Mouth opening wide, its pink tongue flicked out in a yawn. Satisfied every kink had been vanquished, the cougar padded toward the bunk on four silent paws.

Dakoda stiffened. She'd done nothing to agitate the animal,

SOUL OF THE WILDCAT / 35

draw its attention. She kept absolutely still as the feline approached.

It lifted its head toward her, its broad nostrils flaring as it sniffed along her body, beginning at her feet and heading up her legs. The light *chuff-chuff* sound of its breath filled the silence of the cell.

Dakoda realized the cougar was checking her out, doing a little investigating in the only way it knew how. She slowly put out a hand. "Nice kitty," she said.

The cougar sniffed her hand. A low sound emanated from its throat, something strangely akin to a whistle. Head dipping low, he all of a sudden butted against her hand. The tawny head slipped under her palm.

The message was clear: pet me.

Dakoda nodded. "Ah, I see. You want a little loving."

The cougar snuffled, butting her hand for a reply. *Yes.*

Dakoda riffled the tips of her fingers across the crown of the cougar's head. The reddish-brown fur felt coarse, like straw, not soft and silky the way she'd imagined. Its head was short and rounded with powerful jaws and strong teeth. The wound above its left eye was beginning to clot and close. Overall the cougar appeared to be a healthy animal.

Using the tips of her nails, she slowly worked her way toward one rounded, cup-shaped ear. The cougar turned its head slightly, welcoming the long deep scratches across its skin.

She smiled. "Ah, you like that, don't you, boy?" she worked her fingers a little deeper, giving the other ear equal attention. "A good scratching behind the ears would make anyone feel better." Leaning forward, she inhaled the animal's scent. Its odor was musky, feral, dangerous, and dark, hinting of the deep forests it prowled. The smell teased her senses, leading her to wonder how it would feel to roam, wild and free.

A chain saw of enthusiastic sound broke burst out. The cougar purred loudly, responding to her touch.

Dakoda laughed. "My goodness, you sure are a friendly boy."

The cougar yawned, giving her a blast of meat-scented breath. Without warning the big feline did a rolling flop, presenting his tummy for a scratch.

Dakoda couldn't fail to get the hint. Leaning over the edge of the bunk, she reached down. "You want more?" Using a rhythmic motion, she scratched her way down the cougar's chest and belly.

Enjoying the attention, the cougar did what came naturally when a male got to enjoying himself just a little too much. A nice rosy penis came into view.

Dakoda blushed, a feverish heat immediately rising to her cheeks. "Oh, my . . ."

She didn't have a chance to say anything else.

Something bizarre happened.

The cougar started to change. Fur zipping away, its torso and limbs stretched out, muscle and bone unknotting and reshaping. Contorting and unsnarling, paws elongated into hands and feet. The skull reshaped, feline features vanishing, simultaneously taking on a distinctly human cast.

In the blink of an eye the cougar had vanished.

A naked man lay on the floor in its place.

Dakoda jolted, damn near choking on her scream. *Holy shit!* What she was looking at couldn't be real.

Could it?

Gaze fixed on the impossible sight, her eyes widened at the display of his bobbing shaft. Heart skipping a beat, a hot flush spread through her veins. Her cheeks heated. His erection sure looked genuine enough. Jutting toward his abdomen, hard and eager, his cock was quite impressive.

The stranger's hands rose, covering a vital piece of his exposed anatomy. "Sorry." A grin of embarrassment split his lips. "I always get a hard-on when a pretty girl pets me."

4

Dakoda's stomach lurched. Hand lifting, she closed her eyes and pressed her palm against her forehead. "The concussion," she reasoned, barely speaking above a whisper. "It's making me hallucinate."

She was seeing things. Yeah. That's it. Between the trauma of witnessing Greg's murder, the exhaustion of keeping herself in one piece, and a near rape, her trolley had somehow slipped off the track of sanity. Reason was going in an entirely different direction, exploring uncharted territory.

I'm losing it for sure, she thought. *Cougars don't turn into men.*

She inwardly cringed. The idea seemed crazy, even inside the confines of her apparently demented mind. Of course a human couldn't turn into an animal. Magic, hocus-pocus, call it what you will, didn't exist.

A man's voice broke through the curtain Dakoda was attempting to pull around her murky senses. "I don't mean to be a pain in the ass, but I can assure you I'm not a figment of your imagination." A pause. "Though, if it helps, I wish I were. I'd rather be anyplace else but here."

The apparition was talking. To her.

Dakoda lowered her hand. She opened her eyes. Sure enough, the naked man was still there.

For a moment she considered the idea she'd fallen asleep. It made sense her damaged, desperate psyche might conjure up such an extraordinary scenario. It could all just be a creation of her imagination.

Easily explained, easily understood.

But the scene unfolding before her eyes didn't have the surreal, kaleidoscopic quality of a dream. In dreams, the angles were off, odd and vague, stretched and distorted. What she saw now was all sharp and very much in focus.

"You were the cougar," she said, a slight frown curving her mouth. "I know what I saw."

The man sat up slowly, moving with lazy grace as he settled into a sitting position not quite as distracting. "Yeah," he said quietly. "But what do you see now?"

What she saw was enough to take her breath away all over again, and in an entirely different way. The one thing she definitely hadn't been prepared for was a man who looked like he'd just walked out of the pages of a *Playgirl* magazine.

Jet-black hair fell past his shoulders, parted exactly in the middle and surrounding a face that might have been chiseled from stone: high forehead, prominent cheekbones, strong jawline. His wide-set eyes were dark, so black she couldn't find a hint of irises in their depths. His face was lightly stubbled, his mouth generous, full, and sensual.

The telltale signs of a hard and rugged life had etched themselves into his skin. Scars slashed down his shoulders, abdomen, and legs. Knotted and long healed, they hinted at deadly claws and jaggedly sharp teeth.

But it was the color of his skin that really made Dakoda sit up and take notice. The shade might have been compared to that of a copper pot, used for ages over an open fire. A thin gash angled above his left eye, still puffy and tender. The line of his nose also wasn't perfect, as if broken by a foot or the stock of a rifle.

Overall, the effect of viewing him as a whole was stunning. Here was a man who'd lived a hard life, living on the edge as he fought to survive in a land yanked out from under his feet by encroaching civilization.

Assuming he was even real.

Real or not, though, he looked damn good. Larger than life, his masculine presence filled the small cell.

Gazing at him, a final possibility loomed large in the back of Dakoda's mind, floating out of the shadowy recesses like a red-eyed specter. *What if Greg wasn't the only one who died?* Maybe she'd also been hit by the shotgun's blast. And this place was some kind of limbo, a realm where the normal rules of existence didn't apply. Logic certainly didn't.

She looked at the man who'd once been a cougar. "Did I die?" she asked, her voice barely above a whisper.

He grinned. "You're very much alive."

Testing the theory, Dakoda gave her cheek a hard pinch, all too aware of the pain. Would the deceased feel any pain? She didn't think so.

"I'm not supposed to be here," she informed him for lack of something better to say.

His lips pulled back in a familiar, feral smile. "Shit happens to the best of us, babe."

His words were delivered as a verbal slap, snapping her back to reality. Not that it was one she wanted to continue experiencing much longer. As it stood, she was locked in a small cell out in the middle of some godforsaken mountain tract, having been kidnapped to be sold as a slave in some twisted animal act to a private seller. And oh, yeah, her partner had been shot dead right in front of her, gunned down in cold blood by a wanted criminal.

Nothing about this day could get any worse . . . or any more unbelievable.

Suspending disbelief and discounting death, Dakoda eyed the naked man. "Looks like I wasn't the only one standing in front of the fan," she commented dryly.

Amusement sparked in his dark gaze. "Looks like I caught a good portion of shit, too," he affirmed with a smile. He politely extended a hand. "My name's Jesse Clawfoot." If his looks hadn't confirmed his Native American heritage, his surname did.

Tension knotted Dakoda's shoulders as her hand slipped into his. His flesh certainly felt real enough, warm enough . . . firm enough. She felt a twinge of confusion, but shook it off, mentally willing herself to stay focused, alert. The least she could do was offer her name. "Dakoda. Jenkins."

"Nice to meet you, Dakoda." A flash of straight white teeth followed. "I hope you'll forgive me for the rude introduction. I never could resist a good belly scratch."

She pulled her hand away. "So where did the cougar go?" she blurted, close to babbling.

Her question startled him. Heavy brows dipped together. "I don't get what you're asking."

Dakoda wasn't exactly sure, either. Nothing made any sense. But rather than have a complete meltdown, she was trying to work through the matter the only way she knew how. By asking questions and getting answers. She could think about chasing down her errant sanity later.

"You know," she prompted. "You're here. The cougar's gone. Where's the cougar?"

He got it. "I'm the cougar," Jesse said, pointing to himself.

Dakoda didn't believe him. "No, you're not."

Jesse started to shake his head, then shrugged. "I guess you need another demonstration." Repositioning himself on his hands and knees, he assumed the pose of a crouching animal. "Watch me. Try to pay attention."

"I will." Dakoda watched closely. Nothing was happening. All she saw was a buck-ass-nekkid man hunched on the bare floor. "How long does it take?"

Jesse shot her a look of annoyance. "Give me a minute, will you? That crack on the noggin really took something out of me." He crouched lower and closed his eyes. "Come on," he muttered under his breath. "Cat, don't fail me now."

Dakoda watched closely, fighting not to blink an eye.

Then, it happened.

Jesse's body changed, skin budding fur as his features changed and contorted, again taking on the body of the sensuous feline.

A fine tremble shimmied up Dakoda's spine as she glanced around the cramped cell. The Indian had vanished.

The cougar settled on its haunches. Its amber gaze burned with intelligence. Human intelligence.

Dakoda shook her head. "I *am* losing my mind," she murmured. "I've gone mad."

The cougar tossed a saucy wink. *No, you're not,* it seemed to say.

The fine hair at the nape of her neck rose. "Don't do this to me, you fucker," she breathed.

The cougar shifted again, and the naked Indian was back. Dakoda would have sworn she saw the instantaneous second where feline and human met, then separated. How he'd managed it, she didn't know. This time some gut-level sense confirmed the reality.

Her eyes definitely weren't deceiving her.

Jesse Clawfoot could, indeed, turn into a cougar.

He pulled a leg up in front of his body, concealing vital parts from view. "Are you satisfied now?" he asked.

Even though she'd just witnessed his transformation—twice!— Dakoda still had a problem comprehending the entire matter.

She mentally ticked off all the rational explanations again. When those ran out she had . . . what? She wasn't quite sure. One certainly couldn't argue with their own eyes. Looking at him now, she could almost see the power stirring under his skin, see the cougar straining against its imprisonment inside a human's body.

She argued anyway. "But people don't turn into animals. It's impossible. Maybe that sort of magic works in the movies, with the help of computers and a lot of CGI. But in real life?" She shook her head. "No fucking way."

Brow ruffling with annoyance, he frowned. "I just gave you an up-close and personal demonstration," he countered. "How can you not believe when you're sitting here, talking to me now?"

Dakoda studied him for a long moment. Her need to believe squared off with the idea that any life-form capable of shifting its physical shape could not possibly be human. At least not in the sense science explained it. "I'm not sure what's happening to me any more," she finally admitted in defeat. "All I know is I'm not having a really good time."

Looking at her, his gaze chilled. "This day hasn't been a party for me, either," he grumbled.

A long stretch of silence ensued.

"How come you can shift, and nobody else can?" she finally asked. "I mean, if anyone could do it we'd all be running around on four paws. Right?"

Jesse's icy gaze thawed a little. "I can try to explain," he offered.

She nodded. "That would help a lot."

Jesse drew a deep breath. "Imagine the beginning of time, when the Great Spirit was creating the earth."

Dakoda hesitated. "Okay . . ." The problem with that line of reasoning is she didn't believe in God, or a higher power of any sort. As far as she was concerned mankind had climbed out of the primordial ooze. "Wouldn't this shifty-thing go better with Darwin's theory of evolution?" The idea men had evolved from chimps wasn't so far-fetched in her mind. Despite the advances of civilization, Homo sapiens nevertheless continued to act like senseless brutes and beasts.

Jesse considered her skeptical expression. "You aren't buying anything I'm saying, are you?"

Dakoda briefly considered his question before shaking her head. "No, I'm really not into the God and the whole creation-of-the-earth thing."

He stared at her through heavy-lidded eyes. "Well, that's going to make it difficult for me to explain the Tlvdatsi, then. Our traditions are based on the belief in greater spirits, divine spirits."

She spread her hands. "Sorry. I wasn't raised to believe in any higher power." Her jaw tightened. "My mother was too busy shoplifting to buy her crack." Though she didn't intend it, her voice came out tinged with bitterness.

Exasperation drained from Jesse's intelligent gaze, replaced with compassion. "I'm sorry," he said. "Maybe I'll try to explain it another time. When we're not so stressed."

Dakoda snorted. "Maybe I'll try to listen."

Jesse shot her a frown. "There's no need to be a snotty bitch. You're not the only one locked in this place."

She considered his statement. No matter where he'd come from, there were now two of them. Her mind set to ticking. "So we've got two heads, and two sets of hands. Maybe between us we can figure out how to get the hell out of here before those assholes come back."

5

Slipping off the bunk, Dakoda prowled the cell, running her hands through the cracks in the walls, then testing the door. The outlaws had a tried-and-true method for locking them inside. They'd simply shut the door, which opened outward, and slid a thick slab of planking across its face. The staples fixed into both sides of the door assured it would remain shut.

Damn. Crude, but effective.

She groaned. So much for the idea of escape. "I think we're going to be stressed for a pretty long time," she observed dryly. "They've got us locked in tight."

Arms folded across his chest, Jesse nodded with resignation. "And guarded," he added. "Make no mistake. Rusty's out there, and he's got his rifle loaded."

Dakoda winced. At the mention of Rusty and his shotgun, she decided to change the subject. "Would be nice if you could turn into something else," she commented, allowing herself a mordant smile. "Something smaller."

The look on Jesse Clawfoot's face said she was an idiot. "A

cougar's the best I can do, and that's still a tough one for me. I've only just learned how a few years ago." His lips curled. "If it helps, I'd give my eyeteeth to be able to do a cobra and slither on out of here. I'd lay one nasty bite on those fuckers."

She frowned. "I suppose you're lucky you can shift."

Jesse rolled his eyes. "Oh, yeah. I just love being hunted by assholes like the crazy bunch outside. It's bad when the Indian still has to bend over and take it up the ass in this day and age. Destroy our people, take our land, mock our heritage. And what are we left with? Fucking casinos and Kachina dolls."

His words delivered a spiteful kick, rightfully deserved.

Guilt tugged at her conscience. "I'd like to say I understand, but I don't. I have no clue who my people were. I don't even know who my father was. What I do know is your people have a right to survive without fear of being hunted into extinction. As a ranger, that's my job and I want to do it. If I ever get out of here alive, I will see those men brought to justice."

Jesse snorted, his disgust apparent through his chilly, distant gaze. "That's awfully generous of you," he snapped. "But I think we've had enough of paleface justice."

Dakoda felt heat creep into her cheeks. "You might have noticed I'm not so pale," she said slowly. She pointed to her hand. "My skin may be light, but it's still brown." She pointed to her head. "And there's no mistaking this black hair has more than a little kink in it."

He immediately brightened. "I did notice. You're such a pretty shade, like toasted almonds. Your parents must be handsome people."

Great. He'd just compared her to a nut.

She narrowed her eyes, staring him down. The one thing she definitely didn't like to discuss were her parents. Neither of them. "My mother is dead," she said stiffly. "And the only thing I can guess about my father was that he was a dark-skinned man. My mother didn't discriminate when it came to spreading her legs. To her a cock was a cock, no matter the color."

Jesse slowly stood up. "Then you know nothing of your heritage, of your people?" he asked, casting a look that engulfed her from head to toe. Considering he'd been wearing fur earlier, the fact he now wore nothing jarred. Long and lean, his nude body rippled with muscle. Power. Nestled amid a thatch of tight black curls, his penis was impressive even when flaccid.

Dakoda tried not to stare at him as she wiped a layer of sweat off her forehead. She couldn't help it, though. Her body stiffened in instant response as her gaze skimmed every inch. The dim glow from the lantern on the table caressed his burnished skin. Light and shadow danced together, emphasizing his broad shoulders, the ripples of his chest and abdomen and the length of his muscular legs. Obsidian waves shimmered around his face.

Forcing herself to think about anything but how good he looked, she slowly shook her head. "No. Nothing. My mother never said who he was or where he might have come from. I don't even have a name." She inwardly cringed as the words left her mouth. She rarely discussed her parents, yet here she was, spilling her guts. How was it they'd gone from strangers to sharing personal intimacies in such a short amount of time?

Jesse stepped toward her, his face intent. "That must be tough, not knowing who your people are—" He reached out, caressing her cheek with the tips of his fingers. "Or where you belong in this world."

Dakoda's stomach fluttered, her nerves doing a quick little flip. She wanted his hands all over her, wherever there was skin to be caressed.

Something about Jesse attracted her like a magnet. Whether he was conscious of the fact or not, his appeal, his sensuality oozed from every pore. Her pulse fluttered in her throat. She licked dry lips, uncomfortably conscious of her physical reaction to his presence. That same searing primal heat she'd felt earlier in the day, when she'd first spied the cougar. This man had everything she liked in a man; the looks, the build, and the smoking hot body.

Dakoda swallowed over the lump forming in her throat. "It is," she whispered, mesmerized by his touch. "I've always wished I knew . . ." she shook her head. "Something. Anything at all would help."

Taking a deep breath, she couldn't fail to notice the exotic musk of his scent. An image of their bodies locked together in carnal embrace flashed across her mind's screen. As she saw it he was on top, pinning her hands down, conquering her as his hips sank between her spread thighs. Heartbeat taking on a faster rhythm, her teeth clenched. She almost felt his cock—the center of his male power—invading her eager sex with a single hard thrust . . .

Unexpectedly, Jesse bent forward, lips brushing her forehead. "I'll help you find your way," he murmured. She could feel need emanating off his body in waves.

Dakoda pulled back, the nearness of his lips threatening to turn smoldering desire into a full-fledged wildfire. Her skin flushed hot, her clit pulsing. The very power of his presence made her palms slick with sweat. "That's not the way to help me," she breathed, confused by all the undesirable feelings he'd stirred up inside her with just a touch.

Gaze darkening, Jesse stepped back. "Sorry," he started to say. "I went too far."

Nerves more than jangled, Dakoda pressed a hand against her chest. "It's not you," she stammered, trying to make amends. "For a moment I just got a little scared, you know?" Sweating heavily, she fanned her flushed cheeks with a hand. Damn. There was nothing worse than a hot flash brought on by sexual desire. A barefoot walk on the surface of the sun would be cooler.

Jesse sucked in a long breath. "I know what you feel, Dakoda," he said softly. "I want you to know I would never hurt you."

Dakoda squeezed her eyes shut for a moment, not really wanting to think of the implications behind his words. "I can't believe this is happening. It's too unreal to even be believed." She opened her eyes, gazing around the narrow space. "I mean, look at where we are. We're locked up, for God's sake. And—" Her voice wavered. "And I just met you and all I can think about is having sex with you. How freaking fucked up is that?"

He studied her, intrigued. "I don't think it's messed up at all," he said, smiling easily. "Haven't you ever just looked at someone and felt an instant spark of attraction?"

Dakoda tilted her head up to look at him. Her head barely came to the level of his shoulder. Her own willowy five-ten height couldn't even begin to match his. "I feel it," she admitted softly. Every time she looked at him her core began to simmer with yearning. "Too much so. And that scares me more than you could ever know."

Like a magnet, she thought. *It's like I'm being pulled toward him, whether or not I want to go.*

Jesse slid a hand under her chin, tipping back her head. "We won't do anything you don't want to, Dakoda." A deep shudder shook his body. "Though I'll have to admit that's going to be damn hard."

Dakoda didn't answer. The entire day had left a raw wound on her psyche, and she wasn't prepared to deal with anything more complicated than finding a way out. Alive and in one piece would be preferable. Her physical attraction to her fellow prisoner was another obstacle she just couldn't handle at the moment.

A sudden twinge of pressure throbbed behind her eyes. "Let's not make this more complicated than it already is," she finally said, reaching up and rubbing at her aching temples.

Jesse eased back, putting a little distance between their bodies. "I get what you're saying."

Turning away, he snagged one of the blankets off the bunk. "I think this might help." He deftly wrapped it around his waist, tucking it in at the hip so it would stay in place. "Now let's see what we can do about getting out of here."

The distraction temporarily averted, he set to reexamining the chinks in the cell's walls. Unfortunately his conclusion was the same as hers. The space separating the thick logs forming the walls of their cell was less than an inch wide. Not much for ventilation at all. And unless they could both somehow turn into pancakes and slide through the chinks, no chance of getting away, either.

In other words, they were up shit creek without a paddle.

His hands dropped in defeat. "Looks like we're going to be staying in tonight," he observed wryly.

Dakoda's bowels knotted. The unbidden rise of tears blurred her vision. She blinked her eyes hard, sending them away. Damned if she'd cry now. "I don't think I can take much more of this." She wiped her hands over her face, before pressing the heels into her eyes and rubbing hard. Her hands dropped. "There's got to be a way out of this mess."

Jesse made a sound just this side of a snarl, as though the cougar in him wanted to emerge. "I've been thinking about that since I stepped into the trap those assholes sprung on me." He shot her a glance. "I have to admit I was mighty glad to see the rangers coming."

Dakoda took a few quick breaths, fighting to pull herself back together. Having a nervous breakdown just this minute definitely wasn't going to help matters one bit. She needed to stay calm, cool, and collected. She needed to keep her head on straight, and stop sneaking peeks at Jesse Clawfoot's fabulous body. She was supposed to be freeing him, not fucking him.

Though I wouldn't mind the fucking at all.

Dakoda immediately stomped down the thought. Being locked up was distracting enough without having stray fantasies about her fellow captive pop into her head every ten seconds. Looking at him was like putting a shot of straight hundred-proof whiskey on an empty stomach. Intoxicating.

She'd better get a grip on control. Now. Resist the idea of making love to him. It wouldn't be right. Moreover, it wouldn't be professional. She was a ranger, for God's sake. Her job was to protect the endangered species, not molest it.

Dakoda reluctantly cleared her throat. "Unfortunately, the Barnett brothers weren't so happy we showed up." She shook her head. "I honestly thought we had them. All the time we were tracking them, we had no idea they had backup."

Jesse grimaced and rubbed his injured forehead. "Yeah, well, the inbred brothers are sneaky like that. Rusty's always got their back."

Dakoda snickered, glad for a bit of humor to lighten the heavy load they both carried. "Inbred brothers. I like that." She'd believe it, too. "So crazy runs in the family?"

Jesse's hand dropped. "Sure does. These guys know no boundaries, either. If bad is to be done, they will be the ones doing it."

"Such a charming bunch." She frowned. "Is it true we're being sold?"

Jesse sighed "Yes. And I suspect where we'll wind up isn't anyplace good."

Dakoda felt the air drizzle out of her lungs. "Then they know you're more than just a cougar—what you can do?"

Jesse swallowed hard, then answered. "Unfortunately, they do," he spat out bitterly. "The poachers sell us to collectors, people who want unusual animals for private zoos." His mouth turned down. "Or to those who want animalistic lovers." He laughed shortly, but with little amusement. "I guess one thing we can be grateful for is they don't kill us off for our pelts, teeth, and claws. Those poor damn bears don't have a chance."

Dakoda just stared at him, trying to fathom the reality behind his words. It didn't take a rocket scientist to know uncommon objects were valuable on the black market, all highly prized by collectors. People made treks all over the world in pursuit of objects their hearts desired. Were willing to do anything, spend any amount, to make the dream of owning the rare prize a reality.

Imagine wanting a person who could shift into an animal. What an exceptional trophy that would be. To possess something so unique would be like having the keys to evolution itself . . .

A human being who could shift into an animal's form. Live as an animal. Breathe as an animal. Be an animal.

What an extraordinary gift.

Dakoda's pulse raced with each jarring beat of her heart. "These men have to be stopped. What they're doing is wrong on every level."

Jesse Clawfoot speared her with a narrow look. "I'd have to agree on every level," he said wryly. "Except we've got one problem: we're the prisoners, not the other way around."

Dakoda tossed up her hands in exasperation. "But there has to be a way out of this mess for both of us. As long as we're breathing, we're alive. And as long as we're alive, there's hope."

Jesse took a step toward the wall and closed his eyes. "I'm afraid hope is wearing pretty thin for my kind." He rubbed a hand against his forehead. "Our tribe numbers less than seventy. Those who remember the old ways are dying off. Add in the fact that more than a few tribe members have just vanished." He snapped his fingers. "Just like that, they're gone."

Dakoda felt a tug around her heartstrings. "Captured and sold off, no doubt."

Hand dropping, Jesse nodded. "It's a given we males have to roam far and wide to establish our own territory and find mates. That's why I was off the reservation. Through the last few months I could have sworn I'd scented a female."

Dakoda felt her pulse quicken. "You mean one of your race?"

Jesse nodded. "Yes. I'd just gotten a fresh track on her when I stepped into a trap." He lifted a hand, showing the deep rope burn around his wrist. "At least it wasn't one of those claw-tooth traps. I'd have lost my hand for sure."

"That means you lost her, I suppose."

Jesse angled his head, sending a spill of black hair down his shoulders. His hair brushed the tips of his flat male nipples. Dakoda couldn't help but wonder how those tips would taste under her circling tongue.

Suddenly unable to look at her, he glanced away. "No, I'm pretty sure she's still nearby." The tension was thickened between them. He seemed to want to say more, but was holding himself back.

A funny sensation began at the nape of Dakoda's neck. Every time she took a breath, the musk emanating from Jesse Clawfoot's skin teased her. That in turn caused familiar warmth to pool between her thighs, making the crotch of her cotton panties uncomfortably sticky.

More images flashed across her mind's screen as she imagined the raw, sensual pleasure she'd feel when he sank his cock into her eager sex. From the moment she'd laid eyes on him in his human form, the notion of having sex with him had popped into her head more than once.

Thinking about it is one thing, she warned herself. *Doing it is another.*

As though able to discern her every carnal notion, Jesse slowly lifted his head. "And she's definitely in heat," he added softly.

Heat. To become excited emotionally or physically.

That definitely described her state of mind.

Unaccountably thirsty, Dakoda picked up one of the bottles of water off the table. Cracking it open, she took a deep swallow of the tepid liquid. She had a feeling she knew where this was going. "I hope you're not going to say what I think you are," she half croaked.

Jesse's black gaze homed in on hers. "You're one of the Tlvdatsi, Dakoda," he breathed out in sudden confession. "You're the female I've been tracking."

6

Shock pulsed through Dakoda, a dismay so sharp she had to fight the nausea rising from her gut. She gulped. "Surely, you're joking." She shook her head adamantly, feeling nothing but the cold refusal to believe. Suddenly a new twist had been tossed into the equation, adding an entirely new level to their captivity.

She shook her head, unwilling to accept. "That doesn't even make any sense," she countered. "How can you even say I'm one of your kind?"

"Unfortunately, I do know."

Dakoda folded her arms protectively across her chest, as if the move could somehow shield her from the truth. "How?" she demanded.

Jesse gave a quick, rueful smile, tapping his nose with a single finger. "There's a scent, a pheromone, which a female gives off. Most people don't notice it, as it takes a keen sense of smell to recognize."

"I have an odor?" Dakoda pulled a face. "Oh, yuck. How disgusting." She lifted one arm, giving her pit a quick sniff. Oh, yeah, she stank. No doubt about it. A groan filtered past her lips.

Something akin to amusement crossed his face, lighting up his chiseled features. "It's a good odor," Jesse said, hastening to reassure her. "And it's practically the only way we have of recognizing a true Tlvdatsi female."

Dakoda threw up her hands in disbelief. Frustration boiled through her. "But that's just what I've been telling you. I don't know what my heritage is. I don't even know my father's name, much less where he came from."

Jesse sighed. "I don't have to guess, Dakoda. One of your parents has some Cherokee blood and is a descendant of the Tlvdatsi clan. Though I'm not really sure how to explain it, people with our bloodline seem to carry some sort of recessive gene that's been passed down through generations. Most of us live our entire lives not knowing we carry it. It's why those who know how to shift are almost extinct."

"But I'm not a shifter," she protested. "I've never had the urge to turn into a cougar and prowl."

A soft laugh escaped him. "None of us did, Dakoda. When I found out, I thought there was no freaking way on earth that was possible. I may be an Indian, but I wasn't born on the damn reservation or raised in the—" He raised his hands, fingers making quote marks in the air. "—old ways of our people."

Dakoda swallowed, remembering the icy prickle she'd felt when she'd first witnessed Jesse shift from cougar to human. "How did you find out?"

Jesse hesitated a beat, then said, "One of the elders of the Tlvdatsi clan tracked me down. Here I am be-bopping along, doing my thing in college, and some ancient shaman shows up telling me it's time to return to our homeland and reestablish our connection with our ancestors." He was suddenly restless, pacing the small cell. His muscular legs seemed way too damn long for the small space. With each step he took, the blanket around his narrow hips shifted lower. "And then he springs the whole cougar thing on me . . . I'm thinking for sure the old man's been hitting the pipe a little hard, if you know what I mean."

Watching the blanket creep ever lower, Dakoda felt a tremor of yearning down low in her core. A little bit more of their grim reality faded, and she was grateful for the distraction.

Clearing her throat, she cocked a brow toward his waist. "Ah, Jesse, if you don't get a grab on that, you'll be losing your cover."

A grin split his lips as he shot her a suggestive smile. "Anything I got that you would like to see?" he hinted.

Her pulse raced all over again at the pull of his sheer male power, drawing her like a physical force. "I've seen it already," she deadpanned.

"And?"

Dakoda licked dry lips. She'd like to see it again, in an up-close-and-personal way. His presence was making her body ache. He smelled of heat and musk and yet a third unique odor she couldn't quite place, one that insisted on teasing her with its mystery. *Pheromones.* The scent of a male.

She trembled, muscles clenching deep inside at the thought of skin pressed against naked skin. *Not now,* she warned herself.

"And what else did he tell you?" she countered, reluctant to drag her mind away from lustier pursuits.

Jesse huffed, tucking the blanket tighter. "He didn't tell me anything. He showed me. *The shift.*" Eyebrows drawing together in a perplexed furrow, he shook his head. "That was when I considered the weed I'd been smoking must be dusted with some serious hallucinogens."

She frowned. "You're joking, I hope."

He raked his hands through his long hair, skimming the

thick strands away from his face. "About the pot. Yeah. About the old man shifting. No. All I can say is that I became a believer that day."

Dakoda tried to envision herself shifting. She couldn't. It seemed too damn incredible to even imagine. Seeing Jesse manage the feat still hadn't made a believer out of her. There was still the possibility she'd lost her mind, and just hadn't figured it out yet. "I guess anyone would," she allowed.

Jesse gave a slow, wry smile. "He also told me it was time for the gathering, for the Tlvdatsi to return to the mountains and learn the old ways before they died out. Of the seven clans of Cherokees, ours is the last that remembers how to shift."

"So you moved to the mountains?" she asked.

He nodded. "Since I was flunking accounting, I went ahead and dropped out." A scoffing sound escaped him. "Ah, what Indian wants to wear the white man's costumes and count his money all day, anyway?"

Dakoda nibbled her lower lip in thought. "Must have been hard, leaving one life behind for another."

He looked at her a long moment, then shrugged. "Not so hard, really. For the last couple of years we've been working to reestablish the clan and become recognized by the federal government as a legitimate sanctuary for the cougars."

Dakoda smiled. "A whole new line of work."

Jesse rolled his eyes. "A tough one, too. Proving the cougar is no longer extinct in these mountains hasn't been the most difficult obstacle. Keeping the secret that we are the cougars has proven a little more difficult."

She folded her arms across her body. "I guess that's hard to do when outsiders know your secrets."

Jesse snorted. "Tell me about it. Trying to adapt to living in the wild is tough enough without having poachers on your tail, and I do mean that literally." His expression turned tight and grim. "You have to remember, their people have been in these mountains a long time, too, and they're part of the reason we were hunted to the point of extinction. Leaving our homeland was the only way to survive."

Feeling the chill behind his words, Dakoda rubbed her hands up and down her arms. "Now coming back is the only way to survive."

Jesse cast a look around the small cell before scrubbing both hands over his face. Sweat beaded his dark skin, giving it a shiny, sexy gleam. "I'm afraid we won't be surviving long under these conditions."

Dakoda knew she didn't look half as sexy. The moment humidity struck, her hair turned all frizzy and her skin all greasy.

She wiped the sweat from her forehead with the back of her hand. Though the night outside was cool, the air inside the cramped cell was sultry. Her heavy uniform clung to her skin, perspiration patches pooling under her arms and breasts. "I'm sorry we weren't more help, Jesse. Once the reports of cougar sightings were confirmed, we redoubled our efforts to catch poachers."

His hands dropped, dangling uselessly at his sides. "I know." He exhaled, a long breath. "It's frustrating, though. We're all trying to adapt to a new world and there's all these obstacles to jump. Sometimes I wish I'd never learned about our gift. I think I could have lived the rest of my life without knowing the truth."

Dakoda sensed the gnawing of desperate frustration behind his demeanor. The more she learned about the Tlvdatsi, the more she wanted to know. Even if his speculation had no grain of truth, he'd still given her something she'd never had before. Hope.

Always a bastard child with no roots and no heritage, Dakoda had never really felt she belonged anywhere. She had no family who wanted to claim her, call her their own. All of a sudden, Jesse Clawfoot had revealed she might have a family, a legitimate heritage. The father she'd never known might have bestowed a most valuable gift on her—a gift she didn't intend to let slip through her fingers.

"I think everyone should know who they are, where they come from, Jesse." She lifted a hand, pressing it against her chest. "When you don't know those things it feels like little pieces of you are missing inside, like they've been sliced away. You know who you are, where you come from, and now you know where you're going in life." Her vision was blurring; her throat tightened, thickening her words. "Anyone who doesn't know would envy that. I know I do."

Jesse stepped toward her, his face intent. "I can see the pain in your eyes. Not knowing your origins has hurt you deeply, Dakoda." Warm hands cupped her face. "I want to help you find your way, help you find where you belong."

Feeling his touch against her needy skin, Dakoda felt oddly comforted. Though his hands were roughened from the hard work of trying to survive in the mountains, his caress was gentle.

She opened her eyes. Her gaze searched his. "You're not just saying that, are you? Please, don't feel sorry for me because I'm a bastard."

Jesse shook his head, his lips just inches away from hers. "I have no reason to lie to you or to deceive you. I only know what my senses are telling me. You do carry the scent of a Tlv-datsi female."

Without really knowing why, Dakoda stepped into his arms, pressing against the hard planes of his chest. "I wish I could believe that. Desperation can do such strange things to a person's mind. If you told me you could fly, I think I'd believe it." She meant the move to be innocent, one human taking comfort from another, but something about the stiffening in his frame said he read something entirely different into it.

His fingers slid into her hair, tugging her head back. His face moved closer to hers. His gaze collided with hers, simmering with predatory heat. "I *am* desperate, Dakoda," he murmured. "Whether or not you believe me doesn't matter at all. I'm trying to make a connection we can hold on to, something positive for both of us to focus on. If we hang on to each other, we might be able to survive."

There was no way she could answer. The events of the day were still raw wounds etched deeply into her mind and on her heart. His offering was more than a balm, it was a promise things had the potential to get better. His presence, his pledge, offered a sense of peace.

Hope she willingly took and held on to.

Before she could form a coherent answer, Jesse's mouth covered hers. His kiss wasn't the ravenous assault of a desperate soul, but a soft tentative pressure. His tongue brushed the seam of her lips, seeking invitation.

Blood racing at the pull of his sex toward hers, Dakoda willingly opened. Something about Jesse drew her like a magnetic force, as if she could draw from his strength and shift into a cougar right then and there. A honeyed warmth pushed against her fear and fatigue, renewing her reserves of determination and strength.

"Promise me you won't leave me," she murmured against the pressure of his mouth.

For an answer, Jesse's hands slipped lower, traveling down her sides. Big warm palms came to rest on her hips. He pulled her body closer to his. With the shift between them, the blanket around his hips dropped to the floor around his feet. The strong length of his torso pressed against her. His throbbing shaft nestled between them. "I won't leave you, Dakoda," he promised.

Feeling the pressure, Dakoda pulled back a little. She glanced down, eyeing his erection with appreciation. "That thing doesn't give up," she giggled.

A shudder ran though him. "Not when there's a sexy woman in my arms."

"Sexy," she breathed. "You think I'm sexy?"

His grin widened. "Hell, yeah."

"And you're not just saying that because I'm the only woman around?" she teased.

Jesse pulled her back into his arms. "I think I'd better let my body do the talking." He kissed her again, his mouth easily conquering hers.

Allowing him full access to plunder and pillage, Dakoda felt the fine tremble beneath his skin, the quivering sensation filling his entire body as he tried to hold back the full force of his intense passion. A man's mouth might lie, spinning some good tales to get into a girl's pants. But his body definitely could not. A bond, a real connection, was forming between them. One going far past the physical, into territory Dakoda had never dared to explore with any man before. For the first time in her life she wanted to find out what it would be like to give herself to a man in every way.

She wanted to belong.

Catching her lower lip between his teeth, Jesse slid one hand up her torso, palm closing over her left breast. Though covered by her clothing, she felt the caress sear all the way through the material. Her nipple instantly came to life, tightening into a hard little peak. God, she was desperate. It had been too damned long since she'd had sex. As though dulled by all lack of sensation, her senses were slowly awakening, blossoming to brilliant life. Her pulse banged in her throat, echoing the need pulsing in her core.

With a moan, Dakoda eased back. "Whoa," she breathed. "I didn't see this one coming."

A low chuckle escaped him. "I think you did."

Hand leaving her breast, Jesse's fingers fumbled at the front of her uniform jacket, working open the buttons. About half-way down, he paused, giving her a look as if to ask permission.

A wicked gleam danced in the depths of his dark gaze. "May I continue?"

Dakoda's heart tripped against her ribcage. "Don't stop now." Slowly, she drew in a breath, a tremor of yearning passing through her. She needed this glorious man as much as she needed the air in her lungs. On the trail of the female he desired, he'd stalked her down, relentless in his pursuit of what he wanted, what he needed.

I need it, too, she thought. Something else to concentrate on that would offer a brief solace from the tragedy and tension suddenly consuming her life. For the moment they were simply two people who needed each other.

Desperately.

7

Hands trembling, Jesse fumbled his way through the remaining buttons. He slid the jacket off her shoulders, tugging it down her arms. "Man, they sure do put you rangers in a lot of clothing."

Dakoda laughed and reached for her shirt. "They want us looking sharp, even when we're out in the middle of freaking nowhere." She quickly peeled off the layer of clothing, leaving only her plain white bra on. Fancy lingerie was never her style. She preferred to keep her wardrobe simple. "God, I was sure I was going to burn to a crisp in this thing. Khaki or not, it sure isn't comfortable in the heat."

Smiling, Jesse gave a low whistle. "Nice." Using the tips of his fingers, he outlined the cups snugly hugging her breasts.

Dakoda glanced down and frowned. "Sorry there's not much there. I barely made a 32A."

Jesse eyed her breasts. "More than a mouthful is a waste." His hands skimmed down her flat belly, reaching for the top button of her stained khaki slacks. He snapped it open. "Truth be told, I'm a leg man. I like long, silky legs." Her zipper crunched down, the grate of metal filling the small cell with an explosive, erotic weight. He began to slip her slacks down her hips.

Dakoda giggled. "I think the boots have to come off before those do."

Jesse looked down at her boots. He sucked in a breath. "Oh. Guess so." Pulling out a chair from the nearby table, he guided her toward it. "I think I can handle those."

Dakoda sat, sticking out a leg. "Here you go."

Jesse knelt with all the grace of the feline inside him. Pushing up the cuff of her pants, he untied the laces of her heavy hiking boots. "Man, these things must weigh a ton." He tugged the boot off and set it aside.

Dakoda sighed gratefully, wiggling her toes in relief. "My feet were beginning to feel like lead weights."

Jesse stripped off her white sock, tucking it inside the boot. He began to work the top of her foot, massaging each of her toes. "Feel better?" Moving from toe to ankle, he continued stroking the sole of her foot, first gently, then with increased pressure.

As she tilted her head back, a low moan broke from her throat. "Oh, my God. I think I've just died and gone to heaven." His strong fingers felt good, filling her with a sense of well-being. Her aching muscles relaxed, a little of the pain draining away as the tension deep inside her gut slowly began to unravel. It was amazing how the simple touch of another human being could calm and soothe.

Jesse slipped off her other boot, repeating the sensual massage. Making circular motions with his thumb and fingers over the sole of her foot, he applied more pressure as he worked every sensitive inch. The man knew his business when it came to touching a woman's body. "I want to take things slow," he said, glancing up at her. "I want to make sure you have what you need."

Shivers rippling pleasantly across her skin, Dakoda swallowed thickly. Every time his strong fingers caressed the sensitive soles of her foot, she felt the pull all the way to her groin. Burgeoning warmth spread through her. The trickle of desire between her thighs wet the crotch of her panties in the most enticing way. Lust trampled through her, drowning out everything but the enticing man willing to serve her every need. "I–I want to take everything you have to give, Jesse," she stammered.

Once you cross that line, you'll never be able to go back, whispered the small voice of sanity in the back of her mind.

Dakoda didn't care. She had nothing to go back to. No family waited for her to be found and rescued. If she dropped off the face of the earth, never to be seen again, absolutely no one would mourn her passing. In the few brief hours she'd spent with Jesse, she'd found a heritage, a bloodline leading her into a world she could neither dream of nor ever imagine.

Her desire for him surged through her like a hurricane making landfall. Finding Jesse was akin to being lost in the desert and seeing a drink of water in sight. He offered more than a cool oasis of salvation, but an awakening that would take her beyond the physical and into the spiritual. Even though they were in captivity, the world before her was wide and open, as if she'd been blind all her life, and then suddenly given the gift of sight.

She could see what she wanted, clearly and without doubt.

Jesse guided her to her feet. He sat back on his heels, helping slip her pants over the curve of her thighs. An eager tug guided them down her legs.

Touching his shoulder for balance, Dakoda stepped out of the tangled pile. Her pants joined her shirt in the pile on the floor.

Rising to his knees in front of her, Jesse placed his palm on her flat belly. Caressing the line above her panties, he leaned in, pressing his lips against her tingling skin. Nibbling at the softness, he gently eased his fingers into the elastic. A soft tug brought her panties down around her thighs.

He raised his brows in pleased surprise. "Oh, I like a Brazilian wax." His breathing grew uneven, a little labored. "Very ni-iicccee. . . ." He quickly leaned forward. A hot male tongue eagerly probed the folds of her sex.

Dakoda shuddered, then moaned softly. "Oh, my," she breathed, mouth all of a sudden cotton dry. "Surely you're not . . ." Her nipples peaked beneath the cups of her bra. Her limbs felt pleasantly heavy, as though she were mired in a pool of molasses.

Jesse pulled back enough to glance up at her. "Going down on you?" A feral grin split his lips. "Oh, yes, I intend to. Your smell has been driving me wild, and I intend to indulge myself—" He dipped his tongue into her navel, swirling around the shallow depth. "Liberally."

Before she quite knew what was happening, Jesse stood up. Bending, he scooped her into his arms. Giving her a quick heft, he spread her across the table. Stepping back, he eyed her like she was the most delectable of morsels. "Now there's the meal I've been hungry for. I like my meat on the bone."

Not quite sure how she'd landed on the top of the table, Dakoda shivered. She propped herself up on her elbows. "Isn't that from some rock song?"

"Yeah." Jesse dragged her panties down her legs, then flicked them aside. "Alice Cooper. Man, I love that song." As he parted her thighs, a low rumble broke from his throat. His muscles were bunched with tension. His cock arched against his cobbled abdomen in eager anticipation. "Almost as much as I love eating pussy."

Dakoda sucked in a breath as Jesse's head dipped low. A long pass of his tongue between her dewed, swollen labia tore a gasp from her lips. "Oh . . . heavens!"

Jesse lifted his head briefly. "Heaven ain't got nothing to do with this." Disappearing again, his tongue danced around her swollen clit, working the small hooded organ with an expert's touch.

The buzz of climax growing at the base of her spine took her by surprise. Dakoda choked out a strangled laugh. "Keep touching me like that and I'll come."

Jesse peered over the length of her almost naked body. "Oh, I intend to keep doing this until you do." Following up with his threat, he added his fingers to the foreplay. Pressing two fingers together, he delved into her slowly. "Oh, man. It's been a long time since I've felt heat like that."

Eyes slipping shut, Dakoda moaned softly. "It's been a long time since I've let anybody feel the heat."

Thumb working her clit, Jesse's thick fingers stroked in and out of her sex.

The pressure building at the base of Dakoda's spine climbed higher. She shuddered. Tight inner muscles throbbed around his thick fingers. Her core literally ached for release. Pressing against the table, her spine was as rigid as an iron bar. The tingling sensation sped upward, causing the fine hairs on the back of her neck to rise. The first pulse of climax hit her like a punch to the solar plexus.

Throwing back her head, Dakoda didn't try to mask her cry of pleasure as she came. Fingers digging into the rough tabletop, she opened herself up to the glittering sensations spreading across her skin like the silken threads of a gossamer web.

The sensations slipped through her fingers almost too quickly to be enjoyed.

Limp and breathless in the aftermath, Dakoda swiped her tongue across papery lips. "Oh God," she breathed. "That was—" Breasts rising and falling, her words trailed off into satisfied silence.

Jesse's hand slipped away, leaving a curiously cold spot in its wake. Switching his position, he eased down over her. The table was the perfect height to allow him easy access. The heat between her legs suddenly returned, hotter than ever. His cock pulsed between their bodies, snuggling comfortably on the nest of her belly. One stab of his hips would fill her completely.

Soft fingertips traced the line of her jaw, then her neck, passing over the hollow of her throat. "I'm not even close to finished," he warned before tossing her a lusty smile of anticipation.

Hands lifting to his broad shoulders, Dakoda grinned. She wiggled her hips against the thick erection pressing into her stomach. "I would hope not," she breathed, barely suppressing a soft groan.

Jesse's breath stalled momentarily before he regained control. "Not yet," he tsked. "I still haven't gotten to these beauties." He dragged down the plain white cups covering her breasts. Her nipples peaked, a darker, duskier shade of pink. "Don't want them to feel neglected."

Bending low, Jesse sucked one soft nub into his mouth. His tongue caressed the aching tip even as his fingers invaded her most private places.

A waterfall of glimmering sensations slid across her nerves with each suck against her taut nipple, intensified tenfold by the weight of his erection nestled against her belly. Dakoda shuddered, swamped by the sensations rushing through her body like a locomotive gone haywire. Her sex grew slicker and wetter with every glide of his fingers. The scrape of his teeth against her sensitive nipple only added to the insanity.

But it wasn't enough. She needed—no, craved—a more intimate physical connection. Hip to hip and mouth to mouth was the only way they could fully come together.

Hands sliding into his long, silky hair, she tugged him away from her breasts. "More," she grated, desperate for him to take her deeper, harder.

Jesse's dark gaze found hers, lust burning in the depths of his obsidian eyes. "Are you sure?" he grated. "I can stop . . ."

Dakoda shook her head. No stopping now. Not when she needed completion so damn much. "I need everything," she breathed.

Jesse nodded. Catching her behind the knees, he lifted her legs and spread her wide. Springing from its nest of thick curls, his cock arched up against the ridges of his abdomen. Thick veins twined around its length. Glistening droplets of pre-cum seeped from its flared crown.

Dakoda's breath caught in her throat as he angled his hips toward hers. His cock pressed against the opening of her sex, gliding through her labia. She knew he was deliberately making her wait, torturing her with a long, slow entry, rather than one jarring thrust.

Hands bracing her weight, Dakoda arched against the table. "Now, Jesse . . . Please . . ." Strong inner muscles clenched deep inside her core.

Jesse slowly eased inside her. "I want to take it slow," he grated between gritted teeth. "Enjoy the feel of being inside you." Silk-encased steel easily penetrated her creamy depth.

Suppressing a happy whimper, Dakoda wiggled her ass. She was definitely getting more then she'd bargained for. "Oh, I feel you, all right. Every. Last. Damn. Inch."

Seated to the hilt, Jesse bent over and braced his hands on either side of her body to support his weight. Corded biceps bulged with power. He ground his hips into hers. No doubt about the strength in his powerful body.

A low male growl of sensual need rumbled up from his chest. "I want to look in your eyes." The tone of his voice was strangely husky, strained. "And watch you come." His thick penis slid out of her silken depths, only to pump inside again seconds later.

Dakoda wound her arms around him, spreading her palms across the concrete-hard slab of his back. Her legs circled his waist as his hips jarred against hers. She bent her fingers just a little, giving him a taste of pain when she pressed her nails across his exposed skin.

The rasp of a groan broke through his lips. "Oh, someone's showing her claws." His hips slapped harder against hers, delivering one punishing stroke, then another.

Dakoda sucked in a breath, taking in his musky scent. There was something untamed, almost primal, in the smell emanating from his deeply tanned skin. As she searched far into his eyes, his face seemed to blur, briefly taking on the features of the cougar lurking inside his soul. His eyes were aflame with the feral lust of a male intent on conquering his female.

Lifting her head, she sought his mouth, savoring the taste of his wild, raw flavor.

Jesse's lips crushed against hers with voracious intensity, his tongue stabbing deep even as his hips pummeled hers without mercy. Again and again he struck, driving his cock into her ravenous sex.

Shuddering with pure delight, Dakoda instinctively arched under him in an effort to take him even deeper than before. His powerful, ramming strokes seemed to reach all the way to her throat. The sensation of being taken so completely, in such a primitive way, damn near caused her to come right then and there.

Dakoda held on, determined to make the sensations last just a little bit longer. Jesse was riding her hard, as if the hounds of hell were snapping at his ass. Hips moving like a jackhammer, he stroked in and out of her creamy sex. Mercury rising into the red, the danger zone was fast approaching. Heat burrowed at the base of her spine.

Her orgasm came blasting in from nowhere, detonating through her veins with blazing delight. Dakoda screamed as the first explosion rocked her senses, speeding through her body like a rocket gone rogue. Sensation coalesced, an internal pressure cooker charged with erotic energy.

Dakoda felt pleasure roaring in, rising up from her core like a volcano barreling toward eruption. Her senses sprang open, welcoming the deluge of unrelenting bliss. Wave after savage wave of sensation pummeled her senses, lifting her up toward the heavens, then dashing her down again at top speed.

Jesse delivered one last punishing thrust. His body stiffened, and a growl broke from deep in his throat as he climaxed. A hot spurt of semen filled her depths. He collapsed on top of her, adding his sweat-soaked weight to hers. The picnic table beneath their bodies shifted, creaking with annoyance. Fortunately all four legs held firm.

A series of delicious aftershocks resonated through Dakoda, the sensations almost too much to bear. A brief wave of dizziness made her glad to be lying down. Heart beating a drumlike thud in her chest, her skin felt tight, as if too small to fully fit over her bones. Were she to try to stand, she'd collapse like a puppet without strings.

8

A few minutes later, Jesse lifted himself off Dakoda. He panted lightly, body still trembling from the delicious climax they'd just shared. Beads of perspiration coated his skin, lending his flesh a gleaming shimmer in the lamplight. "Damn," he breathed. "That was awesome." His ravenous gaze skimmed her nude body with appreciation. Despite the intense climax they'd just experienced, he wanted more. Once clearly wasn't enough.

Shivering from the abrupt change from warm to cold, Dakoda folded her arms across her bare chest. It was hard to keep her eyes off him. Composed of hard ridges and harder muscle, his body was the epitome of male perfection. Even with the scars marring his bronzed skin, he was glorious to look at.

She nodded. "Very intense." Heart beating in her chest, she kept her words light, easy. The one thing she'd never mastered after sex was the small talk. This was usually the part where she'd begin the motions to slip out the door and head home. Like her mother, she'd never formed permanent attachments to her lovers. It was always easier to get up and go, keep things light and easy on the emotions.

She already knew Jesse was going to be different. Since she'd laid eyes on him, she'd suspected he was something rare. Special. Finding a man she wanted to be with, to embrace on every level, was an entirely new experience. It was also a frightening experience.

If you don't hold on now, she warned herself, *you might never get a chance like this again.*

There was one problem, though. Dakoda didn't know how to do the love thing. Lust, sure. That was simple. Uncomplicated. Easy to walk away from. Love was an entirely different concept. It implied myriad emotions. Emotions she'd purposely walled up and guarded like Fort Knox. Tearing down her inner wall wasn't going to be easy.

But she wanted to try.

Desperately.

Sitting up, Dakoda scooted to the edge of the table, letting her legs dangle over the edge. She felt a little awkward, far more exposed than ever before.

Sensing her unease, Jesse's hands settled on her knees. He gently spread her legs apart, then stepped into the space. Warm palms cupped her face, dipping her head back. Reflected in the lamp's dim illumination, his black eyes looked endlessly deep. The hateful collar still circled his neck, an ever-present reminder of their captivity. "Something's wrong," he murmured. "I can see it on your face."

Fingers circling his thick wrists, Dakoda slowly drew his hands down. "I was just thinking this can't be happening. It seems so surreal that I'm here, with you. We just had sex and . . ." Words trailing off into silence, she shook her head.

Jesse reached out, caressing her mouth with the tips of his fingers. "And it's too much, too fast."

Dakoda hesitated a moment, then nodded. "I've never been good at hanging around long, if you know what I mean," she confessed. "The only thing I've ever been good at is cutting and running off when things get too heavy."

Jesse brushed his fingers over the curve of her lower lip, then her chin. "It's okay to get scared when you're in situations that make you uncomfortable. If it helps, I'm not exactly feeling at home here myself."

Dakoda shook hear head. "This place is bad enough," she allowed. "But what I'm talking now is you, Jesse. When it comes to getting involved with a guy, well . . . I haven't got a very good track record of making relationships last."

His gaze probed hers, darkening subtly. "Are you trying to tell me I'm someone you're—" His throat tightened, briefly cutting off his words. "Someone you're not interested in?" He stepped back, abandoning the intimacy he'd been attempting to nurture between them.

Unable to look him in the eyes, Dakoda dropped her gaze. Looking anywhere but at him was much easier.

I'm an idiot, she thought. Without intending to, she'd already begun to push him away when, in reality, she was trying to let him in.

A lump formed in Dakoda's throat. She forced herself to swallow. "I—I'm not saying the right things," she stammered.

Folding his arms across his chest, Jesse gave her a skeptical look. "They must be right or you wouldn't be saying them," he countered.

Head lifting, Dakoda frowned. "You have to understand how sudden this is for me." Her hand settled on her chest. She felt the dull thud of her heart beneath her rib cage. "When my day began, I had no idea someone like you would come tearing into my life. My God, Jesse. You just rolled over me like a bulldozer, telling me so many wild and wonderful things."

Jesse arched a single thick brow. "And that's so terrible how?" Sarcasm iced his question. There was something else, though, something going deeper than scorn. Dismay also tinged his words, laced with the subtle hint of pain.

Dakoda grimaced, cut by the tone of his voice. A bitter sense of desolation washed through her. "I didn't say it was terrible." The rise of hot tears blurred her vision. She blinked them back, refusing to let a single one fall. "It's just that people under duress tend to form deep, emotional bonds very quickly. How can we be sure what we're feeling is real and not just something we conjured up because we're so desperate to make a connection before we die?"

Jesse clenched his fists. "What we just did felt pretty real to me," he said hotly. The abrupt ferocity in his voice stung painfully. "But I get the idea you're not on the same page."

Dakoda's guts knotted, tight and painful. "What we had was sex," she said bleakly. "This is . . . different." *Way different.*

Frustration boiling to a dangerous level, he stared back at her. "How so?" he demanded.

Talk about putting her foot straight into her mouth. The taste of shoe leather was awful. Instead of making things better, she was steadily making them worse. She needed to slow down. Think.

Dakoda struggled to find the right words, say the right things. "It's just that falling in love is something I've never done before." She raised her gaze, looking him straight in the eyes. "I want to be sure it's right, damn it. I want to be sure it's real." The last few words sped out of her mouth, forced out by desperation.

Jesse Clawfoot looked thunderstruck. "You said you love me?" he repeated dumbly.

A small smile crept across Dakoda's lips. His words held the eagerness of a puppy locked in a pound cage, waiting and hoping the door would open.

Something clenched under her rib cage, a throbbing, forlorn ache. "I didn't quite say I loved you, Jesse." Sweat beaded her bare skin. Now she was shaking. "What I am saying is the potential is there, and it's scaring the living shit out of me."

A brilliant grin split his lips. "Potential is good," he agreed, nodding his head. "I can go with potential." He swiped his hands across his face, brushing back long strands of hair.

Dakoda closed her eyes a moment. Her own hands rose, fingers pressing to her temples. The postsex climax was threatening to turn into a pre-regrets headache.

All through her life, relationships were something she'd deliberately tiptoed around, flirting with, but never committing to. Commitment meant staying in one place, building a life around one person. In her world, that was an alien concept, almost as unnatural as pigs growing wings.

However, running off when things got serious was tiring. So was always holding people at arm's length, never letting any man get close enough to find out more than her name and address. Sleeping over? She'd never done it. Shacking up? Pffttt! She needed her space, the freedom to do whatever she wanted, whenever she wanted. With no consequences.

Just like her mother.

Except her mother's actions had consequences. Terrible ones, etched deeply into Dakoda's psyche.

Feeling emotionally hollow, Dakoda rubbed her temples harder. *Keep running and one of these days I'll be old and alone,* she reminded herself.

Jesse's big hands suddenly covered hers. Guiding her hands down in her lap, he pressed his fingers to the pressure points she'd massaged. Soft, slow circles ensued. "Potential is supposed to be a good thing," he murmured. "Not give you headaches." His touch was familiar, soothing. At least he recognized her need for comfort.

Dakoda's stomach knotted. The feel of his fingers pressed against her temples was comforting. A fleeting, half-conscious image of him picking her up and laying her on the table flashed across her mind's screen.

She released a pent-up breath. "It is good, because I want this to happen."

"At least I've got a chance," he said. "For a minute I thought you were going to tell me the sex sucked."

Feeling suddenly exposed, Dakoda crossed her hands over her breasts. A little shudder of delight passed through her as an image popped into her head. "Sucked isn't the word I'd use to describe it."

Jesse's fingers curled into her hair, tilting back her head. "So what word might be more appropriate?" Strong gentle hands stroked down her neck, over her shoulders, and down her back.

Dakoda's clenched muscles trembled, unexpectedly eager for release all over again.

She dipped her head back. Her lips hovered just inches from his. "Um, one time isn't really enough to base a sound judgment on. In my opinion, it takes a lot more than one orgasm to decide on what the right word would be. I could guess, but why do that when I could find out for sure?"

Jesse grinned. "Sounds like it's back to the old drawing board." Bridging the tiny space between them, he took her mouth with his. She felt his tongue probe the seam of her lips, seeking entry. She opened a little, granting access. His tongue swept in, heating up things deep inside her groin all over again.

Dakoda's senses spun, dizzied by the pull of his sheer maleness. It drew her like a physical force, a shield surrounding her on all sides with reassurance and comfort. It seemed to say as long as she was with him, she'd be safe. Cherished.

Sweet tension began to push away her fear and fatigue, morphing into something far more delicious—and demanding. There was no telling how much more time they had together. Each minute ticking away never to be recovered, more precious and rare than any jewel. Whatever time they had together—even if only an hour more—she wanted it.

Slipping her arms around Jesse, Dakoda explored the hard ridges of his back. She deliberately slid her hands lower, enjoying the feel of her palms over the round curves of his perfectly shaped ass. Rock hard and beautifully sculpted, it was a pleasure to look at and explore.

Jesse's hands settled at her hips, dragging her closer. She felt the subtle motion of his whole being with each movement of his body. He repositioned his hips between her spread thighs. His cock pulsed, eager and ready.

Dakoda felt heat coiling through her core, rising at the thought of his deep, penetrating thrusts into her hungry sex. Liquid warmth spread through her veins.

Without a word, Jesse scooped her off the table. Dakoda wrapped her legs around his waist as he carried her to the narrow bunk. He laid her down on the flannel blankets spread across its narrow surface, then stretched out beside her.

Easing himself up on one elbow, he stroked her hair away from her face. "Not over there," he murmured. "That was just sex. This time I want to make love." He hesitated, throat tightening. "I want to show you I've got more than potential," he finished in a rough voice.

Slipping one hand under his body, Dakoda shifted onto her side. His straining erection pressed against her stomach like a branding iron. Shadows caressed his features, softening the deep black shade of his eyes.

She pressed a single finger across his lips. "Don't make any promises, please. There's no telling what's going to happen to us once the sun comes up. Let's just enjoy the time we've got, whether it's a few hours or a few days."

For now they had the night to themselves. But it wasn't always going to be that way. When the dawn finally arrived, they'd both be plunged back into the horror of captivity. It was possible one or both of them would be taken away. Or worse, killed.

Jesse nodded, brushing his fingertips along the edge of her jaw. His lips gently brushed hers. "Even if it's only one night," he murmured against her mouth. "It's going to be one you'll re-member for the rest of your life."

Dakoda's hand found the ridge between the back of Jesse's neck and his shoulders. She traced it with her nails, then skimmed her fingers down the line of his spine. "Oh, trust me. It's already a day I'll never forget."

9

Jesse raked his fingertips down the length of Dakoda's throat, following with a featherlight caress of his lips. "It's been hell, I know. And if I could wave my hands and make it all go away, I would. If the day had gone right, I wouldn't have walked into the trap, and you guys wouldn't have had to come running to rescue the endangered animal."

Dakoda fingered the small dimple above the crack of his ass. The feel of his hot, naked body pressed against hers threatened to send her thoughts spinning away. "If it hadn't happened today, it would have happened later. The men we're dealing with don't care about life—*anyone's* life—except their own. None of us stood a chance today. I was pretty sure today would be my day to die."

Jesse's hand moved lower. His palm settled in the soft hollow between her breasts. "I can feel your heart beating fast," he said softly. "Are you afraid?"

Dakoda's pulse stalled a second. "Of dying?"

Hand still in place, he gave a tight, quick nod. A single tic moved his jaw. "Yes."

Drawing in a breath, Dakoda shook her head. "I'm not afraid of dying, as long as it's quick." A small shiver began to work its way up her spine. The fine hairs on her neck and arms rose. "I mean, Greg went fast . . . I don't even think his brain had time to register the pain." Horror began to seep back in, creeping in and twisting her guts. She quickly tamped it down. "He was pretty much dead before he hit the ground. I just knew that shotgun would go off a second time, and I'd be on the ground beside him."

"That wasn't going to happen," Jesse whispered softly. "They needed two cougars."

Dakoda gathered herself. "But I can't shift," she reminded him. A thought occurred. "Can I?"

A soft laugh escaped him. His hand slid toward her left breast. Using just the tip of his index finger, he drew slow circles around the jutting nipple. "According to Tlvdatsi lore, at the beginning of man's evolution, everyone had the capability to shift."

Dakoda's breath caught at the delicious sensations his touch elicited. "Really?"

Catching the little peak between thumb and forefinger, Jesse gave her nipple a delicious tug. Each pull of his fingers delivered a torrent of liquid delight straight to her blood. "Yes. But as time and civilization progressed, men's minds began to reject a connection with their animalistic natures. Certain neural pathways needed for shifting atrophied."

Dakoda wriggled on the flannel blankets beneath her body. On one hand, she wanted more information about the Tlvdatsi and their seemingly magical ability to shift. On the other, she wanted him to shut up and put his mouth into motion in far more pleasurable ways. She decided a compromise was in order.

Hand slipping between their bodies, she curled her fingers around his erection. Long and thickly veined, his penis pulsed against her palm, a steel rod wrapped in soft velvet. To give him back a little of his teasing, she jacked slowly up and down its length. "But your people retained the knowledge of how to keep them open?"

Jesse's breath caught on a moan. "Oh, man . . . I can barely think when you're touching me that way."

Another long, slow stroke. "Guess one thing hasn't changed," she teased. "Give a man a hard-on and he can't put two words together."

Jesse gritted his teeth. "Isn't that the damn truth?" Hand leaving her breast, he changed his tactic to delving between her legs. His long fingers slipped between the honeyed folds of her labia. A tip dipped into her creamy depth. "And what about you," he countered with a grin as his finger slipped deeper. "Seems to me you're hot, wet, and very ready."

His touch effectively derailed the rest of the conversation. "So what are you going to do about it?" she challenged.

For an answer, Jesse rolled on top of her. Arms supporting his weight, he settled the rest of his lean body between her spread legs. "Well," he said in a lazy drawl. "First I am going to do this."

He lowered his head, and his mouth closed around the protruding tip of one nipple. Catching it between his teeth, he painted slow circles with his tongue.

Every thought in Dakoda's head scattered. A waterfall of magical sensations flooded her nerves with each delicious caress. "Oh, my," she moaned.

Jesse breathed an enticing sound, but didn't remove his mouth from her aching nipple. One hand slid up her rib cage to fondle her other breast, stroking and teasing the sensitive areola until she whimpered.

Needing an anchor, Dakoda wrapped her arms around his body. Her palms instinctively settled on the soft curve between his back and buttocks. His hips rolled against her slowly as he suckled and teased, sending her into a frenzy of erotic need. He rubbed against her stomach in a most enticing way. If only he'd go a bit lower, then thrust. Entry would be assured.

The first tight curls of orgasm began to weave around her spine, tying up and then tickling her senses with an invigorating delight.

Responding to the move of his hips, Dakoda attempted to inch up higher. "Damn, Jesse." His name came out breathy and strangled. "What you're doing is torture of an innocent pussy."

Muffling his laugh, he cocked a brow. "Innocent pussy?" His hips ground against hers, giving her belly another good long rub of his hungry cock. "Oh, babe. There isn't anything innocent about what you've got between your legs. What you've got there is all sin. . . ."

Dakoda slipped her fingers into the cleft of his rear, inching her way into its warm depth. The tips of her fingers made tentative contact with his tight, puckered anus. She pressed against the tight ring, gently easing just the tip of a finger inside. "Mmm, and heaven is just a sin away." She pressed farther, working her finger into his wickedly tight channel.

Jesse's cock pulsed against her belly, bigger, harder. Hungrier. He closed his eyes, enjoying the feel of her penetration. "Man, oh man," he half-hissed, half-groaned. "No one's ever done that before. Keep that up and I'll come right now."

Dakoda made a circular motion with her finger. "I'd prefer it if you came inside me," she purred.

Jesse shifted. Lifting his weight just a little, he reached between their bodies. His fingers circled his erection, guiding the broad crown toward her damp slit. "You drive a hell of a hard bargain," he grated. "I'm going to pound your cunt until you scream."

Feeling the thick weight of his shaft pressing against her softness, Dakoda lifted her legs, spreading them wide. Knees settling up around his shoulders, she placed her hands on his hips. Glancing through the narrow gap between their bodies, she could watch his body enter hers.

Encouraged by her hold on his hips, Jesse started to enter her. Holding back from a quick, hard thrust, he slowly eased inside her. The silky glide of his organ stretched her rippling sex, penetrating deeper and deeper. His balls, heavy and full, settled against her ass as he slid in to the hilt.

Dakoda wrapped her legs around his waist. Full. She was completely full, every last bit of space crammed with cock. "God," she breathed. "You're even bigger than before."

Hands braced on either side of her, Jesse grinned down. "And you're even tighter." He flexed his hips in a circular, stirring motion. "Damn. There isn't an inch of wiggle room in there. Taking you is like having a virgin . . . the ultimate pleasure."

Dakoda laughed softly. "A virgin, I am not."

Cocking a brow, Jesse pulled out of her. A slow, warm glide of flesh on flesh ensued. He stopped just short of pulling out. "That little move with your finger up my rear gave me my first clue as to the wealth of experience you must have on tap."

Dakoda's fingers flexed against his hips. "Oh, you have no idea the things I've seen . . . and done." She dug her nails in just a little, just enough to give him a taste of her eagerness.

Jesse chuckled softly, a low rich sound emanating up from the depths of his throat. "I hope you might be willing to share some of your, ah, techniques." Taking his time, he pumped back in. His slide felt wonderfully endless.

The tension of being taken so damn slow and easy was exquisite. From what she'd sampled, Dakoda thought his technique was just fine. Dandy, in fact. Trembling with anticipation, she tightened her grip on his sculpted hips. Her aching nipples brushed his chest each time he made an upward or downward stroke.

Biting back a moan, she tilted back her head so she could

look directly into his eyes. "It seems to me that you've got some pretty good ones to fall back on."

"It's about to get better," he promised.

Dakoda didn't think it could.

Jesse proved her wrong.

Angling his head to one side, Jesse's mouth settled on hers. Instead of sweeping in and attacking with his tongue, he caught her bottom lip between her teeth, giving it a long, slow suck. His hips picked up a faster rhythm, grinding against hers in a manner that was more of a sensual waltz than a battering-ram assault.

Dakoda tightened her legs around his waist, willing to let him take all control and lead the dance. One thing was for sure: he had all the steps just right. All the bad things about the day began to mercifully fade away as their bodies moved together in perfect synchronicity, beginning an electrifying onslaught of carnal sensation. Lust boiled inside her like a pot left on the stove too long. Everything inside her felt deliciously molten.

Just when she thought it couldn't get any better, or any hotter, Jesse's kiss changed into something more brutal. Hungrier. A small, subtle shift had taken place, one she didn't recognize until it was too late. His mouth suddenly crushed over hers. His tongue pressed for entry, sweeping in with long, stabbing strokes. Cock pulsing inside her, he began to deliver deep, punishing strokes that jarred her bones.

Gentleness was over. It was time to get down to the business of some serious fucking. He delivered thrust after punishing thrust. His balls slapped her against her ass with each bone-jarring, breath-stealing stab.

All Dakoda could do was hang on for the wild ride.

Jesse lifted his head. Wave after wave of hair spilled over his shoulders, a cascade of shiny black silk. Coils of glowing amber writhed in the depth of his gaze, sizzling with feral lust. "You may have had other men," he growled, at the same time he delivered a vicious downward stab with his cock. "But I'm going to make sure I'm the only one you remember. From now on you belong to me."

Dakoda half-gasped, half-moaned at the ferociousness in his tone. Cock buried to the hilt, his eyes burned with the heat of the predator. Jesse was no longer a man making love to a woman, but a predatory male on the prowl for a female. The instincts and nature of the cougar lurking inside his soul were driving him to claim and conquer her on the most basic, primal levels. He wasn't just mating to procreate. He was mating to survive.

Jesse's hips became a piston, slamming against her with deep, muscular flexes that drove his shaft as far as physically possible. His body collided with hers, each strike delivering a teeth-clattering jolt.

Pinned under his weight, Dakoda writhed helplessly, overwhelmed by the thrill. At the last moment, she arched up into him, taking a last body-shuddering slam.

Slamming down a final time, Jesse ground his hips against hers. Buried to the balls, his pulsing cock blasted liquid flame, filling her womb with a stream of hot semen.

Dakoda's senses shattered into a billion tiny pieces. Energy rushed through her like a current, far too fast for her brain cells to process all at once. Climax arrived in its wake, an uncontrolled explosion of sensation rushing down an endless tunnel. It felt as if her insides were slowly tying into knots, the searing pleasure as pure and bright as a roll of shiny new copper wiring. Arcs of multicolored lights spiraled behind her eyes, turning her brain into a blobby mass. She felt like she was glowing all over, brighter and hotter than a star gone nova.

Clit singing out in delight, Dakoda threw her head back. A long, ragged squeal of unadulterated joy tore past her lips. As she crested through level upon level of incredible rapture, it occurred to her that having sex with Jesse Clawfoot was going to be a very hard habit to break.

10

The feel of a warm body shifting against hers drew Dakoda from the depths of a slumberous inertia.

She opened her eyes, blinking sleepily at the unfamiliar ceiling overhead. Mind fuzzed with the remnants of strange, disjointed dreams and edged with exhaustion, she stared for a moment without any real focus, close to drifting off into the cocoon of soothing unconsciousness.

Her companion wiggled again, snapping her thoughts back into focus. Images of the last several hours flooded her memory, the previous day's horrifying tragedy merging and mingling with the night's sultry passion.

Dakoda sucked in a little breath. His sleek body radiated with feral heat. She could almost glimpse the raw power of the cougar rippling beneath his glossy skin. Her blood began to simmer. Her body ached for the feel of his naked skin sliding against hers all over again. Jesse made love with a fierceness unmatched by any man she'd ever known before. Sex with him was searing, a plunge into the richer, darker side of desire.

"Jesse . . ." she murmured. Through the last few hours he'd

managed to distract her from the grim reality of their captivity, making love to her shamelessly and without restraint. He'd brought her to orgasm not one, or even two, but three magnificent, mind-blowing times. Every place he'd touched still tingled. Muscles she hadn't used in ages ached pleasantly. It was the first time in her life she'd had such a good night in bed with any man.

Her mouth quirked down. Too damn bad they probably weren't going to get the chance to do it again. Tiny slivers of light were beginning to creep through the narrow gaps in the walls. Dawn was breaking, and the day to come wasn't at all promising.

Barely daring to breathe lest she disturb her companion, Dakoda eased herself up on one elbow. The bunk they lay on was barely wide enough to accommodate one, much less two, bodies. For both to fit comfortably meant Dakoda was practically plastered back against the wall. Jesse Clawfoot lay partially sprawled on top of her. His eyes were closed, and lashes longer than any man had a right to have were spread out just above his finely etched cheekbones. Deep in sleep, his mouth was parted just enough to allow the barest hint of a snore to escape.

Catching him asleep and unaware gave Dakoda the chance to see, really see, him for the first time. When he'd shifted into human form, the shock had made it impossible for her to concentrate on more than what was happening at the moment. Now that she had a minute to herself, she could study him without restraint.

Her searching gaze skimmed over his naked form, visually tracing the lines of his sinewy body; from the hard-packed muscles of his arms, to the ridges of his back, then down his long, endless legs.

A small smile of appreciation parted her lips. He was solidly built. And utterly gorgeous. *A man who can shift into a cougar.*

Though she'd witnessed it with her own eyes, Dakoda still found it almost impossible to wrap her mind around the concept. Even though he'd somewhat explained that the ability to shift was centered in neural pathways modern man no longer had any cognizance or control over, she still found the idea hard to grasp. She supposed the key would be in the idea of mind conquering matter, some sort of psi-kinetic ability clearly dormant in most human beings. The fact the Tlvdatsi had managed to retain and use a knowledge dating back to practically the beginning of mankind was amazing.

Careful not to disturb his rest, Dakoda gently traced the knotty ridge of a scar gashed across his left shoulder. He had a lot of them, some more set into his flesh than others. Crisscrossing his shoulders, back, and thighs, the damage indicated he fought often and viciously.

A small shiver tripped down her spine. As a young male, Jesse was fighting for not only a mate but also territory of his own.

The shiver made another trip. *He said he could smell me,* she thought. *A female in heat.*

One of his kind.

Tlvdatsi.

Was it really possible her unknown father might be Native American in origin? Could she really be carrying some sort of recessive gene that would identify her to others of her kind?

At this point such questions were unanswerable. She could guess, and she could speculate. But she just didn't know for sure. The possibility she'd *ever* know for sure was just as remote. Her mother was long deceased, and her father was listed as unknown on her birth certificate. The world viewed her as just another bastard. Society gave little sympathy to people like her, the children of poor, transient, drug-addled women. Making her way, finding her place, was her own responsibility. The path she chose to travel was one she charted.

Somehow, for some reason known only to fate and the heavens above, Jesse Clawfoot had stepped in to point her in an entirely new direction. The route he guided her toward went against everything she'd ever known or believed about herself—and her soul.

Dakoda already knew she wasn't going down without a fight. A single glance at Jesse's skin reassured her that he didn't just turn tail and run, either. He fought and fought hard. Whatever force or fate had brought them together would now pay hell tearing them apart. Somehow, they'd stay together.

Somehow they'd survive.

She just didn't know how yet.

Yawning deeply, Jesse opened his eyes. "Mmm." He snuggled closer to Dakoda. "Now this is a hell of a way to wake up, with a naked, warm woman beneath me."

Dakoda couldn't help smiling. "Don't you mean a squashed woman beneath you?" She wiggled briefly, rolling on her side and repositioning her body to better fit against his in the narrow space. She cocked a leg over his hips to make things a little more comfortable.

One of Jesse's big palms immediately settled on the curve of her rear, bringing her in a little closer. Awakened by the heat of her nearby sex, his flaccid penis stirred with interest. "Now this is something I could take advantage of," he murmured.

Dakoda trembled. Oh, heavens. There was no doubting the sudden achy warmth spreading between her legs. She wanted him again. The minutes were ticking away until their captors would return, but she didn't care. All she could think about was satisfying the sweet ache in her core one more time.

"So take advantage," she murmured against his mouth.

Jesse's hand slowly traveled up her side. Slipping between their bodies, he found and stroked one beaded nipple.

Shuddering in lust, Dakoda pressed her hips closer to his. Gloriously erect, the silky crown of his penis rubbed against her creamy sex. All it would take is one push, and he'd be inside.

Realizing her intent, Jesse held off. "Slow," he murmured, nibbling her bottom lip. His breath was moist, musky, against her needy skin, not at all unappealing. His fingers made a slow circle around her sensitive areola.

Teeth clamping together, Dakoda sucked in a breath. The first pulses of climax were beginning to build all over again. "Please," she moaned.

Pinching and twisting her swollen nipple, Jesse pumped his hips upward. He eased inside her, just a little. Just enough to give her a taste. "You want it," he said, not a question but a statement of fact.

Dakoda's hand automatically curled around the curve of his ass cheek. He was taking his own good time, but she wasn't willing to wait. These last precious minutes were too few, and couldn't possibly last much longer.

"Yes," she breathed back. "I want it all." Fingers digging into the firm flesh, she urged him deeper.

Tugging on her nipple, Jesse relented. He stabbed his rigid cock upward, hard enough to fully penetrate her sex. His eyes fluttered shut, and a low groan emanated from his throat. "Being inside you feels like warm, wet velvet."

Shuddering in raw need, Dakoda closed her eyes, prelude to the spinning of a deliciously carnal fantasy. *If only . . .*

The sudden clatter of rough-edged voices outside shattered the moment. Heavy footsteps drew closer. A curse and grunt accompanied the grating sound made by the plank as it was lifted away from the door.

Desire fled like a rabbit flushed out of the brush by a hound. Bodies immediately breaking apart, both of them struggled to find something to cover themselves with. Dakoda reached for the blanket, flipping it over her nude body. A snarl curled Jesse's lips as he sprang to his feet. The blanket he'd earlier covered himself with lay a few feet away. He barely managed to snag it before the door swung outward on creaky hinges.

The sun beaming in from outside outlined a familiar figure. "Wakey, wakey," a cornpone-accented voice boomed.

Dakoda's breath hung in her lungs, too heavy to easily expel. Waylon Barnett stood at the threshold. As expected, he wasn't alone. His cousin Rusty, ever the bearer of the big firepower, followed closely behind.

Dakoda's eyes narrowed. *The bastard.* He'd killed Greg without thinking twice or showing an ounce of remorse. The thought of leaping off the bunk and tearing him a new asshole loomed large in the back of her mind.

Too fucking bad she couldn't do it. Given the chance, she would love to kick the living shit out of him and then some. If there was any person who was a true waste of good oxygen walking the face of the planet, Waylon Barnett definitely qualified. He could fall off the edge of the earth, and she wouldn't miss him.

Acutely aware of her state of undress and the lack of weapons to back up her vicious thoughts, Dakota kept her back pressed against the wall. The blanket covering her naked body wasn't much, but it was better than nothing. "We're awake," she growled back.

A twisted grin crossed Waylon's face as he stepped into the cell. The small, fetid space reeked of sexual musk. "Well, well, it looks like our male is doin' what comes natural with a nice piece of pussy." A croaky laugh spilled over tobacco-stained lips.

As he wrapped the blanket around his waist, a snarl pressed past Jesse's curled lips, more animalistic than human. "Just what I wanted to see this early in the morning," he grumbled. "A couple of ass-wipes."

Waylon Barnett's insane grin didn't waver. "Watch your mouth, mangy Indian," he countered. "You may be standin' on two legs now, but deep down you ain't nothing more than an animal. Abomination toward God if you ask me."

"You're the abomination," Jesse spat back. "Backwoods, in-bred cracker."

Rusty raised his rifle. "Shut the fuck up," he warned quietly.

Dakoda stiffened. Disaster was just a trigger pull away. "I think you'd better mind your manners," she said, cocking her head toward the rifle.

The smile on Waylon Barnett's face was snaggled and what few teeth he had left were stained brown. "Manners?" he crowed. "That there thing ain't got no manners. He's just a soulless animal." He glanced toward Jesse, still standing naked and proud. "You know where you're goin' to end up, Indian? Right back in a cage where your kind belongs."

Jesse clenched his hands into tight fists. "You wouldn't be talking so big if you didn't have a gun behind you." He cocked his head, eyeing the poacher. "Seems to me I put a few of those scars on your face, Skeet." He flexed his fingers. "If I ever get another chance, I'll get your throat."

Dakoda gritted her teeth. If he was trying to goad them into killing him, he was doing an excellent job. Her heart tripped with slow, thudding beats against her rib cage. She'd already seen her partner blasted to bits in front of her eyes. Seeing Jesse Clawfoot die wasn't exactly high on her list of ways to start the day.

"Jesse, back off," she warned, her voice rough with anxiety. "Now isn't the time or place." You had to pick your battles, and this wasn't one they could reasonably win.

Waylon Barnett sneered. "Better listen to that piece of pussy you're fuckin'," he advised.

Jesse shook his head. "Maybe I don't want to listen," he countered in a voice deadly and low. Arms going stiff beside his body, he lowered his head. Veins suddenly corded around his arms, chest, and legs like thousands of tiny whips. Fur sprouted from his flesh, rippling across his skin the way a tornado whipped across a wheat field. Within seconds the cougar inside him sprang out, ferociously angry and ready to fight.

Before Dakoda could blink twice, the outlaw drew the pistol holstered at his side. Pointing it directly at the cougar's massive head, he expertly thumbed back the trigger. "Just try it, Jesse," he warned. "Somehow I think that fur coverin' you won't stop a bullet." An ugly snarl twisted his lips.

Ignoring the threat, Jesse crouched low and snarled back. Ears pinned back against his skull, his tail snapped back and forth. Narrow amber eyes burned like coals in the deepest pit of hell. Feline lips curled back to reveal deadly sharp fangs. Seriously pissed, he was ready to fight.

But it was a battle he had no chance of winning. The only thing he'd accomplish would be a bullet through the head.

Pulse skidding to a stall, Dakoda choked on a gasp. "No, Jesse!" She glared toward the captors. "Now's not the time."

Backing up his cousin, Rusty raised his shotgun. "Think long and hard, boy."

Waylon Barnett sneered. "You make any wrong moves and it won't be you who pays." His crazed stare swung toward Dakoda. The gun followed, pointed straight toward the center of her chest. "I'll take her out so goddamned fast your head will spin."

Though a low growl of dissent rolled up from his throat, Jesse backed off. He shifted back into human form. "Leave her alone."

Releasing a satisfied grunt, Barnett tucked his weapon away. "Well, isn't it just sweet of you to want to protect that nice piece of poon. Your new owners will be thrilled you're getting along so well." He made a crude gesture for sexual intercourse with his hands. "They're just lookin' forward to some little baby cougars."

Baby cougars? Dakoda licked dry lips. Oh man. Birth control definitely hadn't been on her mind last night when she'd made love to Jesse. Having someone to hold her, touch her, soothe away her fears had taken precedence over the consequences.

But reality was filtering back in with the cold light of dawn, and with it the sinking feeling that was sure to twist her stomach into thousands of knots.

Since she wasn't sexually active, Dakoda hadn't kept up a steady regime of birth control. She'd let her prescription lapse, preferring instead to use an over-the-counter method, when and if needed. She hadn't needed any in quite a while. Now her lapse was coming back to bite her in the ass. At twenty-six years of age, she was right on the cusp of a woman's peak age of fertility. Last night she and Jesse had made love several times, and he hadn't withdrawn once before ejaculation. Caught up in the moment, it had felt like the right thing to do.

Wrong! The single word slammed into her mind like a sledgehammer powering into concrete.

Head dropping, Dakoda's hands slipped to her face. All her blood seemed to be draining away, leaving her with a sudden unwelcome chill. *I can't have his baby,* she thought wildly. *Not in this kind of situation.* She could hardly imagine her child being born a captive in someone's private zoo.

The thought was too terrible to even contemplate.

"This can't be happening . . ." she murmured, more to herself than for the benefit of other ears.

Waylon Barnett snorted, breaking through her misery. "The buyer is comin' this afternoon." Slipping off a backpack he wore, he tossed it at Jesse. "There's something for you to wear. Make sure you have it on. They want to see a real Indian, and by God, you're going to be native out the ass."

Unwilling to take any more orders, Jesse let the pack drop. "And if I don't?" he rumbled.

The outlaw bared his broken, stained grin. He fingered the butt of the gun resting at his hip. "Then I'll shoot you and fuck her," he smirked. "As many times as I want."

11

Jesse Clawfoot curled his lip at the scrap of leather he held out in front of him. "Oh, God, you have to be kidding me." He moaned. "No sane Indian has dressed like this for centuries."

Having managed to get herself dressed, Dakoda sat at the table, digging through the smaller cooler the outlaws had left for their breakfast. What she found inside wasn't promising, but it would fill their stomachs. "What is it?"

Dangling it between thumb and forefinger, Jesse sneered. "Believe it or not, it's a fucking breechclout." Another disgusted huff escaped him.

Dakoda had no idea what he was talking about. "How do you wear it?" Stomach rumbling, she picked out a few foil-wrapped items. Inside she found a half loaf of dark crusty bread, a hunk of hard cheese, strips of beef jerky. More of the trail mix had been tossed in as an afterthought. A half dozen small bottles of water finished the stock of supplies.

She picked up a piece of the jerky, attempting to gnaw through the dried strip of meat. Was it bear, or perhaps venison? Tough as shoe leather, it had a decent enough taste. Someone had taken the time to season and spice it just right with a tangy sauce. Chewing the tough strip, she washed it down with a swig of water. "So are you going to put it on or go naked?"

"I'd rather wear fur." Despite his reluctance, Jesse put the breechclout on. Pulling it up between his legs, he secured it at the waist with thongs.

As he struggled with the unfamiliar clothing, a vision flashed across Dakoda's mind-screen, the lust-driven sensual power of his cock sinking into her . . .

Her clit twitched against the tight rub of her slacks against her crotch. Suddenly her clothing felt too tight, constricting. If asked, she'd gladly whip them off in a second. Her uniform was filthy, dirty, stained with remnants of Greg's blood and her own sour sweat. Always a stickler for fresh underwear, she hated wearing yesterday's panties. At least she'd gotten to bathe a little—if washing in a wooden bucket full of cold water could be called bathing.

She hurriedly cleared her throat. "Doesn't look so bad."

Jesse grunted. "Covers my ass at least." He put on the rest of the costume, which consisted of a pair of leather chaps and beaded moccasins. "I feel stupid," he grumbled.

Dakoda swallowed thickly, attempting to get those very images out of her head. Yes, he definitely looked better without any clothes on, but going around bare-assed and exposed wasn't practical. The more she looked at his beautiful body, the more she wanted another taste of the pleasures she knew he could easily deliver.

She bit off another mouthful of jerky. It was tough, but tasty. "Too bad you can't figure out how to shift and still have clothes on when you return to human form."

Jesse walked over to join her. "Anything decent?" he asked, sniffing around the food. "I'm more than half starved."

Dakoda indicated the jerky. "That's not bad."

He crinkled his nose. "Please, have mercy on my stomach.

You'd think these assholes could go into town more often for supplies."

She nodded. "Riiiight. Considering they have warrants out in Connelly Springs, sure, going to town to buy supplies would make a lot of sense. These guys don't stick their necks out very often, and when they do you can bet it's one of their inbred relatives doing the shopping. I imagine they live off the land as much as possible."

Jesse reached for the bread, tearing off a piece. A chunk of cheese followed. Smashing the two together in a sort of sandwich, he shoved it into his mouth. "Tastes like shit," he mumbled, washing it down with a swig of water. "Be better if it was pizza with a nice pitcher of cold beer."

Dakoda cocked a brow. "I've been slavering for a burger and fries, myself."

Jesse swallowed down another bite. "You know, the only hard thing about returning to live the wild life is you have to leave the modern one behind. I mean, yeah, my ancestors lived on this land, hunted in these mountains, and made their lives here. I know we Indians got our collective asses kicked and then some, but, what the hell, the world goes on, you know. Civilization goes on—and it's a nice place to be, the twenty-first century."

Dakoda blinked. "I think you're trying to say something profound there, but I can't quite catch it."

Jesse reached for a piece of jerky, tearing off a strip of the dry meat. "What I think I'm trying to say is I sometimes think preserving our heritage as shifters is a lot of hooey."

Her brows rose. "Hooey? Is that some Indian term?"

He chewed thoughtfully. "No, but all this embracing our inner animal might be. I mean, come on. Preserving ancient rituals and traditions is one thing, but actually trying to live by them in a world that's left mysticism and magic behind is crazy. There's a reason our numbers are so thin, why we're almost extinct."

Dakoda's throat tightened. She didn't like the turn their conversation was taking. She'd already experienced more gloom and doom than she cared to. Adding another heap to their plates wouldn't help matters one bit. "Why's that?" she asked slowly.

Obviously losing his appetite, Jesse flicked the jerky aside. "Because we just don't belong. What we do defies not only logic but also nature itself..." he paused, taking a breath. "And things that are deviant should die off."

His words sent a cold shiver down her spine. Bile washed up the back of her throat, killing her appetite. "My God, Jesse. That's no way to talk."

He stared at her through an unblinking gaze, his stare fierce and boiling with resentment. "Why not? Assholes can't hunt you if you're dead. Why should we even fight to survive when all they do is treat us like freaks, to be captured and put in cages?" Reaching out, his fingers circled her wrist. "You know what they're going to want us to do, Dakoda? Breed. That's right. We'll be put on display to entertain people's most perverted fantasies. You'll be the woman who fucks a cougar, an animal." Grip tightening, he shook his head. "I don't know about you, but I don't want to live that way. It would be better to be dead."

Dakoda struggled to keep her arm in place, not jerk it away from his hold. Right now he was the only thing, the only person she had to hold on to. Keeping him focused and aware he wasn't in this mess alone was her only chance of survival. If Jesse gave up and did something stupid to get himself killed, she'd be on her own. Contemplating the alternative turned her bowels to icy liquid.

She put her hand on top of his. "Getting yourself killed isn't the answer, Jesse."

His gaze drifted to the ceiling above their heads, supported by exposed beams. "Hanging would be slow," he murmured, licking his lips. "But better than a cage."

Catching the intention behind his glance, Dakoda tilted back her head. "Killing yourself won't be any easier, Jesse."

Jesse's hand slipped away. His touch, so warm and reassuring, left a cold spot in its wake. Pushing away from the table, he stood up. His hands raked through his hair in frustration. "I can't live in a cage," he said, slowly shaking his head. "Being locked up in a cage won't be living, even if I'm with you. If there's a way out, I'll take it." Gaze turning inward, his words trailed off into silence.

Suicide. Just thinking about the word and its definition turned her blood to icy water. The idea of actually climbing up on a chair and then kicking it away, only to dangle helplessly as the oxygen was sucked from her lungs wasn't the slightest bit appealing.

Dakoda grimaced. Considering their present situation, self-extermination would seem like the logical choice. What sane person wanted to live as a slave, a captive to someone else's whims? Maybe it would be the best thing to do. Maybe it wouldn't be as bad as she imagined. For herself, it might not be so bad. But she didn't want to have to watch Jesse die. He was part of an honorable and noble race, a man possessing not only intelligence but also an innate kindness that extended toward others around him.

Last night when she'd been on the edge, when she would have been the one ready to leap, he'd pulled her back from the abyss. Now it was her turn to do the same for him. Somehow they would find a way to keep each other going.

She looked at Jesse, trying to ignore the rush of heat pooling between her thighs at the sight of his lean body just barely covered by a breechclout and leather chaps. He stood still, the muscles in his arms cording as he contemplated his next move. She wanted his arms wrapped around her waist, his big palms settled on her ass as he pulled her hips toward his straining erection.

"Don't think that way," she said, hoping he wouldn't notice the grate of raw arousal in her tone.

He released a long sigh. "I can't help it. I don't want to face what's waiting for us out there." The barest trace of a bitter smile crossed his lips. "Makes me quite a hero, huh?"

"It makes you someone who is human," she countered quietly.

He shrugged. "According to some people, the red man is nowhere near human. Nothing but a damn savage." His words were tinged with recognizable traces of angry self-loathing. "Fuck. In this day and age, we still can't get past the old stereotypes of being godless savages."

She shook her head. "That's not true and you know it."

Simmering with a thousand different emotions, Jesse's gaze bore down on her like a block of concrete. "Do I?" he bit back coldly.

Trembling hard, Dakoda rose from her chair. Her legs shook, barely able to support her weight. Walking over to him, she grabbed him by the shoulders, craning up on the tips of her toes so she could look into his eyes. "Do you remember what you told me last night?"

He shook his head. "Last night feels like it never existed," he stated in a flat, dull tone.

Dakoda shook her head. "It did. . . . and it still does." Her hands rose to his broad shoulders, fingers digging in deep. "You told me if we hang on to each other, we might be able to survive." She pressed her body closer to his, leaving nary an inch between them. "Well, I'm hanging on, Jesse. I'm hanging on for dear life and praying for the best. I'm not ready to let you go, and I'm damn sure not going to stand by and let you kill yourself. I don't care what you freaking Indians say when your backs are against the wall. Today is *not* a good day to die."

Craning higher, Dakoda pressed her mouth against his, holding nothing back as she kissed him with all the fervor and craving rolling through her body.

Just as she'd imagined, Dakoda felt Jesse's hands slide around her hips, catching her rear and lifting her against his hips. Her nipples rose into hard little peaks seconds before he crushed her against his chest.

Taking control, his tongue pressed deeper into her mouth, exploring and then conquering every moist crevice. Dakoda's senses whirled at the absolute erotic intensity driving his response. Her body relaxed as relief drizzled in.

Their kiss broke briefly. "You're incredible," he murmured against her mouth. "Too damn good to be true."

Dakoda nipped his lower lip between her teeth, suckling gently. He moaned in pleasure at her teasing nibble. "I could say the same about you." Together less than a day, they'd already forged a bond delving past the physical and into an entirely different level. She could handle the stresses of captivity as long as she had Jesse. Without him, she would have already fallen to pieces in more ways than one.

Releasing a soft moan, Jesse bent slightly and lifted her body against his. Arms circling his neck, Dakoda wrapped her legs around his waist, locking her ankles together. Their mouths came back together as he pressed her against the wall of the cell, using it as a brace to better hold her weight in place. His cock was like an iron bar, pressing directly against the crotch of her slacks.

Dakoda felt the crotch of her panties grow moister, her sex preparing for the entry of his shaft.

Working a hand between their bodies, Jesse dug under the layers of her uniform. "Damn, you're wearing too much clothing." Finding her bra, he dragged one cup down off her breast. One erect nipple popped free, aching and swollen. Releasing a growl deep in his throat, he tugged and pulled at the hard little tip. "I want you naked."

Suddenly a clamor of men entering the cell shattered the

temporary lull. Letting her go, Jesse rounded on the intruder, a snarl rolling past his lips.

"Well, looks like they're going to be able to perform just fine for our buyer," Willie Barnett chuckled with wicked amusement, rattling the chains he held in one hand. The chains that would attach to the collars both she and Jesse wore. "Time to meet your new owner."

12

Dakoda had imagined the outlaws would be living in squalor not far above that of the cell she and Jesse had been imprisoned in, so she wasn't surprised when confronted with the reality.

The cabins the men occupied were plain and simply constructed, hearkening back to the days when the first white settlers had began to invade the mountains in search of gold. Water was still drawn from hand-powered pumps and electricity was nonexistent. Most of the lamps inside were older standbys, filled with highly flammable kerosene.

The operation was a lot less sophisticated than Dakoda had imagined. The outlaws clearly worked to keep a very low profile, doing nothing that would attract attention to their activities. By keeping it simple, they could pack up and vanish without a trace. It didn't take a professional to guess poaching generated a profit. Animal products, such as hide, ivory, horn, teeth, and bone, were sold to dealers who make clothes, jewelry, and other trinkets. In other countries, animals had religious value and were used as totems and in witchcraft. Many animals were killed for ceremonial purposes.

What these men had stumbled on to was far more valuable, a thing so precious and rare as to almost be priceless.

No doubt they could demand any price—and probably get it.

Dakoda swallowed her fear as she and Jesse were ushered past the outer rooms and into some sort of private inner sanctum. A short Asian man wearing an expensive suit waited for their arrival. Well groomed and manicured, he appeared to be in his late forties. By the look of him, he hadn't done a hard day's work in his life. Head tilted at a haughty angle, he carried a crop, the kind used in horse riding. His smile was straight, and shiny white. Ratlike beady eyes observed everything.

A shiver scurried down her spine. *The showroom,* she thought, casting a glance around the sparsely furnished area. *This is where they sell the merchandise.* Another shiver followed on the heels of the first. *And we're the product.*

Taken from their cell, they'd been led like dogs across the compound. No chance to run, or fight back. Rusty's rifle was trained on their backs with every step they took. He was ordered to shoot first and ask questions later.

Still dressed in the breechclout and leggings he'd ridiculed earlier, Jesse Clawfoot stood stiff and straight. He was doing his best imitation of the silent, stone-faced Indian, saying nothing as he stared off into space. By the look in his eyes, he was a million miles away, far removed from the humiliating proceedings.

Suppressing her anger, Dakota wished she felt as calm and composed. Her trembling knees barely held her weight, threatening collapse at any moment. Tension knotted her guts.

The Asian man smiled. "They are both very nice." He cocked a brow. "Authentic?" He spoke in an abrupt clipped way, his words bitten off into small, precise chunks.

Willie Barnett nodded. "The male is one hundred percent Cherokee, Mister Kamai. Just like your buyer requested."

The man identified as Kamai spoke. "And her? She is native as well?"

Willie Barnett chuckled. Walking over, he caught Dakota's chin, wrenching her head to a better angle. "Look at the skin color an' the cast of her face. She's got a little mutt in her, but most of it's Indian." He showed her the way he would some inanimate object, accentuating her positive points while downplaying the negative.

Kamai made a quick gesture with his crop. "My buyer wants pure blood," he said, his accented voice sharp.

Willie Barnett shook his head. "Do you know how scarce women are in these mountains? Layin' hands on any stray female, Indian or not, is a lucky break." He chuckled obscenely. "You can be happy, though. They seem to like each other a lot. Since we got 'em together, they've been fuckin' like, well, wild cats. That's as good a breedin' pair as you're goin' to get."

Dakoda felt heat creep into her cheeks. Having her sex life set out in front of a bunch of strangers made her feel filthy, degraded. Their captors were discussing her and Jesse as though they were little more than animals, incapable of understanding or thinking for themselves.

Her hold on self-control snapped. "Don't you get that we're human beings?" She rattled the chain attached to the collar around her neck. "I'm a goddamned ranger, or can't you tell that by the fucking uniform I'm wearing?"

Willie Barnett's hand immediately shot out, clouting her soundly. "I warned you about talkin'," he snarled. "Unless he asks you to speak, you don't say one goddamned word."

Dakoda's senses reeled as multicolored stars jetted behind her eyes. Skin burning hot, she tasted blood from the lip he'd split.

Hands clenching into fists, Jesse stepped up. "Keep your fucking hands off her," he snarled viciously.

Barnett easily delivered a second strike, punching Jesse in the solar plexus. "And you keep your goddamned place, animal," he barked back.

Choking out a gasp, Jesse's face hardened. He didn't budge an inch, even though the hit must have been painful. Face twisted with rage, he stood face-to-face with the outlaw. "Don't ever turn your back on me." His voice was deadly and low, the kind you didn't want to ignore. "If I ever get the chance, I'll gut you like a fish."

Barnett's hand shot toward his hip. Drawing the knife sheathed there, he pressed the sharp blade against Jesse's bare abdomen. Handcuffed and chained, Jesse didn't have a chance. "We'll see who guts who."

Jesse's expression was as cold and set as granite. "Do it now, and do it fast."

Dakoda's blood pressure sank faster than a thousand-pound weight in quicksand. If Jesse's plan was to get himself killed, he was doing a damn good job of accomplishing his goal. Apparently staying alive and staying together wasn't part of his plan, after all.

Dakoda wasn't ready to die. Not today, anyway.

She also wasn't willing to stand by and stay silent. Sucking the blood off her busted lip, she spat, sending a wad of phlegm toward Barnett. "Kill us and you kill the sale," she snarled, wiping her mouth with the back of her hand.

Barnett backed off. "If it was just you an' me," he said, sheathing his knife. "I'd go ahead an' take you out." A laugh bubbled from his lips. "But seein' as you're worth cold, hard cash, I guess I'll have to restrain myself. No use killin' the goose just because the gander's in a flap."

Observing it all, Kamai suddenly laughed. "They've got fight. I like that." He gestured with his crop again. "Let me see more of her."

Barnett turned to Dakota. "Strip," he ordered, removing her cuffs.

Dakoda's jaw dropped. "You mean as in naked?" she gasped out. There was no time to consider she'd broken the rules again. Hand cocking back, Willie Barnett delivered another fast, roundhouse slap. "Take off your clothes," he ordered. "Now!"

Her senses were rocked to the core; a multitude of sparks flew behind her eyes again. She should have known her protest would earn her another hit. That didn't make it any less painful, or any less degrading.

Barnett grinned at her discomfort. "If you don't get them off." He patted the Bowie knife like a trusted friend. "I'll cut them off. You won't have a shred left on by time I get finished."

Embarrassment heated her cheeks. She cut a quick glance to Jesse. Gaze skittering away from hers, he slowly nodded. The meaning behind his gesture was clear. *Cooperate.*

But bending for the sake of survival was not breaking.

Sliding off her jacket, Dakoda lifted a hand to the top of her shirt. She fought to keep her hand from trembling, to make her fingers work at her command as she unbuttoned. What the hell? She had nothing these men hadn't seen before. Resisting the order would only make it worse for her and Jesse.

Discarding her shirt, she kicked out of her boots, then stripped off her slacks. Her bra and panties were all she had left on.

"Everything," Kamai ordered, sensing her hesitation.

Dakoda forced herself not to blink when she unhooked her bra, letting it fall away from her breasts. Without bending, she dropped her panties down her legs, then stepped out of them. All she had on was the skin she'd been born in.

Willie Barnett's eyes widened with appreciation. A low whistle escaped his lips. "Oh, that's one nice-lookin' piece of pussy," he leered, rubbing the front of his grimy jeans. "I might still give her a fuck or two before I sell her off."

Dakoda tensed. Her heart pounded in long, jarring beats against her rib cage. She'd scratch out the bastard's eyes before he'd lay another hand on her, even if it meant she'd be put down like a rabid dog in her tracks. Throat thickening with emotion, an unwelcome thought crept into her mind. *Maybe Jesse was right. . . .*

Kamai immediately shot the poacher a contemptuous smile. Displeasure slit his beady eyes. "You fuck her, you keep her," he sneered. The Asian's own intrusive gaze slid over Dakoda's skin like razors. "I want no contamination of the bloodline. If I'm going to buy them for my employer, I don't want to have to abort your bastard child first."

Mouth dry as sand, Dakoda breathed a sigh of relief. She'd already had her go-round with Barnett once. The thought of his big piglike body pressed on top of hers made her want to puke.

Barnett backed off. "The only one that's been fuckin' her is that tomcat," he reaffirmed.

Kamai rose from his chair like an emperor over his subjects. Crop in hand, he circled Dakoda, examining her from all angles. As he walked, he ran the tip of his crop over her skin, skimming her curves.

Goosebumps dimpling her exposed flesh, Dakoda rubbed her hands up and down her arms. She glared at the Asian when he stepped in front of her. Man, she'd love a set of cougar's claws right about now. *All the better to scratch his eyes out,* she thought.

A lascivious glint crept into Kamai's gaze. Reaching out, he cupped her left breast. His thumb brushed the tip of her nipple, bringing it to instant erection.

Repulsed by his touch, Dakoda tasted the tang of burning

acid at the back of her throat. Having taken two hard slaps, she wasn't inclined to take a third. She allowed herself a sneer.

Kamai's thumb slowly circled her areola. "Very responsive," he said approvingly. "Does it make you wet when a man fondles your breasts?"

Forcing herself to silence, Dakoda stared straight through him. Kamai might have warned the outlaw against taking advantage of her. But as a buyer he might think himself well within his rights to liberally sample the merchandise.

She sent a glare his way. *Drop dead,* she mouthed silently.

Kamai ignored her. Like an equestrian inspecting a nice piece of horseflesh, his intrusive touch skidded over her rib cage, then across the flat plane of her belly. Dakoda barely managed to bite down on her scream as his hand pressed between her thighs. Cool, slender fingers located her clit, rubbing slow circles around the small hooded organ.

An unintended moan slipped past Dakoda's lips. "Don't," she gasped hoarsely. "Please—"

A smile crossed the Asian's pinched face. "Ah, she is very damp." He probed, dipping a finger into her sex. "And very tight."

Face burning hot, Dakoda barely heard the man's comments. Just when she was sure she'd go screaming mad, his cold touch fell away. Grunting with disgust, she shifted uncomfortably to cover her exposed parts. She felt sick, diseased by his unwelcome invasion of her most private places.

Kamai nodded his approval. "She will suffice." He turned toward Jesse. "Now the male."

Barnett prodded Jesse. "You heard the man. Get naked."

Mouth twisting with rage, Jesse said nothing as he stripped off the few pieces of clothes they'd allowed. As an act of defiance, he threw each piece toward Waylon Barnett, an expression of utter contempt on his face.

Refusing to cringe under scrutiny, Jesse pulled back his shoulders, standing exposed to everyone's view. "Take a good look," he snarled. "This is everything you'll never be, you little bastard."

Just as he'd inspected Dakoda, Kamai looked Jesse over from head to foot. Though he didn't fondle, he did take note of Jesse's flaccid penis. "Very impressive," he stated with approval.

"Foreign fucker," Jesse gritted under his breath.

Kamai immediately stiffened. Swatting Jesse with the crop, he laughed. "In my country," he said, drawing out each word for emphasis. "You will be the foreigner." Stepping back, he eyed them both. "The flesh is acceptable. Now I wish to see what makes these people so rare."

With the stubbornness of a mule, Jesse shook his head. "No."

Rusty, who had been standing silently behind them, lifted his rifle. "Don't start actin' up now, Jesse," he warned. "Just do what the man asks."

Jesse dug his heels in deeper than an unruly child on the first day of kindergarten. "What are you going to do?" he challenged. "Shoot me?" Given a fair hand-to-hand fight, there was no doubt he'd walk away the winner, but in these circumstances, resistance was futile. However sharp, a pair of claws had little chance against gunpowder and hot lead.

Rusty's rifle moved to the right. "No," he drawled around a mouthful of chewing tobacco. "I'll shoot the woman."

Dakoda almost wished he would.

Push came to shove, and someone had to retreat.

Realizing the ice he walked on was way too damn thin and getting thinner, Jesse grudgingly retreated. "Okay." He held out his hands, rattling the cuffs circling his wrists. "Take them off."

Barnett shook his head. "No way."

Jesse insisted. "I can't shift if anything distracts me." He held out his hands again. "Take them off or nothing happens."

Kamai tapped Barnett's elbow with his crop. "Take them off," he said amiably. "We want no distractions."

Grumbling a string of curses under his breath, Barnett removed Jesse's cuffs. "The collar stays on," he warned. "You try to run and I'll jerk that chain till you choke."

Jesse ignored his warning. Dropping into a crouch, he opened his mouth and curled his lips back from his teeth. For about a minute he looked like a man doing a bad parody of a cat. Then something happened. His white, perfectly normal human teeth began to change, his incisors swelling into sharp fangs that extended as his jaws widened. At the same instant, his eyes narrowed, irises fading from deep black into an amber shade. Tiny coils of energy sparked and crackled in their depth. Seconds later he disappeared.

A huge man-sized cougar sat in his place. Though the animal's eyes were all feline, the intelligence gleaming there was purely human.

Kamai looked down at the huge beast in wonder and amazement. "Fascinating." He clapped his hands together. "I have heard all my life of the shifter races. But to see one with my own eyes . . . I shall tell my employer they will be well worth the price. He has been anxious to acquire a pair since seeing the one owned by Prince Abdul Marhala."

Jesse quickly shifted back to human form, rearing up on his knees. "Three of our tribe have gone missing in the last year," he hotly accused.

Kamai tapped him on the cheek with his crop. "That number will increase significantly, I am sure, once word gets out among collectors of the curious that a whole pack of shifters exists." He looked to Dakoda. "But why should I pay for one that can't shift?"

Jesse quickly shook his head. "She's not one of us," he lied in an obvious attempt to negate Dakoda's worth. "That would make her a useless curio to your employer." He pointed at his chest. "I'm the one you want."

Kamai cut a look to Barnett. Slapping his crop against the palm of his hand, he frowned. "I told you I required at least two shifters. If she can't change, I refuse to pay full price."

Dakoda curled her lip in defiance. "Sorry. I can't. Never have." *Though I wish I could,* her mind echoed. She'd love to have a kick-ass set of claws and fangs to sink into some nice soft human flesh about now.

"That wasn't the deal," Barnett stammered, clearly in no place to bargain.

The expression on Kamai's face hardened. "I'll take her, but I won't pay full price," he snapped irritably.

Dakoda's heart sank. After all, she was witness to not only the outlaws' trafficking in human beings but also her own partner's murder.

Freedom is a word I might as well strike out of my vocabulary, she thought. If push came to shove, she definitely preferred the idea of being a rich man's pet, rather than a mangy outlaw's fuck toy. Her mouth curved into a frown. *At the very least, we'll probably live in a nice cage and eat better meals.*

Though he hastened to put a smile on his face, Willie Barnett wasn't a happy man. "Just take her off our hands," he grumbled. "We'll go two for the price of one."

Kamai started pacing, looking at the captives with an expression of chilling calculation. "I think that would be acceptable." He slapped his crop sharply against his leg. "There are many possibilities for their entertainment value."

"Good enough," Barnett said. "We have a deal."

Kamai smiled thinly. "Yes. We do." Slipping his crop under his arm, he returned to the chair he'd occupied earlier. Elbows resting on the arms, he stretched out his legs, crossing them at the ankle as if readying himself for the show. "In the meantime, I am anxious to observe the mating rituals of these *curiosities* in captivity." He flagged a hand toward Jesse. "Breed her." He cocked his head, smiling with self-induced amusement at his suggestion. "In your animal form."

Dakoda's brows shot up. "Did you just say . . ." Her words were a splutter of disbelief. She wasn't even sure that was physically possible.

And she damn sure didn't want to test the theory.

13

Dakoda lay on her side, staring at the wall. Legs drawn up to her chest, she hugged them tightly, attempting to bring a sense of warmth back into her body. It wasn't working. She was cold. So cold she doubted she'd ever get warm again.

Jesse pressed closer to her, attempting to add his body heat to hers. Hand settling on her shoulder, he bent close to her ear. "I'm sorry about what happened," he murmured. "It was terrible, I know."

Hearing his words, Dakoda squeezed her eyes shut. "That was humiliating," she grated through clenched teeth. Though the images hovered at the edge of her mind, she refused to pull them out of the shadows and look. It was bad enough they'd been forced to strip naked for inspection. Worse still was being fondled like a piece of merchandise, her nude body invaded by an unwelcome hand. But the coup de grace had been Kamai's demand that she and Jesse have sex—with Jesse in cougar form.

Bestiality. The word floated up from the dark morass bubbling in her skull, bringing with it a distinctly sour, sewer-like odor. She reeled at the thought of such a twisted and perverted thing happening between herself and an animal. Even if the animal was Jesse, it was still, well, *wrong* on so many levels.

And anyone who'd suggest such a thing was a sick psycho. Anyone who'd want to watch, sicker still.

There are a lot of sick people in this world, she thought. And she'd had the bad luck to run into all of them in the same place at the same time.

Dakoda opened her eyes, staring at the blank wall in front of her. They were back in the cell. Still prisoners, only their status had changed. The FOR SALE signs hanging around their necks had been changed. Sold. Kamai had purchased them both, paying over a million dollars to acquire his valuable prizes.

A storm rolling in from the north had prevented their immediate departure. Outside the cell, thunder rolled, breaking up the sound of rain beating against the roof. Flashes of lightning emanated through the spaces in the front wall, viciously striking the earth with an electrifying lash. It was night fit for neither man nor beast. Everyone was forced to hole up and wait out the worst.

Unwrapping her body, Dakoda stretched out and rolled over. "It's okay." She sighed in an attempt to relieve her inner tension. "Nothing happened." She looked into Jesse's face, tense and drawn with worry. "Thank you for not doing it."

Palm settling against her cheek, Jesse's agonized gaze found hers. "I really didn't have much of a choice," he breathed, brushing her mouth with his. "There was no way I could perform like a circus animal, on command."

"You sure did piss them off."

Jesse frowned. "Got my ass whipped for it, too."

Dakoda grimaced, remembering the sound of Kamai's crop coming down hard across Jesse's exposed flesh. "How's your back?"

Jesse flexed his shoulders. "Not so bad. I'll survive. I won't like it, but I'll survive."

She looked at him with admiration. Throughout his beating, Jesse had refused to cry out, forcing himself to silence as lash after brutal lash sliced into his skin. He'd borne the punishment of a disobedient animal with pride, refusing to be cowed by the cruel hand of control. "Kamai didn't appreciate your defiance."

Jesse glowered a moment. "It still didn't stop him from buying us," he said, a hint of bitterness creeping into his voice. "We're still not any better off than we were. Once he gets us out of the country, we're goners. Never to be seen or heard from again."

Dakoda propped herself up on one elbow. "It happens all the time, though."

Jesse shot her a frown. "You know, it's hard to believe people can still be bought and sold like cattle in this day and age. What's even harder to believe is that it's happening to me."

She considered his words. "Earlier you said three men from your tribe had disappeared."

He nodded. "Yeah, vanished. Without a trace."

"Kamai mentioned he had seen one of the shifters, belonging to a Saudi prince, I think he said."

His frown returned, doubly fierce. "So what's your point? They're still gone, still captives."

Dakoda pressed a hand on his chest. The thud-thud of his heart beat wildly beneath her palm. "It means they are still alive. And if they're still alive, help can be sent."

Considering her words, he nodded reluctantly. "We still have to get out of here ourselves," he reminded her. "Seeing as we're between the rock and the hard place, that's unlikely to happen anytime soon."

She had to agree. "Right now the odds are definitely against us."

"Speaking of being hard and being against something . . ." Jesse snuggled closer until his partially clad body connected with her fully clothed one. "I have to admit I'm glad I'm not alone. I hate to say it, but it helps having somebody to hold on to. If that sounds stupid or selfish, I'm sorry."

His confession echoed exactly what she'd been thinking.

Dakoda searched his gaze with hers. Her breasts pillowed against his chest, nipples instantly rising to hard little beads inside her snug bra. Heat bloomed between her thighs as she remembered the feel of his cock sliding into her eager depths. "It's not stupid," she said softly. "As much as I hate what's happening, I'm glad you're with me. I think I would have fallen apart and lost my mind if you hadn't been here."

His thumb brushed her lips. "You're strong, Dakoda. A lot stronger than I am."

Her brows rose in disbelief. She didn't feel a bit strong or capable. She felt weak and scared and stupid. Having Jesse to hold on to had been like having a life preserver to cling to. "Oh?"

Jesse's throat worked with emotion. "If it had just been me, on my own, I'd have killed myself for sure." His palm left her cheek. Fingers slipping to the nape of her neck, he adjusted her head to a more pleasing angle. "As it is, you've given me a lot of other things to think about. Nice things . . . ," he murmured, sliding into a slow, wet kiss.

Oh, God, this was what she'd been needing . . .

Dakoda's lips parted beneath his, eagerly welcoming the first invasive caress of his tongue against hers. Though in human form, Jesse tasted even more wild and feral than she remembered, like the untamed wilderness at midnight. The musk emanating from his bronzed skin was a richer, darker odor. The scent teased her nose, arousing her all over again.

God, how was it his slightest touch could turn her into a maniac, ravenous for sex? Every inch of his strong, burly frame pressed against hers, reminding her all over again of the delights of body-to-body contact.

The pressure of need built between them when his hand settled on her ass, dragging her hips closer to his. The brief breechclout he wore barely managed to cover his straining penis. All it would take is a tug at the thin leather ties to get it off. Then he'd have nothing on.

Nothing at all.

The plunk of a big fat drop of water jolted them apart.

Wiping his wet face, Jesse cursed. "Hey, what the hell?"

Cold droplets hit Dakoda on the face. Blinking up at the ceiling above their heads, she saw the beginnings of seepage. The damp planks were swollen and sagging from the deluge outside.

Wiping her face, she sat up. "Terrific. Just want I wanted to do, sleep in a wet bunk." As if it already wasn't miserable and cramped enough in the small cell. "Just one more thing to add to the discomfort," she added, scooting out from under the splats of water.

Jesse abruptly slid off the bunk. "It might be our way out," he said, looking up at the ceiling. "Look." He pointed. "See that?"

Dakoda tipped her head back, following his gesture. The ceiling had sprung a few more leaks, bringing in a steady stream of water. Anticipation zinged across her nerves. Maybe the light at the end of the tunnel wasn't the oncoming train after all. "I see it."

Jesse headed toward the worst of the leaks, one near the table. "A solid roof doesn't leak." Climbing up on the table, he circled one of the exposed beams with his hands, then hefted himself up so he could examine the source closer. "The wood's got some rot in it," he reported with a note of satisfaction.

Realizing the implications, Dakoda scrambled off the bunk. "Is it rotted enough we can dig it out?" she asked excitedly. Now that a glimmer of hope had presented itself, she felt a surge of energy through her veins, a much-needed burst of adrenaline to clear her head and sharpen her senses.

This is our chance, she told herself.

Jesse was working more quickly now, trying to wiggle his fingers between the narrow planks so he could get a hold. "Damn."

"What?" Dakoda moved up behind him, climbing onto one of the chairs to bring herself closer to the ceiling. She reached up, pressing the tips of her fingers against the damp wood. It gave a little. She pressed harder. "I can feel it giving way."

Jesse's hands dropped. "It's wet enough, but the rot hasn't gone all the way through. I need something sharp to gouge with, like a knife of something."

Dakoda pressed her feet against the chair and flattened her palms against the ceiling. "Nothing sharp," she grunted. "We'll just have to try brute force."

Jesse shook his head. "I'm a lot stronger than you, and I can't push through."

Suddenly Dakoda could feel it, the powerful blast of defeat slamming into her, reeking with despair and negativity. *It's no use,* it whispered in her ear. *Greg had no chance. What makes you think you deserve one?*

Shutting out the nagging voices, she growled an obscene curse and went on pummeling at the damp planks above her head. "You're not trying hard enough!" she snapped. "I don't want to be sold into fucking slavery, no matter how nice the cage might be." Bending her fingers, she dug her nails into the wood. A few small pieces of debris scattered across her face. She wiped them away with an angry hand. "If only I had some goddamned claws."

A light instantly went off between them.

Dakoda's hands dropped. "Jesse—" she started to say.

Smacking his hand against his forehead, he cut her off. "I can't believe I am that damn stupid," he groaned. "I'm right on it." Before she could blink, he'd shifted into his alternate form. A huge, tawny cougar sat on the table in the place he'd occupied.

She smiled. "Good going." At last, hope was beginning to become something more than a dim, half-imagined sentiment.

Jesse cautiously stretched upward, balancing on his hind legs. One huge paw settled on a beam for support. His free paw flexed, unsheathing a beautiful set of razor-sharp claws. Aiming toward the weakest point in the planks, he began to hollow out the rotted gut of the plank.

It was slow work.

Layer after layer fell away until a Frisbee-sized hole had been gouged through the ceiling.

Dakoda hissed out a breath of anticipation. "Bigger," she said, stroking a hand down the cougar's damp fur. "It needs to be big enough for us to crawl through."

The cougar abruptly vanished. Jesse held his hand in front of him, bloodied and torn by the sharp shards. "Sorry," he gasped, grimacing through the pain. "I needed a break." A little sigh broke through his lips. "Give me a minute and I'll try with my other hand."

Dakoda nodded. "Okay." Then she winced, realizing that he only had two good hands to work with and one was now out of commission. She glanced up at the hole he'd gouged in the ceiling. Nowhere near big enough to get through. "It's rotted, but not enough. At this rate it'll take all damn night."

Jesse disagreed. "It's the best shot we've had so far." He flexed the fingers of his good hand. "I'll dig until the skin peels away if I have to."

Before she knew what he was doing, Jesse shifted again. Releasing a roar that ripped through her ears, he flung himself at the ceiling. Digging both paws in, he used the leverage of his weight and hind legs to tear away more wood. Larger chunks snapped away, bringing in a torrent of rain.

Bigger. The hole was a little bigger.

Losing his grip on the slippery wood, Jesse fell hard, smashing against the tabletop with a body-shuddering thud.

"Careful," Dakoda warned, pushing the single word out between her tightly clenched teeth. Anticipation tightened her throat, sped up her heart beat. The tension was eating her up inside. "Don't hurt yourself, Jesse."

The cougar ignored her cautions.

Rolling back onto his feet, Jesse's sleek feline form took a second lunge toward at the ceiling. Unleashing another bone-shattering shriek echoing the reverberations of the thunder outside, his claws ripped through the wood like tornadoes eating up a city. More pieces of soggy timber disintegrated under his brutal assault, peeling away layer after layer. Seconds ticked away, spinning into long, jarring minutes.

Fists clenched as she watched the big cat at work, Dakoda could almost taste freedom. Escape would be the icing on the cake.

The hole expanded. Though it wasn't the biggest opening, it was wide enough to squeeze a cat through.

Dakoda clapped her hands with delight. *Or a very slender woman.* "I think we're on our way!" she shouted.

"What the hell do you think you doin'?" A voice savage with anger hollered behind them.

Startled by the intrusion, Dakoda whirled. Moving too fast to keep her balance, she stumbled against the back of the chair. Her ankle twisted out from under her. "Shit!" she cursed as a hot spear of pain tore up her left leg.

Losing her footing, she crashed to the bare ground with a bone-jarring crunch. The impact crushed the air from her lungs. For a moment she lay in a heap, dazed by the fall.

Before Dakoda could even focus her gaze, Rusty barged into the cell. He leveled his shotgun directly toward Jesse. "You'd better climb down from there, boy," he warned, brandishing the dangerous weapon like a shield between himself and the captives.

Dakoda glanced up in time to catch a glimpse of the cougar crouching low on top of the table. His ears were pinned flat, and Jesse's tail whipped back and forth like a kite in a high wind. Amber eyes lit with hate; an ominous growl rolled past sharp fangs.

Rusty took a threatening step closer. "Get down, Jesse!" he warned furiously. "Else I'm gonna blast you to hell and then some."

Unwilling to heed the warning, Jesse crouched lower. A high shrill roar exploded from his throat. His eyes glinted with furious intent. This time he wasn't going to back down.

Even if it cost him his life.

Dragging herself into a sitting position, Dakoda felt another white-hot bolt of pain shoot up her leg. Damn. She'd given her ankle a good twist. For all she knew, she'd broken the bone. Still, this wasn't the time to be thinking of herself. Having been pushed to the edge, Jesse obviously wasn't in any frame of mind to obey Rusty's warnings. He'd taken enough from the poachers.

Dakoda's heart thudded in long, sonorous beats. Oh, God, she doubted she could bear the sight of Jesse lying at her feet, shot to pieces. It couldn't possibly happen again.

Today isn't a good day to die, she thought wildly.

Dakoda threw up a pleading hand. "Don't!" she gritted, her voice rough with panic as she fought to help control the situation. One wrong move could end in tragedy.

Rusty sneered. "Better do what she says, Jesse. You might not be worth nothin' dead, but we can catch another just as easy as we got you."

Jesse immediately shifted. Naked, he continued to crouch on top of the table. "Stay away from my people," he snarled.

Rusty grinned. "Not while they're makin' us a whole hell of a lot of money."

Dakoda tried to appeal to the man's sense of reason. "For God's sake, they're human beings."

Rusty's smile morphed from unpleasantly arctic to a gut-twisting chill. "The red man ain't got no soul," he snapped. "That's why they're still like animals. And beasts like 'em were meant by God to be hunted and killed by man." As if to second his words, a rolling crack of thunder splintered the ferocious storm.

Who could reasonably argue with such insanity?

"He'll mind," she promised. "We both will."

Holding his gun with one hand, Rusty dug in the pocket of his heavy overcoat. He pulled out a set of handcuffs, then tossed them toward Jesse. "You put those on, nice and slow. Keep your hands where I can see them. Once you're hobbled, I'm gonna chain you up. Shift or not, you ain't goin' nowhere."

Jesse caught the cuffs. Glaring with rebellion, he snapped them around his wrists. "Fuck you."

The grate of metal on metal tore through Dakoda's heart. Escape had been close.

Rusty laughed and shot Dakoda a lecherous look. "After I get you all nice and hog-tied, the only one getting a fuckin' is her. I bet she's got one sweet poon, and I intend to get a little taste of it before sendin' her off with that slant-eyed prick."

Dakoda's stomach twisted. Tiny hot prickles of disgust skittered across her skin. *That definitely isn't going to happen!* Saying a quick prayer, she braced herself. She had an instant to make up her mind. Continue to be a victim, or start taking some names and kicking some serious ass.

Anger ratcheted through her. Ass-kicking won.

Acting more on instinct than rational thought, her booted foot shot out toward the toppled chair. Catching it between the slats, she used every ounce of strength she possessed to kick it toward the outlaw.

Her aim was true.

The chair sped toward Rusty's legs, catching him squarely behind the knees.

Struck suddenly from behind, Rusty stumbled forward, fighting to keep his balance—and his hold on the shotgun.

Seeing his chance, Jesse's shoulders flexed, muscle and sinew drawing into action as he launched himself from the table. Blasting forward in a powerful leap, he drove his full weight toward the outlaw. He hit hard, powering Rusty straight into the ground.

Flailing helplessly, Rusty landed hard on his back. He cried out, tobacco-stained lips peeling away from his teeth as he struggled to buck out from under Jesse's brawny weight. He tried to lever the shotgun across Jesse's throat. "Get the fuck off me!" he roared, his eyes blazing like coals from the deepest pit of hell.

Forcing the shotgun away from his neck, Jesse's shoulders flexed with exertion. Holding it tight, he twisted it back on its owner. "No way," he gritted, fighting against the strength of a desperate man. Having suffered enough abuse, he was equally as desperate.

Rusty fought harder, bucking like a bronco set loose on fiery ground. "You're gonna regret this, you son of a bitch."

Jesse's naked body shimmered with sweat as he strained to keep the upper hand against the outlaw. "I don't think so," he grunted. Gathering every ounce of strength, he twisted the shotgun out of the outlaw's grip. Hobbled by the limitations of his cuffed wrists, he somehow managed to hang on to the rifle's barrel.

A snarl rolled from Jesse's lips. "Let's see how you like the feel of this." Cocking the shotgun over his shoulder, he swung hard. His aim was dead-on. The stock made an instant connection with Rusty's temple. The sound of bone crunching against wood was sickening.

Rusty's head lolled to the side, and a moan rolled from his slack lips. Blood oozed from the gaping tear in his forehead.

The abrupt shift into motionlessness stunned. The fight was over almost as fast as it had begun. The storm still howled, cutting the cell off from the rest of the outlaws' compound.

Breathing hard, Jesse slowly backed away from the downed man. Chest rising and falling from his effort, he looked around wildly for another source of danger.

Dakoda relaxed. Rusty's mistake was readily apparent. He'd come alone, believing a shotgun was enough to handle two angry, desperate people. "I think that's it," she ventured.

Jesse turned his head, gaze settling on her. "Are you okay? You fell pretty hard."

Dragging herself off the floor, Dakoda nodded. "That fall was the best damn thing that's happened to us so far," she said, making light of her clumsiness. She winced when she tried to put her weight on her injured limb.

Jesse hurried toward her, offering a strong shoulder. "You're hurt."

Sliding a hand around his neck, Dakota gritted her teeth. "I twisted my freaking ankle." She shifted her weight back on to the leg, persisting through the twinges, ignoring the discomfort. Now wasn't the time to be hobbled by a bum leg. "I'm fine." She glanced down at the unconscious man. "But he's not."

Taking in the damage he'd inflicted, the rifle slipped from Jesse's limp fingers. "Shit," he gasped between breaths. "He's bleeding like a stuck pig."

Dakoda limped over to the outlaw. He reeked of wet tobacco and unwashed skin. It took all the willpower in her not to puke. "There's not enough soap and water in the world to get this man clean," she muttered, breathing through her mouth to lessen the stink. The idea of his hands on her exposed flesh made her skin crawl. She'd sooner jump into a river of boiling acid than endure a single touch of his nasty hands.

Jesse hovered. "Did I kill him?" The barest trace of regret laced his voice.

Dakoda glanced up at him. "You did what you had to," she said softly. At the time of the struggle, it had been kill or be killed and he'd acted on the impulse of the moment. Survival was an inborn instinct, but that didn't make taking the life of another human being any easier.

Using her training in CPR, she quickly checked for a pulse

and heartbeat. "He's alive." She eyed the cracked stock of the shotgun. "He's going to have one hell of a headache when he wakes up."

A sigh of relief broke from Jesse's lips. "I've never killed a man before . . ." His gaze drifted toward the rifle. He started to reach for it. "But in this instance I think I could."

Dakoda caught his wrist. She felt the tension, the anger boiling beneath his flesh. Nerves stretched taut, he was a mass of writhing emotions. "I won't say he doesn't deserve killing," she said slowly. "But we're not the ones to judge whether or not he gets it."

Jesse's gaze met hers. "I guess you're right," he allowed after a long pause.

As much as she didn't want to lay hands on the unconscious man, Dakoda set to riffling through his pockets. "The law will take care of him," she said, digging through the trash the outlaw had squirreled away. She found a small set of keys hiding between a pocketknife and a can of snuff. "And the sooner we get out of here, the sooner we can get some help and make it happen." She dangled the keys. "Give me your hands. No telling how long it will be before they miss him."

The cuffs dropped away from Jesse's wrists. "We need to make tracks." Grabbing the discarded loincloth, he shoved his feet into the moccasins.

Snatching her own jacket off the bunk, Dakoda looked him over. "That's not enough for you to be wearing out on a night like this."

"I haven't got much choice." Jesse eyed Rusty's clothes, visually measuring the man's build against his own. "You think—" he started to ask, prodding the unconscious man with a foot.

A smirk spread across Dakoda's lips. Despite the stink, Rusty's clothing was better than having nothing. "I think he deserves to be left naked—" She dangled the cuffs. "And hog-tied."

14

Exhaustion. Mind-numbing, body-aching, rubbery-legged exhaustion. If they had thought escape was going to be easy, they were wrong.

So wrong.

Feeling her ankle turn for the ten-thousandth time on the rocky terrain underfoot, Dakoda hissed out a moan of pain. "It's no use," she said, collapsing onto the muddy ground. "I can't take another step."

Jesse immediately knelt beside her. "We've got to get as far away as we can, before they find Rusty and come looking for us."

Soaked to the skin and bone cold, Dakoda curled her arms around her body, desperate for a little extra heat. "I know," she muttered through chattering teeth. "Believe me, I know. I just need a minute, Jesse. Just a minute . . ." Close to drifting off, her lids slipped shut.

"Wake up, Dakoda." A firm slap across her face brought her eyes open. "You can't go to sleep here."

"I'm so sleepy, Jesse," she whimpered. "And cold."

Jesse shrugged off his stolen overcoat, pressing it around her shoulders so the folds would fall over her body. The stink of its former owner still lingered in the material, but she didn't care. It was waterproof and warm and that's all that counted at the moment.

"Stay here," he said. "I'm going to look around and see if I can't find a place for us to hole up. We made at least three, maybe four miles, so that should be a good enough distance to buy us a little time." He looked around, attempting to make out the landscape, lit now and again by the flash of lightning penetrating the trees. Being out in the open wasn't safe. Being under a tree during a lightning storm wasn't, either. "The good news is the storm will cover our tracks. There'll be no telling which way we went."

Her lids drifted back down. "Uh, huh, okay . . ." At the moment, Dakoda just didn't care. She'd reached the end of her rope and hung dangling at the end. Her fingers were beginning to lose their grip as she slipped into a dark abyss.

Jesse pressed a small penlight—one of the many objects Rusty had stuffed his pockets with—into her hand. "Hold this. It'll give you a little light." He pressed a quick kiss against her chilly forehead. "I'll be back as soon as I can."

Dakoda nodded numbly. "Come back soon," she mumbled. "Please."

Jesse slipped off into the darkness.

Dakoda pressed closer to the tree, huddling in a mass. Even though they'd made it into a denser part of the forest, they'd still taken a good lashing from the intense rain. Her damp clothing clung uncomfortably to her skin, making her feel twice as cold every time the wind blasted through. Escape wasn't anything like she imagined. Instead of being happy to be out of the cell, she was missing the idea of a roof over her head and a warm blanket to curl up in. It didn't help matters one bit that her ankle felt thick and hot beneath the damp laces of her boot. She was going to pay dearly when she tried to take that boot off.

She sighed. "Nothing I can do but wait."

The minutes ticked away, each one stretching into a longer and longer arc. Ten minutes, twenty, then finally a half hour.

Dakoda fidgeted. Time was slipping away and still Jesse hadn't returned.

Worried, she forced herself to stand, leaning against the thick trunk for support. Her ankle throbbed in protest when she tried to put her weight on it.

She peered around. The gloom around her was thick enough to cut with a knife. Impenetrable. The tiny penlight was no help. She might as well have been shining it into outer space for all the illumination it provided.

A new thought niggled, something she'd been trying not to think about.

What if he doesn't come back? A chill began to creep up her spine. Ten thousand images slammed into her brain, each one worse than the other. Anything could happen on a stormy night in a dark forest and none of them were good.

If he doesn't come soon, she decided. *I'll have to go after him.* She couldn't sit there all night, waiting and wondering. The longer she stayed in one place, the better chance she had of being found and recaptured.

Dakoda hesitated. Leaving would mean she might become permanently separated from Jesse. If she wandered off, they might never find each other again.

She sat back down, pulling Rusty's slicker over her body to make a little tent of sorts. Inside the cavity she created was a little nest, a little pocket of warmth. "I'll just rest a minute," she told herself.

More time ticked away.

A sudden jolt brought Dakoda wide awake. Someone was digging through the coat, trying to get to her. Yanking it away, a blast of cool night air hit her squarely in the face, bringing her instantly awake.

She blinked, but her eyes were slow to focus in the gloom. A figure loomed in front of her, vaguely familiar.

She fumbled for the penlight he'd left in her care. "J-Jesse!?" she stammered, attempting to pull her wits together and stuff them back into her skull.

He knelt beside her. "It's me." His long hair whipped around his face and shoulders, tugged by the wind's violent gusts. "Sorry I was gone so long. I got lost a couple of times."

A corner of her mouth turned up. "Some Indian you are. Thought you guys were born trackers."

He chuckled. "Yeah, well, contrary to popular belief, not all Indians are country boys in tune with the land of their ancestors. I was born in the city and I need a map to get around just like anyone else." Another soft laugh. "It would also help if I had night vision. Most of where I'm going is a guess."

Stiff and achy, Dakoda clambered to her knees. Every joint and muscle in her body sang out in protest. She gritted her teeth against the pain and forced herself to ignore it. "Did you find somewhere we could hole up?"

Jesse knelt, slipping a shoulder under her arm so he could help her rise. "Actually, I did. I think you'll be pretty happy, too."

Leaning against his solid frame, a flicker of hope sparked in her head. "A cave?" she asked, envisioning a nice snug hole to crawl in and curl up.

"Better." His voice carried a tone of achievement.

"Better would be me at home, in my own bed," she groused.

He pounced on that one the way a cat would a tasty morsel. "Better would be me, at your house, in your bed," he hinted.

Dakoda lifted her chin. "Is that all you think about, getting in my pants?"

A soft laugh wafted through the wind, caressing her ears. "All the time," he chuckled.

She flashed the tiny penlight in his face. "Can we just go, you damn horny toad?"

"Cougar," he corrected through a grin. "Horny cougar."

Urging her forward, Jesse led her through a thick area of trees and other weedy brambles. Dakoda's bum ankle ached with every step, but she forced herself to concentrate on walking. Jesse already had enough on his hands without worrying about a cripple.

Somehow, they pressed forward. Nothing was familiar. Nothing recognizable. Every tree and bush looked like the last, stretching on endlessly. These mountains truly were the middle of nowhere.

Despair rose. It seemed like they'd walk forever on a trail that would go on and on until they just collapsed and died from exhaustion.

"Are you sure this is the right way?" she grunted between painful steps.

Jesse nodded. "It's here, I know," he muttered.

"What?"

He all of the sudden came to a halt. Lifting his arms, he pointed toward a tangled mass. "There."

Dakoda's gaze followed the direction he indicated. "Am I seeing . . . ?" she started to ask. Eyes snapping open, exhaustion drained away as familiar lines were illuminated through bright flashes of lightning.

He nodded. "It's a plane. One of the wings has snapped off and the belly's tore up a little, but otherwise it's intact." He caught her ice-tinged hand, squeezing her fingers with his larger, warmer ones.

She smoothed her tangled hair away from her face. The wreckage was the best thing she'd ever seen in her entire life.

Tears pricked at her eyes. She blinked them away. Now wasn't the time to get all sentimental. "Crashed, no doubt."

"No doubt," he agreed. "Bad for them. Good for us." He tugged her forward. "And wait until you see what's inside."

They headed for the plane, taking care to pick their way through the rubble of downed trees and other scattered debris. The last thing Dakoda needed was another broken ankle.

After plummeting out of the sky, the plane had clearly skidded across the tops of the trees. The force of the impact had completely torn off one wing and bent the other. The cockpit was smashed, something the pilot couldn't possibly have survived. It had come to a rest on the ground upright, minus its landing gear.

Jesse wrenched open the side hatch. "I couldn't believe it when I found this," he huffed, pulling himself up into the opening. "It's like manna from heaven." He bent and held out a hand for Dakoda. "Coming?"

She nodded and gave him her hand. "Gladly." Jesse hefted her inside. She dug in her pocket, flicking on the penlight he'd left with her, shining it into the black, yawning void.

One look told her the plane wasn't for passengers. No, this big old baby was stripped down and outfitted for hauling cargo. A series of storage bays lined the walls, leaving the middle aisle reserved for the main portion of the shipment. Square bales wrapped in black tarp and duct tape were stacked one atop the other. There must have been a hundred, maybe more.

Dakoda's eyes widened. "Is that what I think it is?"

Jesse grinned. "Yep. Marijuana." He looked around. "I'd say some drug dealer somewhere is a very unhappy man."

Dakoda flashed the penlight around. "How long do you think it's been here?"

Jesse cocked a thumb toward the front of the plane. "Judging by the look of the bodies still strapped in the seats, they've been here quite awhile. Didn't take long for all the little beasties in the forest to make a good meal of the remains."

Dakoda shivered, grimacing at the thought. "I don't think I want to see." A thought occurred. "I don't suppose the radio works?"

He shook his head. "That's the first thing I checked. It's smashed."

"Just our luck, which really seems to suck lately." She shined the thin beam around. "I'm surprised they haven't found the wreckage."

"Even if they have, there's nothing they can use here." Jesse kicked a bale. "Unless you're a drug dealer or jonesing for a doobie, it's all pretty worthless."

Dakoda sighed. "Guess you're right there." Struggling out of the borrowed overcoat, she lay it aside. Taking a seat atop the bales, she stretched out her legs. "Well, at least we've got a roof over our heads."

"That's a plus," Jesse agreed.

She looked around. "What's in the storage?"

He shrugged. "Don't know. Haven't had time to look."

She handed over the penlight. "Might as well."

Jesse set to rummaging through the bays, which doubled as seating for the plane's passengers. He flipped up one flat top, shining the light inside. "Oh, this is good."

Dakoda heard the sound of broken glass shifting. "What is it?"

Jesse dug some more. "Booze," he said, pawing through a carton stuffed with straw. "Most of the bottles are broken, but . . . Ah!" He pulled out an undamaged bottle. "Pay dirt. Looks like our smugglers dealt in more than weed."

Feeling a twinge at the back of her throat, Dakoda licked her dry, chapped lips. "Heaven be praised. I could use a drink about now. What is it?"

Jesse handed the bottle over. "Looks like Mexican tequila, worm and all."

Dakoda scrunched up her nose. "Tequila ain't my favorite thing," she said, cracking the seal and catching a whiff of the distinctive scent. "In this case, I'll make an exception." Putting the rim to her lips, she tipped back her head and took a healthy swallow. The tequila burned all the way down her throat, lighting a fire in her belly. Warmth began to seep into her chilled system. Various aches and pains throughout her body settled down into a dull throb.

"Hey, take it easy," he warned. "You're drinking on an empty stomach. Too much and you'll pass out cold."

Dakoda handed over the bottle, wiping her mouth with the back of her hand. "Don't remind me that I haven't eaten much today. I'm so damn hungry the worm in that bottle is starting to look good."

Jesse took a quick swig. "Let me see what else I can find."

He dug through some more bins. "More damn alcohol," he groused, slamming the lids shut. "Don't drug smugglers have to eat?"

Dakoda pointed to another row of bins on the opposite wall. "How about those?" She started to rise, but trying to put pressure on her ankle sat her back down. She winced, a breath of air escaping through her teeth in a hiss. "Damn, I think getting off it was the worst thing I could have done."

"Just stay put and I'll do the looking," he said, waving her back down.

He switched sides, digging through more bins. He lifted a couple of thick heavy-looking parcels out of one. "Well, here's the parachutes they obviously didn't get to use."

"A lot of good those will do," she groused.

He set them aside. "More good than you think, actually. They'll make quite a snug bed for us tonight."

Dakoda sipped a little more tequila. More warmth spread through her, delivering a contented glow. "Good idea," she nodded. "Looks like that Indian sense is beginning to kick in."

Jesse moved to another set of bins. "Last set." He opened them up and shined the light inside. "I wish I could say things were looking up for us."

Dakoda craned her neck to see. "What is it?"

Frowning deeply, he reached inside. "Unfortunately it isn't anything we can eat." He pulled out a small carton, shining the light across its face: .9MM LUGER AMMUNITION. "Looks like our drug dealers came prepared for trouble."

Dakoda closed her eyes in dismay. Through the last few hours she'd been feeling woozy, trying to ignore the growls and rumbling deep in her stomach. Knowing Jesse was probably just as hungry, she hadn't complained. They'd been denied further meals as punishment for not performing for Kamai. A hungry animal, he'd said, would perform better.

She pressed a hand against her stomach to stay the growl deep inside her gut. "Any guns there?"

Jesse pulled out a couple of leather pouches. "I'm going to guess this is the firepower." He unzipped one of the pouches and took the weapon out. "Just what I thought." He made a quick check of the magazine and slide with the confidence of one used to handling a firearm. "Loaded and ready for action," he announced.

Dakoda cocked a brow. "You seem to know what you're doing."

Jesse returned the gun to its pouch. "I can handle myself," he said. "If it comes to them killing me or me killing them, you can be pretty much assured I will pull the trigger first."

She nodded. "In this case, I would have to agree." In the back of her mind she was sure she could shoot Skeeter Barnett down without hesitation and smile as she did it.

Jesse did a quick rundown. "So we've got our drugs, our

booze, and our guns. Pretty much everything you'd expect a smuggler to carry."

"Nothing else?" Dakoda asked plaintively.

He shined the penlight into the bin again. The small beam was losing its bright, cutting edge. The batteries clearly wouldn't last much longer.

Jesse showed her the white box marked with a big red plus sign. "And here's where you believe there is a God after all. What every good drug dealer needs to have on hand. A first-aid kit."

Dakoda grinned despite herself. "That's better than nothing."

"Don't forget, we have something nice and warm to wrap ourselves in," Jesse reminded. "Just give me a minute and I'll get us all settled in."

15

Jesse set to work, rearranging the belly of the plane into a campsite. Restacking some of the marijuana bales, he hollowed out a good-sized space in the center of the shipment, leaving a single layer as padding against the bare floor. Ripping open the parachutes, he unfurled the nylon material, spreading it out to form a layer of bedding.

Hands on his hips, Jesse surveyed his efforts with satisfaction. "Your castle awaits, my lady."

Tequila clutched in one hand, Dakoda slid over the waist-high bales and lowered herself into the space. Though half the size of the cell they'd earlier occupied, it was a hell of a lot cozier. Giving a little sigh of relief, she sank down on the bale-padded floor. "Oh, man. This is the first time I've felt safe since all this shit began."

A particularly strong gust of wind hit the plane, giving the wreckage a good shove. "At least we're out of the storm," Jesse said, climbing in with the first-aid kit. "Just a minute and I'll take a look at your ankle. Still bothering you?"

"Yeah, in the worst of ways." Bending a leg, Dakoda clawed

at the laces of her boots. The water had swollen them tight and thick, making them difficult to handle. "I'd like to get these off," she groused. "My foot is killing me."

"Let me." Clenching the penlight between his teeth, Jesse used the tip of his stolen pocketknife to pry the laces apart. Untying them, he eased the boot off Dakoda's foot, and then her wet sock. His fingers gently probed her ankle, swollen to twice its normal size.

Stretching and wiggling her cramped toes, Dakoda leaned back against the bales. "Is it broken?"

Manipulating the area, Jesse shook his head. His touch heated her skin, causing the hair at the nape of her neck to rise with pleasant anticipation. "I didn't make it to med school, but I don't think so. You twisted it pretty bad, though. Best thing for it now is to stay off it." Reaching for the first-aid kit, he snapped it open. "Let's see here . . ." He pawed past a roll of sterile gauze for an elastic bandage and adhesive tape. "This ought to stabilize your ankle." He handed over the light. "Keep it steady so I can see what I'm doing."

Holding the penlight for him, Dakoda watched him unroll the elastic, then carefully circle it around her swollen ankle. As he bent closer, his scent assailed her senses, lush and wildly exotic. He smelled of the storm and his own musky heat. Knowing how he tasted, how his hard muscled body felt on top of hers, sent a tremor up her spine.

No time to be thinking about that, she warned herself. With a roof over her head and a belly full of intoxicating tequila, her mind was beginning to drift toward other things. A curiously familiar numbness was spreading through her body. She was more than a little tipsy. It was easy to imagine making slow, sweet sensuous love to him atop the silken material.

Pushing the forbidden thoughts away, she cleared her throat and tried to remember what the subject was before she'd veered off track.

"Looks like you've had some medical training," she commented, noting he took care to make sure the circulation wasn't cut off. As a junior ranger she'd taken several courses on wilderness survival. She had a rough idea which plants were edible, which were poisonous, and how to stay hydrated when drinkable water wasn't readily available. Stumbling onto the wreckage was a stroke of luck.

"Actually, I have," he said.

"Oh?" Braced by the stretchy material, her foot instantly felt a hundred percent better. Another swig of tequila helped even more.

Jesse used a few strips of tape to secure the bandage. "I worked as a lifeguard at the college pool." He shrugged. "Went through a couple of training courses. For a while I thought I might switch and study to become a paramedic."

Her brow wrinkled. "I thought you were studying to be an accountant."

"*Was* is the key word," he reminded. "I never graduated."

She shook her head. "Somehow I don't see you as a bean counter."

"Honestly I don't either." A low laugh broke from his lips. "Thanks to my uncle, I had a job on the reservation, working in the casino after I graduated. Nice salary, good benefits. I'd have been set for life."

"Do you regret leaving all that behind?" Dakoda asked.

Jesse thought a moment. "On good days, I like living in these mountains, being wild and free. On bad days—like now—I miss the conveniences of a normal life."

Dakoda nodded. "I guess there are advantages to both."

Jesse sighed. "Our tribe would have more advantages if the wheels of the federal government didn't grind so exceedingly slow. I am sure the powers-that-be think we're just a bunch of crazy Indians out here running wild with the big cats."

Dakoda stifled a giggle behind her hand. "All the while not knowing you *are* the big cats."

He reached for the bottle of tequila. "And not many of us left at all," he said, after taking a quick sip. "It's really an ability that's dying out. Somehow our tribe held on to the old knowledge, but I don't know how much longer we'll have it. The elders are dying off, and the next generation has been seduced by modern technology and beliefs."

"I can see where it would be difficult to hang on to such an ability in today's world. Who could believe such a thing without seeing it with their own eyes?"

Jesse took another thoughtful sip, grimacing as the strong alcohol hit his stomach. "No one would, and that's the point. We've got to manage to hang on to our fading heritage without letting the outside world know we exist. Can you imagine the media frenzy if something like this got out?"

Dakoda winced. "I wouldn't even want to imagine it," she said.

"Neither would I." Jesse patted her foot, then helped her take off her other boot. He sat them up on the edge of the bales. "That's taken care of. Now let's see if we can't do something to take the edge off the pain." Looking in the first-aid kit again, he dug through some antiseptic wipes and antibiotic cream, finally coming up with a plastic container of plain old aspirin. He shined the light on its label. "It's expired." He tossed it back in the box. "No good."

Dakoda lifted the tequila bottle. "Guess this will have to do."

He watched as she took another stiff drink. "Is it helping?"

She wiped her mouth with the back of her hand. "I don't know, but I don't care." Her voice was more than a little slurred.

"Better slow down," he cautioned. "Don't want to wake up with a nasty hangover tomorrow."

Hunger was getting the better of her. She finally had to open up and spit it out. "I don't suppose there's something to eat in that damn kit," she asked. "I hate to complain, but I think I'm about to pass out."

Jesse shook his head. "Medical supplies, yes. Food, no. We're shit out of luck on that count."

She pressed a hand to her woozy forehead. "Guess I will have to pass out then." Unconsciousness might be more merciful at this point.

Jesse grinned. "Not so fast. Help might yet be on the way."

"What are you going to do," she groused. "Go out and catch us something to eat?"

"If it weren't storming, that would be an option," he said. "I'm a pretty good hunter on four paws. In this case, however, I think we'll have to thank our old friend Rusty for our snacks."

She brightened. "Snacks?" She gave him a suspicious look. "You been holding out on me, Jesse?"

"You had the coat while I was gone. For all I know you gobbled up everything." Standing up, he reached for the outlaw's overcoat.

Dakoda perked up. She'd been too busy trying to stay warm to think about riffling through the coat for something to eat. It simply hadn't occurred to her to look. "What are you saying?"

Jesse flipped open the coat, showing her its inner pockets. "Turns out old Rusty is a true mountain man. He's stuffed every pocket with items you'd need in a pinch." He pulled out a handful of foil-wrapped packets. "Dehydrated, high-calorie food bars."

Dakoda had to restrain herself from making a grab for the precious items. "I don't care what it is, as long as you can eat it."

He laughed and handed over a couple of the bars. "You can. It says on the side of the wrapper they're edible for five years."

Dakoda tore through the plain silver wrapping. The food bar inside was dry and hard. She took an experimental nibble, breaking off a bite between her teeth. Chewing slowly, she cautiously swallowed down the mass. "Not real good," she commented, taking another bite. "But not real bad. Tastes like one of those Danish butter cookies, except without the flavor."

Jesse tore off a chunk of his. "A really dry butter cookie," he agreed, washing his bite down with a sip of tequila. He eyed the worm floating at the bottom of the bottle. "I may yet consider that dessert."

Shoving another bite in her mouth, Dakoda squinched up her face. "Oh, yuck. I think I'll pass on the insect." She chewed slowly, careful not to rush and gulp down her food. The last thing she needed was a bellyache.

He laughed and winked. "A half hour ago you were ready to wrestle me to get it."

Finished with her first bar, Dakoda ripped open another packet. "That was before I got my hands on these. I'm pretending they're biscotti and that I have a nice hot cup of coffee with extra cream and sugar to dip them in." She devoured the second bar, which tasted vaguely like apples and cinnamon. By the time she'd swallowed the last bite, the hungries had begun to subside, leaving her with a warm, contented feeling. Her head still swam pleasantly from the alcohol she'd consumed, just enough to blunt the unpleasantness of their present dilemma.

Tomorrow the pressing problems of escape and survival would return. But for now those things were temporarily put aside. By some grace they'd managed to stumble into a safe haven, however temporary. *Thank the drug dealers for that.* No telling how long had passed since the plane went down. Out in the middle of nowhere, most wreckage took years to discover, if it was found at all.

"Missing the comforts of home?" Jesse asked, jarring her out of her thoughts.

She blinked, startled by the question. He had an uncanny way of homing in on what she was thinking. "Honestly? I am. I'd give my eyeteeth for a hot shower. I don't think I'll ever be completely warm again."

Finished with his meal, Jesse leaned back against the stacked bales. "I wonder if this shit's any good."

Dakoda's brows rose. "You mean, smoke it?"

He poked his pocketknife through the plastic covering. "Smells decent." He reached for the breast pocket of his borrowed shirt, producing a roll of cigarette papers. "And our man Rusty liked to make his own." Picking out some of the marijuana, he expertly rolled himself a thick joint.

Dakoda frowned. "You've got some experience there," she noted dryly.

Jesse beamed and lit up with his borrowed cigarette lighter. The end flared red when he took his first puff. "College, man. The parties, the chicks, the keggers. Shit, those were the days." He inhaled deeply, then sent out a stream of smoke.

The cloyingly sweet odor of the marijuana singed Dakoda's nostrils. She waved a hand in front of her face, chasing the tendrils of white smoke away. "That does bring back memories." She frowned. Unfortunately they weren't very good ones.

"You toke a few?" he asked, offering her the joint.

Dakoda shook her head, declining. "I used to have a little problem with the stuff," she admitted honestly. "I did more than my share and then some."

His brows rose in surprise. "You don't strike me as the party hearty type."

She allowed a dry laugh. "I was the type through most of my teenage years. You could say I was a chip off my mother's block, following in her footsteps."

He considered the joint he'd rolled, letting it burn. "Did your mom do a lot of drugs?" His question delivered a hard jolt.

Dakoda's mouth thinned, the beginning of a snarling come-back. Somehow she held the impulse in check, swallowing back the bitterness. His question was entirely reasonable. She didn't have to give him a detailed history. A short, sweet answer would suffice. "Let's just say my mother wasn't going to win any parent of the year awards. The only time she was clean was when she was in jail, and even then she managed to get things smuggled in. Saying she had a bad drug problem doesn't even begin to describe my mother's addictions."

Jesse must have sensed her tension and discomfort in the presence of a drug she'd once indulged in with little regard for the damages it would do to her mind, or her status as a juvenile delinquent. Licking his thumb and forefinger, he extinguished his smoke.

He flicked the butt away. "You said a few things earlier, about your mom and the fact you didn't know your father. Sounds like things were rough when you were a kid." His voice had lost the playful tone, becoming serious.

For just a moment Dakoda considered changing the subject. Then she shook off the impulse. Hiding her past was the same as running from it. Instead of being ashamed of where she'd come from, she should be proud she'd overcome the handicap of having an irresponsible parent.

She drew a long breath. "Listen, I'm going to tell you the truth," she said, going flat out and straight ahead. "My mom was nothing but a whore, a druggie, and a petty thief. I never saw much of her because she was usually in the slam, or off party-ing. My dad—" She shrugged. "Like I told you. She probably didn't know him long enough to even get his name. More than likely, he picked her up as a twenty-dollar trick, and never even knew he'd made a kid."

Jesse held up his hands in a defensive gesture. "Whoa! I think I'm detecting a little bitterness there."

"You could say I'm a little pissed," Dakoda agreed, at the

same time wondering why her inner anger would choose to rear its head just now. She usually tried not to let the past intrude on the present, yet somehow the bad old days had a way of creeping in when she least expected their arrival. "While other kids were going to school, and bringing cookies their moms baked, I was shacked up with whoever she could shove me off on. I can't tell you how many men we'd lived with by the time I was fourteen."

A low whistle escaped him. "Damn. I'm sorry. That must have been tough."

She laughed shortly. "Hey, it's the card I drew being born. I guess I'm lucky. Of all the kids she got knocked up with, I'm the only one she didn't abort or give away." Feeling a knot forming in the back of her throat, she lapsed into silence. In her mind the past should be dead and gone. Poking through the graveyard of memories wouldn't do her any good.

Jesse leaned forward, reaching out to brush her tangled hair away from her face. "She must have known there was something special about you, Dakoda. You were the one she held on to."

Suddenly unwilling to be the recipient of his pity, she pushed his hand away. His touch held too many implications, things she wasn't sure she was ready or able to deal with, no matter how attracted she was to him.

Bile simmered, creeping up the back of her throat. She forced herself to meet his gaze without blinking. "You don't know what you're talking about!" she snapped without thinking. "You think that was a good thing, being dragged around like so much garbage?" She regretted the words the instant they sped past her lips, but it was too late to take it back.

He slowly shook his head. "I'm not saying it was a good thing. What I am saying is that what happened in your past made you the person you are today. People don't become rangers just because they have a whim. You've obviously

worked hard to get where you are, and you did that by not letting the past hinder you."

She slumped back against the bales. Her vision began to
blur, her eyes pricked by the rise of tears behind her lids. "I'm
sorry I snapped at you." She blinked away the offending mist
of emotion. "I can't take credit for doing all the hard work,
Jesse. The last man my mom hooked up with before she
crashed and burned is the one who ended my career as budding
criminal. Ash. Ash Jenkins. He took care of me when no one
else wanted me."

He nodded his understanding. "So you did have someone
good in your life?"

Dakoda nodded. "Yeah. Ash was a cop. He forced me to
straighten up, get clean, and fly right. How he ended up with
my mom, I'll never know. I think it was his desire to rescue a
lost soul. He always believed people could change. Too bad
some people are rotten to the core."

She closed her eyes a moment, allowing the memories in.
These were the good ones, the ones she was happy to remember. It was easy to picture her stepfather. A big, burly man, he
could kick ass with the best of them, then just as easily turn
around and save a tiny kitten out of a drainpipe. Just being a
good human being wasn't enough for Ash. He believed to serve
and protect his fellow man was the best pursuit in life. In that
belief, he was an extraordinary man.

"You said *was*," Jesse commented quietly. "Did something
happen?"

Remembering how her stepfather had died, Dakoda felt her
stomach clench, then commence a backward slow roll. It was a
little more than ironic the two men she'd valued as mentors had
both been shot down in the line of duty.

Forcing her eyes open, she sucked in a quick breath through
her teeth. Though they'd turned off the little penlight to pre-

serve the batteries, she could still make out Jesse's figure between intermittent flashes of lighting. She was glad he couldn't see her clearly, tell how close she was to crying.

"He was killed," she finally said, jaw tightening around the toughest three words in the world to spit out. "Some punk with a gun and an attitude. They never caught the little bastard."

Jesse's dark gaze met hers. By the illumination of the flickering lightning his eyes danced with unnatural glimmerings. "I'm sorry," he murmured simply.

"Don't be." Feeling as limp and spent as a wet dishrag, Dakoda scrubbed both hands across her numb face. Her eyes were scratchy with exhaustion, and every bone in her body ached. "Let's not talk any more." She sighed. "All I want to do now is lie down and rest my eyes for a little while."

Jesse grunted his assent, then gave a yawn and a stretch. "I have to admit I could use a little nap myself." Standing up, he started to strip out of his clothes. Rusty's flannel shirt had turned out to be a tad too small for him, and the material was tautly stretched across his broad shoulders and chest. The cuffs rose at least two inches above his wrists.

Catching a flash of naked skin, Dakoda felt her stomach make a quick backflip. "What are you doing?" The temporary resentment she'd felt against him faded away. *Must be nice to be such a free and easy spirit,* she thought, *carrying no baggage through life.*

Spreading the shirt over the top of the bales, he kicked off his shoes. "Getting out of these wet clothes." The borrowed jeans followed. A little too tight, they clung to every curve of his ass and hips. He wrestled them down his legs, then stepped out of the mass. Because the jeans had been snug, he'd had to discard the breechclout to get them on. Shirt and jeans gone, he was back to the state he seemed to be most comfortable in.

Buck-ass naked.

16

Dakoda couldn't help staring. God, Jesse Clawfoot was a beautiful man. His nudity was mesmerizing, erotic, and enticing. There was something magical about him, in the way his slightest touch sizzled over her skin. It was as if he held some inner electrical charge, and her body completed the connection that would make the power surge. If she looked close enough she fancied she could almost see the glow radiating inside him.

She held out a hand. "I think I need a little help." A tremor ran up her spine. His waiting body promised all kinds of carnal pleasures.

Pleasures she was too weak to resist. More to the point, his touch was a pleasure she didn't want to resist. He knew just how to make love to her, giving her all the delightful gratification she could handle, and more.

Jesse's fingers curled around hers. His grip was firm as he lifted her to her feet. "Careful there," he breathed. "Try not to put your weight on your ankle."

Dakoda leaned against the hard plane of his chest. The brush of damp lace cups against her sensitized nipples tormented her.

The first heat of desire trickled between her thighs. Need swamped her like the waves of a storm-tossed sea. "Thanks," she breathed.

"No problem," he murmured into her hair.

She struggled with the zipper of her jacket, barely able to make her hands work. Damn, she didn't think she'd had that much to drink, but apparently she was mistaken. The thing confounded her.

Jesse took over. "Let me," he offered, one corner of his mouth turning up in a suggestive smile. Metal on metal crunched. He slipped her jacket off her shoulders, draping it over the edge of the bales. "Now your shirt."

Dakoda's head tipped back. "Okay," she breathed. Her legs quivered, close to collapsing under her weight. Fearing she would fall, she held on to him tighter. All she wanted was for him to hold her, love her . . .

His fingers plucked at the front of her shirt, slowly undoing each button. A moment later Jesse slid her shirt off her shoulders. Her bra followed. Cool air caressed her bare skin, sending a spray of goose pimples across her exposed flesh.

His breath hitched. "Damn, you're so gorgeous." He shifted closer, running the tips of his fingers across the curve of her collarbone. "Every time I get close to you, I get hard."

Feeling the heat emanating from his eager body, her mouth curled. She might have said something similar about her own physical reactions. "What are you going to do with all that surging testosterone?" she breathed in a coy voice.

His featherlight caress swept up her neck, gently tipped back her head. "Well, I can think of a few ways to ease the tension," he said. "That is, if you're not too tired to submit to a little friendly molestation."

Dakoda leaned into him. The tips of her nipples rasped against his bare chest, sending a delicious shiver of anticipation shimmying down her spine. Somehow the outside world always seemed to fade away when they were together. When his arms were around her, embracing her, everything felt good. Right.

"Molest away," she breathed.

Dakoda didn't get a chance to say much more. His mouth settled on top of hers, the beginning of a slow and gentle kiss that rocked her senses. Arms circling his neck, she willingly opened for him as his tongue pressed against the seam of her lips. Granted entry, he eased his tongue into her mouth, conquering with a silk-warm stroke. He tasted like tequila, an enticing flavor that made her entire body quiver.

Closing her eyes, Dakoda let him lead in the sweet, slow dance their bodies knew so well. His lips charted a new course, lower, tracing the soft curve of her chin, then nibbling along the pulse beating frantically beneath the surface of her skin.

Dakoda shivered as Jesse's big palm cupped the curve of one breast, his thumb sweeping over the pebble-hard tip. "Feel good?" he murmured, catching her bottom lip between his teeth and giving it a gentle tug.

"Umm, yesss. . . ." Dakoda's pulse thrummed behind her temples, each pounding beat keeping time with the anticipation coiling deep inside her core. Her body ached, her nipple peaking as he tugged and rolled the sensitive tip.

He brushed another soft kiss against her lips. "I want you," he breathed into her mouth. "But only if it's something you want, too."

Dakoda gasped out a strangled giggle. "It's all I've been thinking about all day," she confessed, her tongue loosened by the alcohol she'd consumed. Slipping a hand between them, she curled her fingers around his jutting erection. "Judging by the size of this, you have, too."

Jesse moaned softly, slipping a hand between her thighs and rubbing slow circles against the crotch of her slacks. "All I want is to slide into that warm, tight cunt of yours."

"Need to get these pants off," she mumbled, trying to keep

one hand on his magnificent cock while working the button of her slacks with the other.

Jesse caught both her hands. "Slow down." He pressed her back against the stack of marijuana bales, settling her butt on the edge. "You just relax and I'll take care of the rest."

Dakoda clenched her teeth. Relaxing was the last thing she had on her mind. "I'm not sure I can wait," she gritted. "I'm already creaming my panties." Though she rarely talked in a raunchy or racy way during sex, somehow it felt right with Jesse. He truly brought out the bad-girl side she'd kept bottled up and stifled for so long.

For the first time in her life she was able to recognize and enjoy her sensuality. Men had taken her body before, used her, sometimes even abused her. She'd taken it, because that's what women did. Shut up and spread their legs, praying to get the fucking over with minimal damage.

As she'd gotten older, she'd gotten tired of getting nothing out of sex. It was easier to cut off her emotions and access to her body, rather than endure a man panting over her. Being alone and on her own was easier, less complicated.

Jesse Clawfoot had tumbled her right back into that pit of complication and confusion. Except this time, instead of being sickened by the touch of a man, she found herself eagerly yearning for his touch, for the passion he ignited deep inside her soul. She hungered for the feel of his mouth on hers, hungered for the feel of his hard, turgid shaft sliding into, pummeling her ravenous sex.

For the first time in a long time, Dakoda Jenkins was going to let herself go wild.

Jesse gave her another slow kiss. "Let's find out just how wet you are." Sucking in a hiss between his teeth, he skimmed his fingers in the waistband of her khaki slacks. "I love the way these fit around your hips," he said, unsnapping the top button under her navel. "They hug every curve of your ass."

Her zipper crunched down, the sound barely heard above the roll of thunder and patter of hard rain striking the plane. She started to move away from the bales, help him push down her slacks, when he stopped her.

"Just lean back," he murmured in her ear.

"What are you going to do?" she breathed, lungs heavy with anticipation.

"Something like this." A seeking male mouth descended on one tented nipple.

Dakoda gasped, then moaned as his tongue circled the hard little peak, scraping against sensitive inner nerves with each velvety tug of his mouth.

Her fingers tangled in his thick black hair. "Oh, Jesse," she moaned. "That feels . . ." The words disappeared, overtaken by yet another series of moans. She had barely had time to think about what he was doing, when he added another sensation to the mix. The parts of her brain governing rational thought dissipated under a wave of carnal appetite.

Still suckling at her breasts, he slipped one hand into her slacks, working his fingers under the elastic band of her panties. Thick fingers found her aching clit, rubbing gently against the small hooded organ.

Dakoda instinctively rolled her hips against his massaging fingers. Using his other hand to brace his body above hers, Jesse moved from one eager nipple to the next, suckling the sensitive tips.

As delightful as it was, though, she wasn't hot enough. Craving the feel of his cock sliding into her honeyed depths, she lifted his head away from her breasts.

"Take me," she grated, one hand pushing eagerly at the impediment of clothing around her hips. "I'm so damn hot I can't stand it."

Fingers still caressing her clit, Jesse looked down at her. Flashes of lighting illuminating the plane's shattered cockpit reflected the desire burning in his intense gaze.

"Not yet," he protested hoarsely. He deliberately slipped a finger through her dewy labia, stabbing into her depth. "I still haven't had my dessert."

"Eat the freaking worm," she grated.

He laughed, his voice a little hoarse from the strain of holding himself in check. His erection pulsed against her hip, hard and hot as a branding iron. "Oh, I'm going to eat, all right," he teased. He slid his finger a little deeper, then slowly withdrew it. "All I want."

"Damn you," she bit off.

Planting a series of warm kisses over her abdomen, Jesse eased to his knees. He tugged her slacks and panties down her hips, easing her feet out of the pile.

Catching one leg behind the knee, he lifted it over her shoulder. "That's much nicer." His voice held an edge of carnal intent.

Draped over the bales, Dakoda gasped out a strangled giggle. "I can't believe I'm having sex in a wrecked plane on an illegal shipment of weed." She giggled again, something entirely out of character. She never giggled. The tequila had certainly loosened her inhibitions. "It doesn't get any better than this."

Jesse planted a small kiss above her Venus mound. "Oh, it's about to get better," he promised. "A lot better." Tilting up her hips, he spread her wide. There was no part of her he couldn't see or touch as he wished. She was totally, wholly exposed.

"See anything interesting?" she asked, feigning indifference.

"I see the sweetest pussy a man could ever have the pleasure of laying eyes on." He dragged in a deep breath. "God, I love the scent of you. You don't smell like other women."

Dakoda propped herself up on her elbows. "What do I smell like?" she asked softly.

Jesse's throat tightened as he swallowed. "Like everything that's pure, wonderful, and fresh . . ." His head dipped. His mouth circled her clit, his tongue gently probing the little nub packed with billions of sensitive nerve endings.

Feeling the invasion of his mouth on her most sensitive center, Dakoda arched her back against the bales. Her thoughts suddenly went sideways, tumbling like a stack of cards caught in a high wind. Releasing a growl of hunger, Jesse began to nibble her softest spots, licking and sucking at her labia. As he suckled and teased, one hand slipped up to find a full breast. While his mouth encircled her clit, his fingers pulled and rolled her hard nipple.

Lungs losing oxygen, Dakoda gasped as the first climax roared through her. She shuddered, delight zipping through her like a rocket blasting into outer space. Propelled by the incredible release of intense tension, searing pleasure sped through her body.

She collapsed back against the bales, limp and shuddering in the aftermath of climax.

She didn't have time to think as Jesse slipped his arms under her body, dragging her down to the floor. The silky material of the parachute caressed her bare skin.

Supporting his weight on his elbows, Jesse stretched out on her. His hips settled snugly against hers, his erection resting against her belly. "I love watching you come." He brushed a spicy kiss against her mouth, giving her a taste of her own musky cream as he fingered the tip of one sensitive nipple.

Pleasantly relaxed, Dakoda's hands slipped around his body; his skin was so familiar under her touch. "I want some more," she breathed, grinning. "I'm still hungry."

Jesse lifted his hips, pressing the tip of his shaft against her slit. Resisting the impulse to take her with a single hard stab, he eased the thick crown of his penis inside, just enough for her to feel the penetration.

Gritting her teeth, Dakoda's palms slid to his ass. Her fingers curved, nails digging into his sun-burnished skin. The last thing she wanted for him to do was control himself, restrain his natural inclinations. She wanted him to enjoy himself as much as she had.

And more.

She started to stroke him, seeking out the place where a man would feel the most pleasure. He moaned, his buttocks tightening as her fingers stroked his tight anus. "Jesse," she pleaded, lifting her hips to take him a little deeper. "Don't hold back."

Giving in to her plea, he slid a little deeper, acting with relentless control. His expression was tight. "I don't want to come too fast," he gritted. "You're so damn tight I can feel every ripple around me."

Breath catching in anticipation, Dakoda lifted one leg, giving him a tap of the rear with her foot. "It's your turn," she murmured, giving his ear a little nibble. "Get on and ride, cowboy."

Jesse took her at her word. "Here goes," he warned, gaze smoldering with hunger. The leash holding his desire in check snapped, allowing his body the freedom to act as it wished. The muscles in his neck and shoulders strained, as taut and tight as rope. Giving a quick thrust, he impaled her. His hot shaft pulsed inside her, stretching and filling every last inch of her sex.

Mouth crushing down on hers, he began to pump. His hips collided against hers. His thickly veined erection pulled out of her in an endless, wet slide, only to spear back in again a second later. His body was all sinew and muscle, working in a synchronicity that bordered on perfection.

Insides boiling with need, Dakoda tangled her fingers through his thick hair, drinking in his taste, his scent, the sheer delicious glory of him. His tongue thrust deeply into her mouth, even as his cock stabbed into her again and again.

She shivered, electric with intense arousal. Driven by desire, her fingers dug deep trenches across the concrete slabs of his back. Climax rose like the storm troopers of an enemy army gathering on the horizon. Her pulse throbbed at her temples with every beat of her heart, deafening her with the rush of blood through her veins.

Cursing under his breath, Jesse reared up long enough to catch her wrists, pinning her arms down.

"Watch them claws, you vicious little hellcat!" He held her down with absolute control, even as his hips ground against hers with grueling force. Primitive lust vibrated beneath the surface of his sweat-slick skin, his alpha dominance over his female assured. His shift into an animalistic authority over her made the moment exquisite.

Perfect.

Dakoda writhed beneath his weight. Had it been any other man but Jesse, she would have fought his attempts to restrain her. The steely hardness of his cock kept her hips pinned against the floor as surely as his hands did her wrists. It was excruciatingly delicious to feel his strength overtake and then overcome hers. The wind outside rocked the plane, matching the intense rhythm of their bodies.

Jesse was sweating and shaking, fighting not to come. He was going to hold off until the last possible second, make her take every punishing stroke he could deliver, and then some.

The sensations coiling inside her aching sex were erotic and mesmerizing at the same time. Every thrust Jesse delivered grew in intensity, pushing, filling her with the heat generated by the friction of two bodies in lust.

Giving one final, mighty thrust, Jesse surrendered his control, slipping over the edge. Throwing back his head, he released a great, earsplitting bellow, almost like that of a great cat roaring out its pleasure. His cock surged, blasting a flood of hot semen straight into her womb.

Perceptions splintering into a billion shards, Dakoda came

with quick, powerless, excruciating need. Her orgasm went off like an atom bomb in the desert, tearing through her with the force of absolute destruction. Shredded down to the last molecule by the sheer intensity of pleasure, she could do little but lay beneath his slick weight as tremor after tremor coursed through her.

They shuddered in the aftermath. Jesse's face was buried in the crook between her shoulder and neck. His breath warmed her skin, chilled now in the aftermath of intense physical activity. The tangle of his thick hair webbed his features, spilling like a glittering black waterfall over his shoulders and back.

Dakoda shifted under his body, relieving some of the pressure of his weight. Pressed chest to chest, she felt the steady rhythm of his heart as she watched the rise and fall of his breath.

He continued to pant in short, quick breaths. "Should I move?" he mumbled sleepily against her skin.

"No," she murmured. "Stay."

Tightening her arms around him, Dakoda drew in a deep breath. A strange, unfamiliar ache filled her. Emotion crept through her mind, reviving the sentiments she'd long ago dug a hole for and buried. It was time to take a chance. Really open her heart and let a man into her life.

Jesse Clawfoot was that man. His scent was on her, marking her as his. At last, after a lifetime of searching, she'd found her place in this world.

She closed her eyes, a new sense of contentment filling a void in her heart. She sighed, surrendering to the tug of exhaustion beckoning her toward the realm of dreamless sleep.

I could seriously fall for this man, was her last pleasant, hazy thought.

17

There was something more than a little frightening about being lost in the middle of nowhere, not knowing which way to go or what danger the next hour might hold.

After two long days spent hiking due north, Dakoda was beginning to suspect what she hadn't dared say aloud: They were lost. Not that it mattered much. With her ankle still giving her fits and twinges, they hadn't managed to get very far very fast. They also didn't seem to be any closer to a territory she or Jesse recognized. Every damn tree, rock, and bush looked the same as the last.

Exhaustion nipping at her heels, Dakoda finally did what she'd been aching to do for hours. She collapsed.

"That's it," she huffed, trying to catch her breath as she lowered herself onto a half-rotted log. She felt rotten in just about every way a person could feel rotten, and then some. "I can't take another step. I am officially given out."

Jesse took her not-so-subtle hint, dropping in his tracks and stretching out on the cool ground. "I have to admit I'm ready for a rest, too," he huffed. "I've never been so damn tired in my life."

Untying the laces of her boot, Dakoda slipped her foot out of the lead weight with glacial slowness. Still wrapped in its elastic bandage, her ankle was holding her upright, but just barely. She really needed a day or two off her feet, but that luxury just wasn't an option. Her feet felt like they'd fallen off miles ago, leaving nothing but little stumps at the end of her legs.

Though she'd been in reasonable physical shape at the beginning of this unwelcome adventure, she'd soon realized her idea of athletic and the mountain terrain's idea of athletic were two different things. Muscles she didn't even know she had ached, throbbing with the heat of intense exertion.

She looked around for a sign of something, anything, remotely familiar. Nothing came into immediate view. "Any idea where we're at?" This deep in the mountains, most of the region was prime and virgin, untouched by any outside development. Untouched also meant most of it was unmapped and unexplored. If both of them were to drop dead of starvation, chances were their bodies would never be recovered.

Jesse sat up, shaking his head. "I'd like to say we're on reservation land now, but I haven't seen any of the markers indicating the territory we're in. Could be we've passed them by. If so, we won't be alone much longer. We keep the boundaries pretty well patrolled."

"How many acres of land did you say belonged to the Tlvdatsi?" she asked.

He shook his head as if to clear his thoughts. "About eighty-five hundred," he said. "A little over thirteen square miles. That isn't a lot, even when traveling on foot."

"If we're even on your people's land," she pointed out. "You were outside Tlvdatsi territory, on state park land as near as I can figure. That's eighteen thousand acres right there."

The South Mountains were the highest and most rugged

chain of the isolated mountain ranges making up North Carolina's Piedmont region. Erosion from numerous rivers and streams had given the heavily forested mountains a series of narrow ridges and valleys. The mountains stretched out over a hundred thousand acres or so, and were still sparsely populated. The possibility of running into another human being was about as likely as locating a needle in a haystack. No one knew they were out here but the poachers—and those were the people they most definitely didn't want to encounter a second time.

"So you think we're still on state land?" Jesse asked.

She shook her head. "It took almost the entire day for the Barnett boys to get us to their place, which I'm going to say is part of privately held land. It wouldn't be hard for them to have a sliver to themselves. Most of the South Mountains remain in the hands of private owners."

He gave a small embarrassed smile. "So in other words, you don't think I know where I'm going?"

She had to ask point blank. "Do you?"

"Sometimes I think I do," he admitted. "Then other times I'm not so sure."

Dakoda massaged her toes, which looked as thick and plump as grapes. Too bad they weren't edible. Food was the only thing she thought about, day and night and every second in between. "Guess there's nothing your inner cougar can tell you about directions," she commented dryly.

Jesse considered. "While it's true the cougar could move a heck of a lot faster than the slow Indian on foot, the brain side of that cougar is still the same. If Jesse's lost, the cougar's lost."

Well, at least he was honest. Most men wouldn't admit they didn't know up from down under the threat of death.

"Some wild beast you are," she snorted. "Here I've been thinking you had some inborn animal instincts and it turns out that you're just useless."

He shrugged and laughed. "That's me."

Dakoda took off her other boot. "I don't know if I can go any more today. I passed famished hours ago and now I'm just plain ravenous. If I don't get some real food in me, I'm going to faint. Seriously. You won't be picking me up off the ground the next time I go down."

Smile vanishing, Jesse's face took on a serious cast. "I've got to admit wild berries and roots aren't doing it for me, either." He tugged at the waistband of the stolen jeans. "Couple of days ago these were so tight I couldn't breathe. Too bad Rusty didn't pack his pockets with more meal bars. I could use a dozen or two right now."

Dakoda agreed. "Bad as they tasted, they were better than nothing." She eyed his lanky frame. It didn't take a lot of looking to see his lean frame had thinned a bit. When he'd first taken the jeans, they'd hugged his firm ass and muscular legs like a second skin. Now they were looser, baggier. The amount of energy they were both exerting was peeling the weight off their bodies at a tremendous rate. Though there was plenty of fresh water to be found in the little rivers running through the mountains, finding something edible—and filling—was a little harder.

She glanced down. Her own clothes were getting baggy, too. Amazing how fast stress and a little starvation could take the extra pounds off. If a ten-course meal were to suddenly fall out of the sky, she doubted there'd be enough food to satisfy her. It felt like her stomach had already eaten a hole clear through to her spine.

"We have a gun," she ventured quietly. "Maybe we should shoot something."

"We could," he agreed slowly. "Are you any kind of a shot?"

"I've had target practice, of course," she admitted. "But as for shooting to kill, I've never done anything like that. You?"

"I've killed my share of game with a hunting rifle." Climbing to his feet, Jesse pulled out the pistol they'd borrowed from the deceased smugglers. "Never killed anything with a handgun, though I suppose the principle of aim and fire is the same." He checked the magazine, loaded with bullets. "The ammunition was dry when we found it, so it should be good. Still, you never quite know. I'd hate to pull the trigger and have this puppy blow up in my hand."

Dakoda shook her head. "Let's just go back to what we agreed, then. Self-defense, only. We won't use it unless we have to."

He tucked the gun away. "I can agree to that. As for the food, well, I guess we'll just have to break the no-fire rule. I don't know about you, but I hate my birds raw."

She scrubbed her hands over her face. "Did you say we could have a fire?"

"Honestly, I don't see how we can go much longer without one. I know we don't want to give away our position if those guys are on our trail, but if they're out after us, I don't think they'd do without one themselves, especially with the nights as cool as they are. The one good advantage we have is the storm wiped out all traces of our escape. There was no way we left any tracks behind. They can only guess."

Dakoda sighed. "If we're going the wrong way, maybe they are, too."

Jesse started to strip off his shirt. "Meanwhile, we've got to keep ourselves as strong as possible. If there's one thing I can do, it's hunt. But I'm better on four paws than I am on two feet."

She hesitated. "Jesse . . . are you sure that's a good idea?"

Draping his shirt over a nearby branch, Jesse kicked off his moccasins and started to shimmy out of his jeans. "I know we said we'd stick together, Dakoda. But if we're going to eat better, I need to shift. I'm faster and can cover more territory when I'm a cougar."

Feeling the bottom drop out of her stomach, Dakoda licked dry lips. Oh, man. Jesse was naked again, and looking just as hot as she remembered. The heat in her gut coiled around her insides, bringing back pleasant memories of the night they'd spent in the plane making love. Two days had passed since they'd last had an intimate moment, something Dakoda found herself daydreaming about with more and more frequency. Thinking about sex was a lot more realistic than thinking about food. She had a much better chance of getting some.

She shook her head, chasing away the fantasy. First necessities, then luxuries. As much as she didn't like the idea of Jesse going off alone, the idea of staying together and staying hungry was just as unappealing. No, she was going to have to let him go, and hope he wouldn't meet something out in those woods that was bigger and meaner than a cougar.

Or little and more poisonous, her mind filled in. That timber rattler they'd encountered earlier in the day had almost planted its nasty fangs right in the middle of Jesse's leg. It was just the time of year when the snakes began to emerge from hibernation. The fact that they were active during the day didn't make walking any easier. The snakes blended in perfectly with the dead leaves and other debris littering the ground. Though naturally docile and not a threat to humans, the snakes would react with violence if disturbed. Jesse had only avoided a venomous bite by moving a little bit faster than the snake.

She shuddered at the idea of what other sort of critters they were likely to meet. Staying out here any longer than necessary wasn't exactly appealing, but it sure did beat being sold into slavery as a curiosity.

Dakoda put her boots back on, lacing them tight. "What can I do while you're gone?" she asked, needing something to keep her mind occupied in his absence. Just sitting around waiting didn't appeal to her. She liked to be busy, and contributing the aid of her two good hands was someplace to start. As for her ankle, well, she'd managed to tough it out almost two whole days. She'd just get a little tougher.

Hanging his jeans beside his shirt, Jesse looked around the place they'd stopped. Overhanging trees offered a cool retreat from the worst of the day's heat. Water winding through the mountains on its way to the Catawba River had cut deeply into the terrain, forming rugged and steep slopes. Nearby, a thin stream trickled down a short incline, draining into the belly of a rocky little reservoir. The recent summer rains had filled it to overflowing.

Jesse nodded with satisfaction. "I think this will do as our campsite for the night," he said. "We've got water and there's enough rocks and wood for you to make a fire while I'm hunting. I shouldn't be gone very long, just enough to snag a nice fat grouse." He handed the precious lighter over to Dakoda. "Keep it as smokeless as possible. The trees will dissipate most of it, but we still don't want to give away our location to anyone."

Fumbling to keep a hold on the lighter, Dakoda nodded. "I can make it smokeless."

He grinned. "A benefit of that ranger training, I suppose."

It was hard not to stare at his beautiful muscular frame. Dakoda made herself look anywhere but at that delicious cock nestled in a dark thatch of curls. "I did have some training in surviving in the wilderness," she said, her voice going a little more hoarse than normal. She shook her head, clearing her throat. Hopefully he would mistake desire for fatigue. "Though I will admit I was a little bit better supplied. That will teach me not to sign up for the extreme survival classes. Learning first-hand has been hell."

Jesse lifted a chiding brow. "Considering we've been though hell, I'd say we've done pretty good," he said quietly. "And once we get some solid food in us, we'll do better."

Dakoda smiled in agreement. If she had to be stranded in the middle of nowhere, she was glad Jesse Clawfoot was her companion. Somehow he had a way of putting things into perspective without totally depressing the hell out of her. "Food will be welcome."

"Guess I should get going," he said. "The sooner I do, the sooner we eat."

"Okay."

Before she could blink an eye, Jesse shifted. The familiar outline of a feline stood in his place. Dakoda's breath caught at the ease of his change, so smoothly done that one could scarcely tell when his human self vanished and the big cat appeared. It didn't matter. Either way he was beautiful, a true wild creature of nature. Whether he wanted to admit it or not, Jesse belonged in these mountains. They were the life, the strength of his people.

Giving a brief roar of acknowledgment, Jesse pushed his tawny frame into motion. Dashing off through the trees, he quickly disappeared through a nearby thicket at top speed. The chances were good he'd soon be able to flush some wildfowl or other small mammal out into the open.

Anticipating his success, Dakoda set to work. She wanted to have a good, hot fire going by the time he returned.

18

Taking off her jacket and stashing the few items they had in a shady spot, Dakoda rolled up her sleeves and went to work. With almost four days' wear, her uniform was a filthy mess. She eyed the river, considering a quick dip. She'd never been so filthy in her entire life.

I'll get a bath later, she decided. First some food, then some play.

Locating a clear spot under the trees, Dakoda raked away all the debris on the ground, raking a patch down to bare earth. Finding a slightly curved stone, she used it as a hand tool to dig a shallow hole in the ground, about a foot wide and almost as deep. She circled the small pit with stones, then lined the bottom and sides. Once they heated, the stones would double the temperature of the fire. A larger, flatter stone provided a perfect surface to prepare food on.

Finding wood dry enough to burn clean presented a bit of a problem. Recent rains had drenched the area, leaving everything a little damp. Smoke was caused by damp wood. It took some scouting around to find something she thought she could use. She didn't pick up a lot of tinder, instead choosing average-sized pieces that would burn out completely and quickly. A log would smoke too much, as would twigs, leaves, or needles. Her goal was to keep it small, hot, fiery, and dry with no debris.

Once she located enough to fill the pit, Dakoda set to getting the fire going. Since using kindling was out, she did the next best thing, adding a sprinkling of tequila over the wood. The liquor was highly flammable and would act as an accelerant. Having drunk almost half a bottle a few nights ago, they'd decided to hang on to the rest for medicinal purposes, adding it to the first-aid kit. While starting a fire wasn't exactly the way they'd decided to use it, Dakoda decided hunger was a definite potential emergency.

I want to eat, she thought. *The sooner the better.*

It took only minutes to get a cheery fire going. The wood burned clean, giving off almost no smoke. An occasional light breeze fanned the flames, causing them to snap and crackle in the pit.

Tossing a few extra pieces into the pit, she decided to see what she could add to the day's meal. The mountains could provide quite a bounty to the knowledgeable hunter. Only the stupid would starve.

She set to digging around the bases of the trees and bushes, clearing away leaves. Her search turned up a cluster of mushrooms with broad round caps.

Edible or not?

Dakoda examined her find. During survival training, she'd learned how to discern the edible from the poisonous. She already knew to strictly avoid any parasol-shaped mushrooms with white gills and any little brown mushrooms. Round or pear-shaped mushrooms were sometimes safe to eat.

Picking one, she examined the bright orange cap. Smooth and hairless, it became wavy at the edge. Encouraged by the look, she broke it open. The flesh inside was firm and white, tinged with yellow and smelled fruity, like apricots. There was no sign of insect infestation or other decay.

Pay dirt.

"Hot damn." She gathered the mushrooms up and carried them to the nearby stream, washing away the dirt and grit. Speckled brook trout darted beneath the surface, indignant at the disturbance. "Man, what I wouldn't give to have a nice fishing pole about now."

On her way back to the fire she spotted another possible source of nutrition, a smattering of Queen Anne's Lace. The umbel of tiny white flowers looked vaguely like a crown. But it wasn't the flowers she wanted, but what was underneath. Wild carrots.

As she unearthed the tiny, tender roots, a bit of trivia about the plant crept into her mind. The crushed seeds of the plant had long been used as a natural contraceptive by native women.

The possibility she could become pregnant was one she'd refused to think about these last few days. As a single, unattached woman, she'd decided to decline the use of a contraceptive. If and when she met someone she wanted to sleep with, she could easily go back on birth control. What she hadn't foreseen was that she would meet a man she wanted to have sex with—in a circumstance where not even a condom could be had. At the time the belief death was imminent had spurred her passion on. She'd clung to Jesse for comfort and support during their first harrowing night together. The consequences that might arise from their lovemaking hadn't been a concern at the time.

Now, they were.

Dakoda did a quick bit of calculation. "Shit," she breathed. "What if I'm pregnant?" Her mind whirled in near panic. It was true she and Jesse seemed to fit together now, but what would happen when they returned to the real world, to the paths they'd been walking before one overlapped the other?

It didn't take a genius to figure out imprisonment automatically forced people into an alliance. In this case, they had shared the desire to escape captivity. How could she be sure her feelings for Jesse were real, and not just the psychology of a victim at work? Was it possible she was really falling in love with him? She understood lust, a purely physical, hormonally driven craving that was easily satisfied. Love was different, way outside her sphere of experience. Singers composed songs, poets wrote flowery odes, writers even wrote romances where happily ever after was the rule. Real life was different, though, and some else's emotions were a messy thing to deal with.

Running away was an easy solution. It had worked for years. Now, there was noplace to go. And in having to stop and face herself, Dakoda had to admit she was tired of holding men at arm's length. Jesse had done more than mesmerize her with his fantastic body. He'd wormed his way into her life, coiling around her heart and tying tight knots. Inescapable knots.

Every morning they awoke together the first thing she wanted to do was make love to him. Even though they were out in the open and exposed to all sorts of danger, she somehow felt safe, content even, curled in Jesse's protective embrace.

She hadn't seriously cared for a man since Ashton Jenkins, and he was a father figure, not a lover. She believed she wasn't the kind of woman destined to fall in love, since she'd never wanted to stay long with any man—a remnant of her mother's bad habits. Truth be told, she just didn't have enough faith in her own staying power. It was easier to pick up and run than it was to commit. If she ran first, she wouldn't be the one who got hurt.

But are my feelings for Jesse real? she asked herself. Damn, if they didn't feel that way. The way her gut clenched when she believed he was in danger . . . The way she craved his touch . . . The way she looked forward to evening's fall, so they could find a safe, warm nook and curl up together . . . Desire rose inside her like slow, rolling thunder.

Oh, hell! Dakoda knew then she'd been bitten by the love bug. It was the real thing and she was in deep, way over her head and struggling to keep afloat. She wished she felt more secure with the realization. But considering the complications of starting a new relationship under such duress, all she felt was confused and more than a little bit lost. It would have been pure and absolute bliss if her mind could slow down, but it couldn't. One thought inevitably led to another.

Well, that answered at least one question. As for the other, it was probably best not to mention the possibility of a baby until she was absolutely sure where she stood with Jesse. Giving him something else to worry about when they were still in such deep trouble wouldn't be fair to either of them. They were both physically and mentally stressed, under a lot of pressure. Those weren't exactly the ideal circumstances for making a baby.

She sighed. "I'll pull a Scarlett, and think about it tomorrow." Finished gathering the cache of carrots, she washed and carried them back to camp. Right now it wouldn't do any good to think beyond the present. Each hour of each day was already enough of a challenge to get through. There was no reason to pile on the complications when there weren't any to deal with.

Yet.

Dakoda sat back on her haunches, pleased with her haul. She hoped Jesse would be, too. Who would have guessed a thoroughly modern woman who didn't have a single skill in the kitchen would be able to settle into domesticity so easily? In her world, any thought of cooking usually involved a frozen entrée and a glass of wine.

Her stomach rumbled, reminding her it would soon need an infusion of real food and not just nibbles at carrots and mushrooms. She was trying to hold off eating them, hoping to add them to whatever Jesse might bring back. He'd been gone a long time. Even in his cougar form, there were a lot of dangerous things he could run into. One wrong step down a jagged ridge could break a bone. Not to mention the fact cougars weren't the only dangerous predator living in these mountains. Black bears and bobcats, not to mention the timber rattlers and other crawlies like centipedes.

A crash of brush alerted her to his return. He pushed through a hedge of growth, trotting into the little clearing. A nice fat brown rabbit dangled from his mouth.

Setting the rabbit down on the grass, Jesse shifted back into human form. "Damn, that little bastard could run," he said, heading toward the stream. He walked with a lithe and feral grace, perfectly at home in this wilderness. His male beauty was spectacular. Simply stunning.

Wading into the cool water, Jesse doused himself from head to foot, rinsing the sweat and grime off his deeply tanned skin.

Speechless, mute, and strangled with need, Dakoda stared with pure admiration as the water sluiced over the hard planes of his shoulders, trickling down his back to caress the curves of his finely molded ass. He looked magnificent when he lifted his arms, brushing a mass of long, dark, soaking tendrils away from his face. For a moment she could have easily mistaken him for a water spirit rising from clear sparkling depths.

A slow burst of heat spread through her core when he walked back on shore, striding toward her like a god about to conquer his chosen virgin. Snagging his jeans, he slipped them on, then shoved his bare feet into his moccasins.

Enjoying the view, Dakoda grinned up at him. "Feel better?"

Jesse walked over to the fire she'd built. "Much," he said, eyeing her handiwork. "Looks like you've been busy."

She poked the fire with a stick and added more wood. "I

found some mushrooms and wild carrots. Not much, but it'll add to what you caught."

Jesse retrieved the dead rabbit. "I have to admit I'm hankering for a good hot meal. Just need to skin it and get it ready for roasting." He pulled out the stolen pocketknife, unfolding a sharp blade.

Dakoda gulped at the thought of the rabbit's guts spilling out before its skin was ripped away from its body. "Anything I can do?" she asked, eager not to witness the entire process. While she had no objection to eating meat and frequently partook of a nice cut of steak or a plump chicken breast, she'd never been up close and personal with regard to the slaughter of said animal.

Jesse looked up from the carcass. "If you could find some thick green branches to make a spit out of, that would be great."

Dakoda nodded. "I think I can manage that." She trotted off before the urge to vomit hit full-force. Aside from nibbling some mushrooms and carrots, her stomach was empty and she didn't want to be caught dry heaving.

19

Having a squeamish stomach wouldn't do when it came to living in the mountains. A person had to be tough, rawboned, able to take the materials at hand and fashion them into the necessary tools for survival. Killing and preparing an animal for eating played a big part of daily survival.

Dakoda wasn't sure she could do that at all.

The fantasies she'd spun around joining the Tlvdatsi way of life suddenly seemed less enticing when put into such a perspective. Though she wasn't a sissy when it came to roughing it, she still remained a city girl at heart. She couldn't begin to imagine her life without modern plumbing and a grocery store down the street. Living on the edge day after day would begin to wear on her nerves.

Thank God she hadn't put her foot in her mouth with regards to Jesse. The door was always open, an easy out if she needed it. Surely he'd understand why their two ways of life didn't mesh . . .

Her brow wrinkled. *There you go again*, she silently chastised herself. Running every possible scenario straight into the ground. Nothing had happened yet, no solid decisions needed to be made just this second. When they did, she'd deal with them. Until then, she needed to stop driving herself crazy with *what if . . .*

"Just deal with *what now*," she muttered.

Finding a tree with a few good thick branches, she began to break them off and strip off the bark. Green and flexible, the long strips of bark would make good ties. Working with her hands gave her time to think, something she seemed to be doing too much of already.

I'm not sure I could stay here with Jesse.

Her idea about considering things another time was beginning to look like a good piece of advice. No reason to say or do anything that would put either of them in an awkward position. After all, she had a career to pursue. And she'd gotten along fine without a man in her life for quite a while. Once things returned to normal it was entirely possible she and Jesse wouldn't have a thing in common. Lust wasn't enough to build a relationship on. The sex would eventually wear thin.

Then what? Another messy breakup?

No thanks, her mind filled in.

Finished with the branches, she carried them back over to camp. She crouched beside him, bringing her into disturbingly close proximity with his half-naked body. Close enough for her to lean forward and plant her lips on his if she wanted to. The memory of their sultry nights of lovemaking swirled through her skull with hurricane force.

She cleared her throat. "Will these do?" she asked, trying to act like anything but sex was on her mind. Every damn time she got close to him, all she wanted to do was drag him down and have sex with him. The man's magnetism was like an invading disease, giving her a dizzy head, swimmy stomach, and trembling legs.

Yeah, he definitely had something potent going on there.

Jesse nodded. "Perfect." Having prepared and cleaned the rabbit, he set to fashioning a spit and propping it over the fire to test its distance from the flames. Making a few adjustments, he pronounced himself satisfied. "This ought to do just fine." Impaling the rabbit through and through, he set it over the pit to cook.

The flames licked hungrily at the rabbit's raw flesh, causing the meat to sizzle like ham in a frying pan. The delicious scent of roasting meat began to fill the air.

Dakoda leaned close and took a deep breath. "That smells like heaven." The aroma of the meat seasoned by the wood brought to mind images of barbeque and tall glasses of ice-cold freshly brewed tea, two of her favorite things in summer. Saliva rose in her mouth even as her stomach rumbled with impatience. If she'd known the rabbit was going to smell this damn good, she'd have gutted it herself. The idea of country living was a little more appealing when a solid meal was in sight.

He grinned. "Glad you think so. By the look on your face a while ago, you'd have thought I was skinning a rattlesnake to eat."

Dakoda froze. A residual shiver of terror over the timber rattler incident shimmied down her spine. "You would eat a snake?"

His grin widened. "Of course. I have several times. They're quite tasty, if a little bit fatty."

She frowned. "I suppose you're going to tell me it tastes like chicken."

"Actually it does." Using the tip of a stick, Jesse turned the carcass so the other side would roast evenly. "You ever eat rabbit?"

Images of sweet little fat bunnies swept across her mind's screen. She quickly shook her head. Wild rabbits were quite different from pet-store rabbits. They were meant to be hunted, eaten. "No, I can't say that I have," she said slowly. "It's not on the menu of the places I usually dine."

"No French restaurants for you, huh?"

Tension uncoiling a bit, Dakoda had to laugh. "I don't get into places like that very often. In fact, never. My idea of dining out is grabbing a pizza or a burger and fries from the drive-through."

Jesse rolled his eyes. "Oh, God, don't mention pizza. I haven't had a slice in years. Man, I wish one would fall out of the sky right about now."

She rolled her eyes at the ridiculousness of the request. "While you're at it, wish for a pitcher of dark German beer to go with it."

Jesse picked at the mushrooms and carrots she'd laid out on the flat stone. "Guess these will have to do," he said, munching a carrot. He chewed thoughtfully, then swallowed. "Would be nice if we had some dip. Ranch would be good."

She considered his comment. "Do you miss living in a more hospitable world?"

Lifting the cooked meat off the fire, Jesse smiled ruefully. "Honestly? Every damn day, sometimes twice a day," he said, carving the meat into smaller pieces to cool. "I mean, it wasn't like I was born in these mountains. Sure, this is the land of my ancestors and I've got some crazy bloodline that lets me turn into a cougar, but do I really belong here?" He shook his head. "Shit, it's a question I've asked myself over and over."

"You mean, to shift or not to shift?" she asked.

Jesse smiled ruefully. "Yeah, something like that."

Without quite knowing what prompted her, Dakoda decided to do a little subtle digging. "You ever think of leaving?"

"You mean go home, back to a real life instead of spending my days running around on four paws?"

She nodded.

He looked at her a long time, his mental wheels clearly turning. "I would go back in a heartbeat—if I had never learned to shift. But now that I have and now that I know what I really am in this world . . ." He shrugged, looking around at the rugged landscape surrounding them. "How could I ever leave? I mean, you don't see a lot of cougars trotting on the asphalt." His hand touched the ground, palm flat against the earth. Their gazes locked candidly for a moment. "Like it or not, this is where I belong."

"Oh, that makes sense." Dakoda's throat involuntarily tightened, barely allowing the words to escape.

Her brain betrayed her, circling back around to the exact subject she'd promised herself she wouldn't think about. She'd entertained the notion of luring him away from the mountains, but his words blew the idea right out of the water. He spoke bluntly and honestly. The implications behind his last statement clearly affirmed any woman he would be interested in would have to be one willing to join his beyond-the-ordinary lifestyle.

Her heart thudded dully in against her rib cage. *At least I know where things stand.*

Living in the mountains with a cougar? It was too damn far-fetched to even think about. Once this misadventure had come to its end, the best thing to do would be say good-bye, then move on. The human world and the feline world just wouldn't come together in her mind.

A feeling of dismay tied her guts into knots. This was not good. Not good at all. The logistics of their entire situation were getting too problematic, and she hated complicated.

Stop that! she warned herself sharply. That's what she wanted to do right now. Stop thinking. Stop breathing. Stop being. The world needed to grind to a halt so she could get off and take a break. Otherwise she'd soon be picking her nose and drooling, a dim-witted lump of nothing useful.

Lifting her hand, Dakoda pressed her palm flat against her

forehead. This entire stupid mess was beginning to give her a massive headache. A dull thud beat at her temples. "Excuse me while I have a small nervous breakdown." The statement had nothing to do with anything they'd been discussing. Or did it? She wasn't sure any more.

Brow furrowing with concern, Jesse cleared his throat. "Are you okay?" A strong warm hand settled on her arm. His essence flowed over her, permeating her skin until she felt him in her blood, all the way to her bones.

The chemistry between them was undeniable. Just looking at him bought a distinctive sexual edge into play. Carnal energy practically snapped in the air between them.

Oh, man. He was so big. And so damn strong.

Dakoda jumped violently at his touch. Her insides contracted hard. She panted. Heat began creeping into her cheeks. Desire shuddered though her all over again. Her hormones were all over the place. Maybe it wasn't a pregnancy she'd better worry about, but a monthly. There was no telling how out of whack her cycle was from all the nervous tension.

Shaking off his hand with feigned nonchalance, she snorted inelegantly. "I'm fine." Her eyes abruptly filled with tears, swimming with misery, fatigue, hunger, and just plain frustration. "I'll feel better when I get some food in me."

Jesse looked at her closely, but made no comment about her uncharacteristic lapse into tears. His gaze briefly dropped to her mouth as if he were contemplating kissing her, but then darted away, leaving the impulse unfulfilled. "Right. That makes sense." He picked up a slice of meat and held it out for her. "I think it's cool enough."

Dakoda accepted the meat, pinching it between thumb and forefinger. She gave it a quick sniff. "Smells good." Her experimental nibble turned into a mighty mouthful. Finding the meat more than palatable, she shoved the entire piece into her mouth. Closing her eyes, she chewed, savoring every tender bite.

Jesse watched her closely. "Good?"

She swallowed. "Oh, God, yes. It's delicious."

He handed over more meat. "Eat up."

Dakoda set to stuffing her mouth with the delicious hot food. "Thanks. I feel like a glutton."

Jesse chewed a mouthful of his own food. "It does taste good after those terrible meal bars."

"Wouldn't want a steady diet of those things," she said between bites. Finished with the meat, she swallowed a few more mushrooms to top off her meal. She patted her stomach. "That's the first time I've felt alive in days."

Jesse grinned. "Good. Then it was worth the effort." He yawned and stretched. "And now what every great hunter needs after a hard hunt and nice meal is a nice long nap in the sun." He eyed the grassy bank of the river. "I think I'm going to take a few minutes and sun myself."

Dakoda laughed. "I suppose you're going to leave me to clean up the mess." She frowned and shook a finger in mock disapproval. "Typical male."

Jesse laughed. "Why don't you join me? Stretch out a few minutes and just rest in the sun."

The idea of lying down beside him pushed her body into the feverish range. It wasn't a bad idea at all. Just an impractical one at the moment. As she'd worked, she'd caught a whiff of her own odor and the scent was, frankly, offensive. There was no way she'd be cuddling up with him until she'd had a good wash. Her skin literally felt alive with creepy crawlies.

She shook her head. "First I need a good head-to-toe wash."

He brightened, raising a brow. "Oh. Can I watch?"

Walking over to the edge of the stream, Dakoda sat down to take off her boots and socks. "If you must," she said, giving him a grin. The attraction between them flared, making her head spin.

Gaze raking her with salacious wickedness, Jesse grinned

appreciatively. "Oh, I must," he echoed with a laugh. "Absolutely."

Dakoda laughed. "You flatter me." She felt the dampness between her thighs at the thought of his cock sinking into her hungry sex.

She eyed his lanky frame. *Oh, yes. That would be perfect.*

After all, Jesse wasn't the only one with a hankering for dessert.

Though she hadn't believed the day could get any better, she was about to find out just how good it was going to be.

20

Standing up, Dakoda quickly stripped down to bra and panties, spreading her clothes out on the clean grass to air. Washing would be impractical at this point. They'd have to be thrown away as soon as she could replace them.

Jesse drank in the sight of her like a thirsting man. "Can I have sex with you if I flatter you some more?" he asked.

She stepped forward, kneeling to put an experimental hand in the water. Though the day was warm, the water flowing down from the mountains was icy cold. She shivered. "Brrr. Going to make for one hell of a cold bath," she said, trying to keep her teeth from chattering.

Stripping out of his jeans, Jesse stretched out on the warm grass. Rolling onto his stomach, he folded his hands under his chin. The curve of his shoulders and back made a nice path to the curves of his apple-firm ass. "The water's cold year-round," he informed her.

Dakoda couldn't help remembering how he'd looked when he'd stepped out of the water. With his rippling muscles, ridged abdomen, and lean hips he was pretty much what she'd imagine male perfection to be.

Taking a deep breath, she mentally manned up and plunged straight into the water. *Holy shit!* The first shock of ice cut right to the bone. She considered dashing right back out.

Dakoda persevered. Teeth clenched tight, she kept walking until the water was waist deep. The bottom wasn't jagged, but the rocks were a little slippery. Her nipples were tight little buds beneath her bra.

Taking a breath, she lowered herself until the water came to her shoulders. It took a few minutes to get used to the temperature, but once she did she barely felt the cold. One palm scrabbled to find a stone with a coarse surface. Finding what she wanted, she ran it lightly over her skin, sloughing away the layers of grime. Since she had no real soap to use, this was the best she could do. Simply wetting the skin would still leave her with a layer of grime once she dried off.

Finished with her body, Dakoda dunked her head under the water, rinsing out her long hair. When her hair got damp it curled into tight little ringlets, almost impossible to pull a comb through. It was a snarled mess, and she'd probably have to cut it off when they reached civilization again. There would be no way she could salvage the mass of tangles. The best she could do was try to rinse off her hair and tie it back up in a bun.

Done with her bath, she splashed back toward shore. She flopped down beside Jesse on the warm grass. Rays of direct sunlight warmed her skin. The heat felt great after enduring the icy chill of the stream.

Jesse lifted himself up on an elbow and looked down at her. "Oh, man, the way that wet bra and panties cling to your skin is about to drive me crazy."

Dakoda glanced down. Sure enough, the white cotton had gone transparent, offering about as much cover as plastic wrap.

So much for trying to maintain a little decency. She might as well have stripped naked. It wasn't like Jesse had never seen her in the buff.

She started to unhook her bra.

Jesse stopped her. "Let me, please."

Gut throbbing with need, Dakoda nodded. Just the thought of his touch caused her body to respond with a surge of red-hot lust.

Catching one strap, Jesse slowly eased it down her shoulder, peeling the wet cup away from her left breast. The rounded flesh came into view, tipped with a cherry-tinted nipple. He fondled the erect tip gently, causing it to pucker briefly before tightening again.

Dakoda caught her breath. "One of these days I'm going to turn the tables on you," she murmured, "and put my lips around your delicious cock."

Jesse traced a single finger around the nubbin, lightly at first, then with more pressure. "I'm looking forward to it. But first I need to take care of something. . . ." A second later his mouth descended, teeth scraping against her soft areola.

Dakoda moaned, arching her back against the ground even as Jesse ran the palm of his hand over her smooth belly. He slipped his fingers under the elastic of her panties, probing the soft rise of her mound. Her thighs opened, welcoming his caress.

Barely able to catch her breath, she gasped. "I want you inside me," she murmured. She wanted to feel the undulations of his body on top of her, to feel his surging heat stab into her with thrust after brutal thrust. Claiming her.

Making her his own.

Jesse raised his head long enough to smile up at her. "It's coming," he promised. "I want to make you hotter than hell." Lips returning to her breast, he slipped his fingers through her damp labia, slowly easing a finger inside her creamy sex. He clearly preferred to be the one giving the pleasure rather than receiving it, a trait of the alpha male.

That was something she'd like to change.

Not that she had a chance at the moment. Not with Jesse's tongue stroking her nipple and his hand making all kinds of arousing moves below her panty line.

Dakoda's breath raged past her lips as she felt his first penetration. Adding a second finger to the first, he pumped into her rippling core. Strong inner muscles clenched, holding him tightly. A soft moan rolled up from deep in her throat. "Damn you," she breathed. "I'm already hot enough." She spread her legs wider, granting full access.

Jesse's fingers slipped away. "Oh, I have to take advantage of this." Pushing himself off the ground, he repositioned himself on his knees between her spread legs. He hooked her panties and pulled them over her legs.

Palms tracing along the insides of her thighs, he kept her spread wide. "Oh, this is how I've wanted to see you. Out in the light, without a stitch on."

"I still have my bra," Dakoda reminded through a gasp.

He unsnapped the front hook, pushing the wet material away from her other breast. "Not anymore." Arched up toward his abdomen, his erection was rock hard.

Her body throbbed with tremors of desire, and he hadn't even really done anything yet. "What are you going to do now that you've got me naked and willing?"

Jesse's big hands circled her hips, lifting her to the perfect angle for penetration. The tip of his cock pressed against her creaming slit. His crackling gaze locked with hers, the depths of his eyes smoldering with untamed lust. "I'm going to fuck you hard and fast." He entered her with a single thrust.

The slide of his length into her waiting softness just about did Dakoda in. She exhaled on a breath of surprise. His penis felt like a bar of molten steel, penetrating her to the very last inch.

Fingers digging into her skin, Jesse pounded her like a sledgehammer striking concrete. It didn't take long for her to realize today's lovemaking wasn't about love at all, but pure sex. The desire of the male to claim the female. There were to be no soft words or caresses of foreplay. Just raw brutal need spurring him on.

Jesse's hips moved against hers, unrelenting in the force or brutality of his desire. A hungry male smile curled his lips. Each hard strike of flesh on flesh tore a whimper from Dakoda's straining throat. Every stroke took her breath away.

Orgasm arrived like a star gone nova. Dakoda felt herself go rigid as his cock scraped every nerve ending inside her clenching sex. He stroked her repeatedly, barely giving her a second to realize she was melting and contracting around his shaft. She heard herself begin to cry out. She wanted to scream his name but she couldn't get enough oxygen in her lungs to help form coherent words.

Jesse never stopped pounding her, never stopped pushing her closer to the dark abyss of pure pleasure. There were too many sensations to process, each streaking by at light speed. Her brain overloaded. Shorted out. There was nothing left but Jesse, delivering stroke after brutal stroke of pure white fire.

Dakoda reached for the sensations, desperate to hang on to them as long as possible. They slipped through her fingers like sparkling grains of golden sand. The tidal wave of climax built, sweeping her away into an endless void.

Just as she hit the edge, Jesse pulled out of her. She gasped in surprise when he rolled her onto her stomach and then pulled her up on her hands and knees. "Deeper," he growled. "I want to go deeper."

Dakoda didn't think that was physically possible. She was

wrong. Jesse pressed the velvety tip of his penis against her slit, slipping through her dewy labia the way a hot knife slid though butter. Her nipples ached for the scrape of his teeth, the pull of his mouth suckling at the pebbled tips. She lifted a hand, twisting one nipple viciously for her own satisfaction. A hot coil of gratification snaked down her spine.

Jesse rolled his hips, each tight lunge taking him deeper than before. He pulled back, barely allowing the broad round head of his crown to peek out, before shoving his thick length right back inside. "Come with me," he grated, delivering one final jolt. His rough command startled. The message was apparent: he was in control to the very end. The way he fucked her was unmistakable.

In the cougar's world he was the male, her lord and master. She would submit, as nature intended. Each stab of his rigid cock burned, forcing her closer to the pinnacle of an absolute erotic meltdown.

Dakoda opened her mouth to protest against his dominance, but nothing coherent emerged. The sensations boiling through her core simply felt too damn good. "I–I, oh, God . . ." A sob broke from her lips, but she couldn't say another word. Jesse's cock surged inside her, spitting a stream of liquid flame.

Taking a grab at the euphoria pouring over every nerve ending, Dakoda caught the glittering wave, seeking to master it even as it attempted to sweep control out from under her feet.

One of Jesse's hands slipped around her body. His probing fingers found her clit, rubbing intense circles into the center of the small hooded organ. His touch felt more electric than ever before. "Take it all the way," he urged. "Enjoy the beast raging inside." His hot breath burned against her ear. His commanding touch seared her to the bone.

For a dizzying instant, Dakoda could almost imagine herself as a cougar, paws pounding the ground as she ran alongside her mate. Her heart thudded wildly against her rib cage—wild with craving and yearning for something she couldn't quite yet grasp.

At the last possible second, she let go, enjoying the fierce power of a mind-blowing orgasm. The shock of ruthless delight stole her breath all over again.

Giving a contented sigh, Jesse slowly disengaged their hips. His half-flaccid penis slipped away, leaving a cold spot in its wake. The breeze winnowing across the grass cooled the heat generated between them. "God, that was great," he said hoarsely, panting hard between each word.

Dakoda huffed. "Glad you think so." Arms and legs giving out beneath her weight, she collapsed facedown onto the ground. Cheek pressed against the soft grass, she lay gasping and shivering. The crushing waves of pleasure slowly receded, each lapping sensation growing weaker and weaker.

Though she'd been with men who tended to get a little rough from time to time, Dakoda had never had a man claim her in such a way. When they'd made love previously, he always played the gentle, humble lover. Today was different. He'd come after her in ruthless pursuit, determined not only to mark her with his scent but also to dominate and control her in every way.

He'd done it, too.

Like a branding iron against naked flesh, he'd burned his essence onto hers, so deeply that for an instant their two separate bodies seemed to become one, undulating with perfect synchronicity. Dakoda would've sworn for a moment their minds had touched, allowing her to feel the same sensations he did when in cougar form.

Awesome. It was just fucking awesome with a capital A. With that in mind it wasn't at all hard to imagine what it would be like to completely embrace his world. To give herself up to his primitive, carnivorous lust for the rest of her life.

And, God, it was so damn tempting . . .

Jesse stretched out beside her, pulling her into a light embrace. Lifting one of her legs over his hip, he snuggled his body closer to hers. A fine sheen of sweat covered their bodies. His hand came up, slipping behind her neck and angling her head. Lips nibbling hers, he was about to slide into a kiss when an ear-shattering yowl tore apart the sultry afternoon.

Acting with split-second timing, Jesse bolted in front of her. He hit the ground on his hands and knees, skidding a little as he smoothly transformed his shape from man to cougar. His change came none too soon. Another cougar burst through a nearby thicket, charging toward them at top speed.

Still too dazed to fully comprehend the source of the terrifying screech, Dakoda's eyes widened at the sight of a second cougar. By the look on the big cat's ferocious face, it had come to fight.

"Jesse, look out!" she shouted as the strange cougar surged across the clearing. Sweating, she scurried around to find her clothing, needing to cover her naked ass.

A series of thunderous roars split the air as the two cougars came face-to-face, anger boiling through them as each big cat released howls resembling battle cries.

Ears pinned back against his skull, Jesse acted first. He roared, leaping toward the intruder and closing his fangs around the other cat's neck. The two great animals fell, rolling together, a writhing heap of flying fur and razor-sharp claws. The screeching emanating from both huge felines was chilling, battering against her ears with vicious ferocity.

Pulling on her slacks and fumbling into her shirt, Dakoda realized that the other cat must have scented her female musk.

"Wait a minute," she muttered, putting the pieces together. If the cougar was drawn by her scent, that must mean it was one of Jesse's tribe mates. They were fighting over her like a prize to be possessed, a trophy in a world where willing females were in very short supply. Jesse was trying to defend his claim on her. The other cougar was determined to take it. Between the two of them, they were trying to impress her with their male prowess.

Angered by the stupidity between two dumbass males, Dakoda swore under her breath and grabbed a good-sized flexible stick off the ground. *I'll give 'em each a piece of my mind.* Stick held out like a bat, she sped toward the massive cats. The sooner she broke them apart, the less damage would be done.

It vaguely occurred to her she should be afraid of two tangling cougars fighting for pride, passion, and a piece of her pussy. Fear wasn't on the agenda, though. She was pissed. In the animal world they might clash for the right to mate, but in the human world the female decided who the hell she was going to fuck.

At least this female did.

Wading into the fray, she whacked the nearest cat on one fleshy haunch. "Stop it!" she shouted, delivering a second and then a third smack. "I won't be fought over like a piece of meat." Brandishing the stick like a mother after two naughty boys, she broke the two big cats apart. A few minutes later both sat side by side, as docile as kittens.

Dakoda stood with her hands on her hips, glaring down at both. "Shift," she ordered. "I want to look at people faces and not cat ones."

Both cougars disappeared, slipping back into human form. Two naked men sat in their place, not an unpleasant sight at all. Though she recognized her cougar, Dakoda had no idea who the young stranger might be. Shorter and stockier than Jesse, he wore his brown hair in a strange cut, shaved on both sides of his scalp with just a strip down the middle of his head. Though short on the top of his head, he'd allowed the hair hanging down the back of his head to grow back, braiding it into a long tail of sorts. A smattering of stubble covered his face, much too youthful to belong to a full-grown man. He looked to be nine-teen, or maybe twenty, tops. With his intense brown eyes and sun-burnished skin he was still a sight to behold. The Tlvdatsi were proving to be a beautiful people.

Jesse's naked body gleamed with sweat and blood as he checked a vicious scratch on his forearm. "Damn, Robin, that fucking hurt," he groused.

The other man shrugged. "Sorry, man. I was lost in the cat, you know?" He turned his unblinking gaze on Dakoda. "Ah, man, I knew I smelled a female." His grin widened. "Nice body, too."

Dakoda followed the line of his stare. Of course her shirt was open and her tits were hanging out. In her haste to dress, she hadn't bothered with underwear, doing her best to cover herself before the two immature idiots ripped each other apart. No wonder she'd been able to break up the fight so easily. She was giving the men quite a distraction.

Feeling heat creep in to her cheeks, she buttoned her shirt. "I just washed," she mumbled with more than a little embarrass-ment. "Surely the smell isn't *that* strong."

The newcomer smiled. "Oh, believe me. Once you get a whiff, there's no mistaking hot p—"

A low growl rolling past his lips, Jesse delivered a hard jab to his friend's rib cage. "Back off," he said through a cold stretch of his lips. "She is taken." There was no mistaking the posses-sive tone behind his warning.

Dakoda felt her heart give a particularly hard thump against her ribs. "I'm not taken," she said quietly. "I make the decision of who I'm with or not."

The stranger's eyes brightened. "Then there's always hope," he quipped.

Jesse elbowed him again. "Right now she's with me, so fuck off, chump."

The other man held his hands up in defeat. "Okay, okay, man. You don't have to rub it in. I get the message. You got her, you're hanging on. That's cool. All's fair."

Dakoda sized up the opportunistic young man. "And just who are you, anyway?"

The young man scrambled to his feet. Fully exposed in every way, he appeared to be comfortable with his nudity. "Robin, ma'am," he said, politely introducing himself. "Robin Huskey. I'm Jesse's cousin."

"Twice removed," Jesse grumbled, standing up. "Where did you come from, anyway?"

Robin shrugged. "Just out loping around the land."

Jesse huffed and rolled his eyes. "In other words, you're avoiding work."

Robin gave his cousin a light punch on the arm. "Actually, I'm not the only one, Jesse. Joseph's been looking for you for days now. He's pissed, too, man. We're not just supposed to run off without letting someone know."

Jesse shot Dakoda a surreptitious look. "I had things on my mind," he grumbled under his breath.

Dakoda knew exactly what he had on his mind. S-E-X. As much as he could get, and as often as he could get it. His verbal jabs at Robin were just as possessive as his blatant lovemaking had been earlier. He had mapped out his territory, and now he was defending it.

Typical male.

Dakoda broke into the argument. "Excuse me, guys. I'd like to finish getting dressed." Reclaiming her discarded clothing, she headed behind a copse of trees to change. The last thing she wanted to do was show more skin. Having one horny cougar on her tail was bad enough, but dealing with two would be just a little too much. Despite her checkered past, she wasn't into threesomes.

Still, she had to be more than a little pleased when she remembered how Jesse had rushed into the fight, fangs bared and ready to tear up some ass. Had it been any other man, Dakoda probably would have been pissed off beyond reason or recovery. But it was Jesse, and she found there was something poignant in watching him back another man down in her defense.

Deep down, Jesse was a decent and honorable man. But at his core he was utterly dedicated to the survival of his people in these harsh mountains. Were the choice between saving the life of his cousin or hers, she had no doubt he'd choose Robin. Despite the intimacies they'd shared, she was still an outsider in his world.

She'd stumbled onto the secrets of the Tlvdatsi by accident. Even though Jesse claimed she carried the genes of such inside her own body, she still didn't feel any sort of a connection with the knowledge. It was sort of like being born with a certain skin color. Though she was aware of it, there wasn't really much she could do to change it.

Safely covered from head to toe, Dakoda stepped out from behind the trees. Her knees were still a little shaky from the incredible sex coupled with an equally incredible scare, but she'd supposed she'd survive.

She found the two men sitting by the fire, deep in discussion. Jesse welcomed her with a bright smile. "Everything okay?" he asked.

Dropping down beside him, she nodded. "Fine."

Jesse's hand slid around her waist, his palm resting lightly against her back. He move wasn't very subtle, unmistakably sending the message they were very much a couple to anyone who had eyes and mind enough to connect the dots. He'd have been less obvious sending up smoke signals. "I was just telling Robin about our little adventure with the friendly neighborhood poachers," he said, briefly filling her in on key points.

Robin agreed grimly. "This is some serious shit. Best to get back to camp and let Chief Joseph know." His eyes flashed with anger, with the hot vigor of a young man ready to make war. "It's time their atrocities against our people were stopped once and for all."

Dakoda's body automatically tightened, gathering tension. "Not to mention mine," she reminded quietly. "That was my partner they gunned down."

Robin skimmed the remnants of her uniform. "I'm sorry for the loss of your partner, but I am glad you were there to help my cousin."

Pursing her lips, Dakoda glanced away. The meal she'd recently consumed all of a sudden felt like lead in her gut. She swallowed hard to keep the food down. "Thanks," she choked, fighting to clear her throat. "We were just trying to do our job." What else could she say at this point? She didn't even know where the poachers had buried Greg's body.

Looking from one to the other, Jesse's dark brows knitted with frustration. "We've all suffered enough." He turned to Dakoda. "Robin tells me we're about a week from our settlement. It's going to be hard travel, but there will be two of us to take care of you, plus any more men we might meet on the way. Do you think you can handle it?"

Dakoda lifted her chin with determination. "The sooner we get going," she said resolutely. "The sooner we'll reach home base."

21

The sun was just beginning to disappear behind the mountains when Dakoda set her eyes on the Tlvdatsi settlement. The sight nearly took her breath away.

Her first impression was that she'd somehow glided through a rip in the fabric of time, stepping back at least two centuries into the past. The outpost looked like a couple of blocks had been lifted straight from some Hollywood set depicting life in the old West. A series of neatly constructed log cabins were set amid corrals and other pens for livestock. There were a multitude of horses, cows, goats, chickens, dogs and even a few fat, lazy barn cats. A nearby waterfall fed into a pond of clear, clean mountain water.

Dakoda's head swiveled, trying to take in every little detail as they walked toward the cabins. In choosing to break away from the established reservations and form their own settlement in the mountains, the Tlvdatsi presently lived much like their ancestors had, with few modern conveniences. Expansion into the twenty-first century was coming slowly, but surely.

A week's hard travel had taken its toll, both physically and emotionally. Her clothes were torn and filthy, little more than rags, and despite the fact that two men had been on the prowl for food, she'd lost at least ten pounds, maybe more, from the intense exertion of hiking through areas where trails didn't even exist. No wonder the men preferred to travel in their cougar forms. It was a hell of a lot easier for the big cats to slip through the tangle of brush than it was a human on two legs. She'd often found herself wishing she could slip off her human coil and morph into a leaner, faster body.

A small group of tribesmen began to gather around, curious about the newcomer in their midst. Both of her companions had chosen to stay in cougar form for the last leg of the journey, which meant Jesse had abandoned the clothes he'd borrowed. Dakoda had hung on to the clothing, though. She wasn't too proud to wear the extra layers on cold nights. Snuggled between two furry cougar bodies, she'd stayed quite warm and comfortable.

One of the men broke away from the group, walking out to meet them. As he approached, Jesse and Robin shifted back to human. By this time Dakoda was accustomed to seeing them walking around buck naked, without a hint of embarrassment. Once she'd gotten over the sexual connotations behind their nudity, she'd found herself quite comfortable with seeing them without so much as a stitch on.

The man walking toward her was a taller, broader version of Jesse. This, she recognized, must be his brother, Joseph Claw-foot, acting chief of the Tlvdatsi clan. As he met the group, the chief folded his arms across his chest like an angry parent about to scold an errant child. His face brewed a combination of anger and relief.

"Jesse, Robin," he said tightly. "I see you have returned home, and brought a visitor." He eyed Dakoda's ranger uniform, frowning severely as he recognized the implications. An outsider, an outsider representing the white man's law, had come onto their land. "You both know it is expressly forbidden to bring an outsider into camp without permission."

"Aw, cut the Big Chief crap, Joe, and give us some slack. She already knows we can shift. And if you'll take your head out of your ass for a minute, you'll be able to tell for yourself she's one of us." He paused, then added, "One of the very few females—which we were all told to welcome with open arms."

Chief Joseph's face softened. "It is true we receive women with open arms." He looked at Dakoda, addressing her for the first time. "You are welcome in our camp."

Dakoda nodded, without offering her hand. "Thank you, Chief. I am honored to stand among your people." Even though she was the law, she had no authority on these people's land. As a tribe recognized by the federal government, they had their own rules, regulations, and laws to abide by—and their own methods to back them up.

The chief's nostrils flared. "You do carry the scent of one of our own," he said slowly. "Therefore I hope these two young men who accompany you have not unduly accosted or coerced you into doing something you didn't wish to do." He pierced each young man with a stern look. "They have been warned about venturing off our land in pursuit of the fairer sex."

Dakoda quickly shook her head, hastening to explain. "That's not quite what happened, Chief. My partner and I were in pursuit of poachers, when we discovered they had trapped a cougar."

Hearing her explanation, Joseph's dark eyes began to brew thunderclouds. "The Barnett brothers," he spat bitterly.

She nodded. "Yes. Unfortunately, in our attempt to take them into custody my partner, Gregory Zerbe, was gunned down by Waylon Barnett. I was myself taken hostage and locked in a cell with your brother, who subsequently revealed himself to be more than a cougar." Her mouth quirked down as she imagined giving the same report to any of her superiors. Tell the truth and they'd look at her like she'd lost every marble in her

198 / Devyn Quinn

head. She'd quickly be put on administrative leave and sent to a psych ward as soon as possible.

"That must have been quite a shock for you," the chief said, watching her reaction closely.

Dakoda shook her head. "Not half as much as seeing my partner murdered in cold blood." Mouth suddenly going dry, she shuddered. "I'll admit it was an incredible thing to witness, but once I got over the shock, I was damn grateful to have someone on my side. It was through our imprisonment that we learned the cougars are sold to private owners wishing to own, ah, unusual animals."

Chief Joseph nodded. "We are aware of what the poachers are doing to our people," he said quietly.

His admission hit her like a blast of icy water. "Then why haven't you gone to the authorities?" she asked, stunned.

The chief didn't look encouraged. "The laws outside this land have little meaning to us—or the men who hunt us. The white government doesn't care about preserving our heritage or our people. To them we're just interlopers taking good land away from the development of more vacation resorts. In a matter such as this, one so sacred to our very hearts, we fight for ourselves. And we welcome no outside interference." He directed his gaze toward Jesse. "My brother is aware of the dangers that can befall us. And when he gets stupid and careless, he gets into trouble."

Jesse's head dropped at the verbal thump. "It wasn't like I went out that day, asking to get caught."

"Yet you went outside our boundaries, and you got yourself trapped," Joseph reminded. "Though I know the call of the cougar in your heart, as a cat you have no defense against men walking on two legs and carrying guns. Our only answer is to arm ourselves as they have. If that means you must deny a part of your nature, then so be it. Finding a mate isn't worth your freedom, or your life."

Jesse hitched a shoulder, mumbling something unintelligible beneath his breath. "Yeah, but you have your woman . . ."

Though his words were rushed and mumbled, Dakoda couldn't be exactly sure what he'd said. Though she had yet to see a female face among the crowd, it helped knowing there were women around somewhere. She wanted to talk to a Tlvdatsi female, ask a few questions, and explore a few concepts that had been brewing in the back of her mind for the last few days. Asking a man wouldn't work. She wanted to talk to another female, woman to woman.

Meanwhile, there was another matter she had to handle. As a ranger. Not as a woman or as one who'd recently uncovered her lost heritage, but as a member of law enforcement.

"You might not advocate taking a legal stand against these men, Chief," she started to say. "But since they killed my partner, I'm afraid I'm going to have to go after them—with or without your sanction."

The chief looked conflicted, but held firm in on the stance he'd taken. "You are within your rights to do so," he answered tightly. "But you must find a way to do it without involving my people or bringing our secrets to the outside world. Moreover, you must also do it without betraying your own knowledge that you belong among us."

Talk about the rock and the proverbial hard place. Between these two crushing forces, she'd be ground down to bonemeal.

In the interest of securing the cooperation she needed to get back into town and make contact with the authorities, Dakoda decided a path of diplomacy might yet be the best course to follow. There was no sense in alienating the Tlvdatsi with the uniform she wore. She would do better to rely on the common bond of bloodline.

I am one of them, she reminded herself. It would also give her a chance to better understand and explore their world. Perhaps in understanding more about her heritage, she could better comprehend her own feelings, the impulses and desires that had driven her to flee close ties throughout her life.

Dakoda couldn't miss the tension in his stance. "I'll do my best to honor your request," she said quietly, breaking the silence between them. "In the meantime, I would wonder if you have a cup of hot coffee. I could certainly use the caffeine, and it would give us a chance to talk."

Chief Joseph's face broke into a wide grin. "Forgive me. I have been rude." He held up an arm, indicating one of the nearby cabins. "My wife will be more than glad to loan you a change of clothes and get a meal into your belly."

Jesse rubbed his hands together. "Anything Kathryn can whip up sounds good to me."

The chief caught his brother's arm. "Getting dressed first would help. When you are decent, you can join us." He eyed Robin. "As for you, your father wants you home, as soon as possible."

Robin nodded. "Yes, sir." He scurried off, shifting and disappearing into the shadows lengthening across the land.

Jesse glanced down at his naked body. "Hey, I may be nekkid, but I'm always decent." Nevertheless, he trotted off toward one of the cabins.

Dakoda couldn't help watching as he walked away, admiring the grace in his casual gait, not to mention the delicious sight of his ass when viewed from behind. He had the cutest dimple on one cheek, one she'd been hankering to take a little bite out of.

She shivered, remembering how it had felt to have sex with him. They hadn't touched each other since Robin had joined them, agreeing it was unfair to be together when her scent was so strong. Jesse had explained how it could drive a man wild, until they were ready to fight, to kill, for the right to claim a female. Holding on to the human side when the cougar called was almost impossible for some.

Having agreed, Dakoda had to brutally suppress the memory of his hard frame pressed against hers. Five long days of hell, aching for his caress, for the penetration of his cock into her hungry sex. She almost hadn't been able to stand the tension, to the point of giving consideration to the idea of letting both men have their way with her. But although the idea appealed, she wasn't sure she was ready to take the step toward multiple partners. She knew it was common practice in a society where females were scarce, and to share her favors would be considered a gift to the men she chose.

Given the curious gazes following her and Joseph as she walked, she wouldn't lack for a choice in partners. To her surprise, many of the faces she glimpsed didn't look a bit Indian to her. Along with some white faces, she spotted a few blacks and Hispanics. Apparently the gene carried by the Tlvdatsi traveled through many races and colors. With her own light brown skin, she'd fit right in.

Chief Joseph couldn't fail to notice the look she gave his brother. Lifting a single brow, he bent close. "You've been intimate with him?" he asked in a level voice meant to be heard by no other ears except hers.

Dakota threw him a shocked glance. Oh, hell. She hoped she hadn't worn the expression of a starving mongrel drooling over a piece of forbidden steak. "Is it that obvious?"

Joseph's gaze was fixed on her, watching her closely. "I'm afraid so."

"It's true we've been together," Dakoda admitted slowly. "And I won't deny your brother has a certain attraction."

Joseph's brow climbed higher. "But?" His voice was neither cold nor judgmental.

"But in the time we've been together, he's dropped a lot on me with regards to what it means to be a part of the Tlvdatsi clan. It's not enough to know who you are—what you are capable of—it's an entirely different way of life."

"One you're not sure you're ready to embrace?" he asked.

With a sigh of relief, Dakoda dropped the pretenses. She had a feeling the chief expected her to speak her mind freely and without restraint or the worry of offense. "Exactly. I mean it's all so . . ."

"Strange?" he finished.

Dakoda had to smile. She couldn't help but like this straight-talking man who clearly had the best interest of his people in mind. Considering the many obstacles they faced, he was probably more than right to be cautious of outsiders—even an outsider who carried the thing these men were so desperate to obtain: A pussy.

As harsh as the judgment was, it was also a true one. The whole of the clan's survival depended on these men finding suitable women to join their lives. Otherwise the bloodlines that made shifting possible would die out. Were that to happen, their people's last ties with the old ways would also become extinct.

Dakoda scrubbed her hands across her face as she met the chief's penetrating gaze with her own. "Strange doesn't even begin to describe what I've stumbled into this last week."

The shit was hip deep.

And still rising.

22

Dakoda watched as Kathryn Dayton-Clawfoot bustled around her kitchen, preparing the evening meal. She worked efficiently, gathering the items she wanted and putting them into an order that would produce enough bounty to feed a bevy of hungry people. She'd already refused any help, saying a guest should sit and relax.

As Kathryn tended to the food, Dakoda looked around the neat, cozy cabin. Oil-burning lamps were positioned throughout the room, providing a soft and welcoming glow, in addition to the fire crackling in the nearby hearth.

The kitchen and living room were an open arrangement, decorated with heavy old-style Americana furnishings, including a picnic table covered with a red-and-white checkered cloth, along with matching benches. The ancient stove shared space with a more modern cabinet and sink arrangement, an odd combination of old and new that somehow meshed together just fine. A bedroom and bathroom completed the cabin's space, an arrangement of perhaps six hundred square feet. It was small, but quite comfortable.

I could live in a place like this, Dakoda thought approvingly. *It's nice. Very homey.*

Kathryn slid a pan of freshly mixed biscuits into the oven portion of a wood-burning stove. "My goodness," she said, fanning a hand in front of her perspiring face. "If I'd have known we were going to have company, I would have made something better than plain old leftovers. Just give me about twenty minutes and the biscuits will be done. At least those will be fresh." She gave the pot bubbling on top of the stove a stir with a big wooden ladle.

Dakoda drew in a deep breath, taking in the hearty scent of a rich meaty stew. She'd watched Kathryn peel extra potatoes, carrots, and onions to add to the leftover venison, as well as add a dash of salt and pepper. As far as she was concerned, it wasn't leftovers at all. An extra day's cooking usually tenderized the meat and thickened the broth, locking in the flavors.

"It smells great," she complimented, taking another sip of hot black coffee laced with lashings of sugar and real cream. "You don't have to go through any special trouble for me."

Setting the heavy iron pot to a side of the stove where the food would be kept warm but wouldn't cook anymore, Kathryn beamed. "Oh, but I do. You don't know how good it is to see a new face around here, especially another female. Even though our tribe has grown these last few years, I'm afraid the men still outnumber the women ten to one." Wrapping a pot holder around the hot handle of the tin coffeepot brewing on the stove, she walked over to refill her own cup. "More?"

Covering the cup with a hand, Dakoda shook her head. "I think three cups is enough. One more and I'll be jittery all night."

"Must have been tough spending a week out there with almost no supplies." Tossing the pot holder aside, Kathryn sat down across from her. "I still can't believe those bastards were going to sell you and Jesse."

Sipping her coffee, Dakoda nodded. "It's not an experience I want to repeat anytime soon," she agreed.

"Nobody wants to see those lowlifes coming." Kathryn curled a lip in disgust. "I had my own run-in with them, one I don't care to remember."

Her words piqued Dakoda's interest. "Really?" By the look on the other woman's face, it hadn't been pleasant. But then again, Dakoda couldn't imagine a single pleasant thing about the Barnett brothers. If any men deserved to be behind bars, those two were prime candidates.

Kathryn shivered as if her skin were crawling with lice. "They caught me alone when I was working with a team from the Wildlife Resources Commission to verify sightings of cougar. I got separated from my group and had to spend a night alone. Of course, those sons of bitches came into my camp and made themselves welcome in a most undesirable way, if you know what I mean."

Dakoda knew exactly what the other woman meant. No further details were required. She licked dry lips, nodding in concurrence. "Those sick fucks tried to rape me, too," she said quietly. "Jesse stopped them."

Kathryn briefly closed her eyes. "If it hadn't been for Joe, I probably wouldn't be here today." Her admission carried enormous tension. "As shocking as it was, I have to admit seeing a pack of cougars arrive and tear hell out of those two was the best sight of my life."

Dakoda's pulse started to pound. "Do you feel safe here now?" she asked. "I mean, don't you worry they'll come back?"

Kathryn shook her head. But her lips trembled a little before she pressed them together. As confident as she wanted to appear, it was clear the experience still brought back bad memories. "The boundaries of our land are pretty closely guarded. The Barnetts and their vermin cousins know not to venture onto reservation property."

Dakoda nodded her understanding. "But when you venture out, it's a whole different ball game?"

"It's a war between them and us," Kathryn admitted slowly.

Anticipation ratcheted up another notch. "Yet you don't go to the authorities?"

Kathryn sighed deeply. "It doesn't work that way, Dakoda. These are a separate people of a separate nation. As small as it is, they have the right to govern and protect themselves as they see fit. Just as the Barnetts hunt us, our men strike with their own retaliations. The law you represent doesn't exist in these mountains. It never will." A roll of her shoulders indicated a shrug. "Though I don't always agree, that's just the way it is."

Dakoda tapped her mug with a fingertip. "Another thing you've had to adapt to, I suppose." She knew most law enforcement problems on the reservations stemmed from limited resources and jurisdictional confusion. The Tlvdatsi settlement was geographically remote and involved enormous tracts of land unmarked by any boundaries. Local authorities like her were also limited in their ability to effectively operate on tribal lands.

On the other hand, tribal law enforcement members were hampered by their limited authority over non-Indians—they could detain, but not arrest, non-Indians on their reservation, but they really couldn't pursue non-Indians off-reservation. As it was, the Tlvdatsi didn't appear to have anyone functioning as a peace officer.

It was a frustrating stalemate between the Indians and the outlaws, and even though she was stuck right in the middle, neither side welcomed her presence.

Kathryn made a strangling motion with her hands and laughed. "And still adapting every day. Sometimes the last few years have felt like centuries." She reached for the coffeepot, refilling her own empty mug. "Anything else I can get you while we're waiting for the biscuits?"

Glancing down at the fresh clothes Kathryn had supplied, Dakoda shook her head. "No, thanks. You've been great." Though Kathryn was a little taller, the two women were roughly the same size, allowing Dakoda to decently wear her borrowed jeans and blouse with comfort. "I do have to admit I wasn't expecting a real bathroom with running water. Soaking in a hot bath was heaven." She'd been relieved when offered the chance to rest and clean up before dinner, spending at least half an hour just soaking in the old iron tub. It had taken at least half a bar of soap to remove the layers of grime and stink from her skin. With many good graces, the chief had recognized her fatigue and withdrawn to give the two women time to get to know each other. She already knew he'd want to talk further.

And she already knew what she'd say in return. She had a feeling the chief wasn't going to be pleased.

Neither would Jesse.

Brushing a stray blonde lock from her perspiring forehead, Kathryn laughed. "It wasn't quite so modern when I first came here," she explained, her blue gaze twinkling with the memory. "When I agreed to marry Joe, I insisted on some comforts, and that included hot running water and better plumbing. The water is pumped from a nearby well house powered by an electric generator. We even have a freezer out there now for storing meat and other perishables. I can't tell you how good it's been to have."

Dakoda nodded. "I can imagine it's been a godsend."

Kathryn rolled her eyes. "Oh, you don't know what a fight it was to get these few concessions. Most of the men were against bringing in any sort of conveniences. They wanted to live in the old ways, like their ancestors."

"Jesse mentioned their desire to stay close to the land several times," Dakoda murmured.

Kathryn laughed and shook her head. "Having Tlvdatsi blood myself, I'm all for preserving our heritage. But I'm also a modern girl, raised in the city. And as much as I like camping out and living off the land, I do have my limits. As do other women, who I explained wouldn't be so willing to join this clan if they thought we were a bunch of treehuggers eating roots and berries and living in tents."

Dakoda nodded. "I have to admit I see your point exactly. It's a lot to ask a woman to embrace something like, ah, like this. It's more than a whole different way of life, it's a whole different way of looking at yourself and your place in the world."

Kathryn lifted her mug, taking a deep drink of her coffee. "It's tough," she admitted. "Especially when it comes to the point when you realize you're either going to embrace it, or that you've got to let it go and walk away."

Dakoda gazed at the woman sitting across from her. A tall, cool blonde with a sun-freckled face, Kathryn looked as if she'd be more at home sunning on a tropical beach than living the rough life of a pioneer woman in the mountains. Kathryn had obviously adapted. Long hair pulled back and braided down her back, her clear skin was untouched by any cosmetic, as were her hands. Her clothing was just as simple—jeans and a man's flannel shirt and a pair of heavy leather boots. To make the shirt a bit more feminine, she'd tied it around her slender waist, revealing a beautifully flat abdomen.

"You adapted," Dakoda said slowly, trying to feel her way along carefully.

Kathryn smiled. "It wasn't easy, but I pretty much knew what I wanted once I met Joseph."

Dakoda fingered her empty mug, absently noting it was handmade and not store-bought. "Did you have any idea about... what you were?"

"If you're asking if I knew about the shift, the answer is no. I didn't. I did know I had a little Cherokee in me; my father's people came off the reservation in Oklahoma some generations ago. But that was about as much as I knew about my own Native American heritage. I mean, who isn't a Heinz 57 now? I've got German, Irish, Scots, and some Russian in my family tree. It just so happens that one of my forefathers carried a gene stretching back to the beginning of creation."

As a person not grounded in any firm religious instruction, Dakoda still had more than a little trouble believing some big entity in the heavens scooped up a handful of soil and created life. "You honestly believe it goes back to the creation of mankind on earth?" she asked.

"I do." In her two simply spoken words, Kathryn seemed absolutely sincere.

"Why?"

Kathryn nodded, serious and unsmiling. "Because I've seen the truth during my mind walk."

Dakoda's brow furrowed. "I remember Jesse saying something about it." She shook her head. "He tried to explain the origins of his people, but I really wasn't into it at that exact moment. My brain was kind of blown at the time, you know?"

"Your mind wasn't blown," Kathryn corrected. "Just closed. There was a time when all men's minds were open, and aware of all the gifts our creator granted to humankind. But as time and beliefs changed, our minds shut down and the faculties we used to shift became dull and blunted. Through time the ability to change our shape began to die out."

"Obviously all of them didn't die off."

Kathryn agreed. "Some few people were able to hang on to the old knowledge and pass it from generation to generation."

"And the Tlvdatsi are such a people?"

Kathryn smiled. "Of course. You've seen the shift with your own eyes, so you know the truth. You're just not able to see it in yourself yet." She reached across the table, patting Dakoda's arm. "Once you take the mind walk, you'll know without doubt."

Dakoda resisted the urge to draw her arm away. For a moment she harbored a feeling of distrust. They way Kathryn spoke sounded much like the spiel one would give when trying to indoctrinate a new recruit into some kind of whacked-out cult. Desperate people, lonely people, lost people, were inclined to believe anything—embrace anything—in order to achieve a sense of belonging. Of the people she'd met so far, they appeared to be well educated and well spoken. They were obviously far removed from the dirt-poor superstitious country bumpkins living in rural areas of other sparsely populated states.

Dakoda didn't consider herself to be desperate or lonely. A little lost, perhaps, but she'd come to believe she was carving a place for herself in this world by following in Ash Jenkins's steps and entering law enforcement. It was entirely chance that she'd chosen to become a ranger and work in these mountains. Had her choice been chance, or some buried instinct bringing her back to the land of her father's ancestors?

She didn't know. And until she did, she wouldn't be making any firm decisions concerning Jesse Clawfoot unless she was absolutely and positively sure. At this point she wasn't willing to let a few rampant hormones rule her head, or stop her from her duty of pursuing Greg's killers and bringing them to justice. Whether or not the clan liked it, the white man's law was about to come down on the Barnetts' heads with full force. The Tlvdatsi might have their own way of handling the poachers, but she had another. And that was just the way it was going to have to be.

My way or the highway.

23

There wasn't much time to think about it, or talk more. The front door flew open, bringing in Chief Joseph and Jesse. Both men headed toward the table.

Standing up, Kathryn frowned at her husband and brother-in-law. "Wash your hands before you sit at my table, please," she commanded, retrieving her pot holder and heading toward the stove to check her baking. She pulled a pan of perfectly golden-brown buttermilk biscuits out of the oven.

"Smells good, honey," Chief Joseph said, offering his wife a quick peck on the cheek. "Can I do anything?"

"Set the table, please," Kathryn answered juggling the hot pan. "We were so busy talking I didn't manage to get it done."

Joseph headed toward the cabinets holding the dishes. "A good conversation, I hope."

Kathryn shrugged. "Just girl talk, my dear," she quipped lightly. "Nothing you guys would be interested in."

One look was all it took for Dakoda to recognize a couple still very much in love with each other. The envy bug bit. Just a little. Just enough to sting.

She swallowed her discomfort and stayed quiet, instead focusing on the family banter going on around her. That was something she'd never had. Even when her mother was married to Ash, they'd spent more times battling it out than kissing and enjoying a quiet dinner. When she was a kid, mealtime usually involved her staggering-drunk mother tossing a few dollars her way and telling her to find some food.

The bug came back and bit again. This time the sting was deeper, more painful.

Dakoda ignored it, propping her chin on her elbow. *These people actually like each other.*

"We're always interested in anything you girls have to say," Jesse broke in, drying his hands on a towel hung beside the sink. "There's so few of you around to do that talking. We're happy if you'll just let us look at you and bask in your beauty."

"Flattery isn't going to get you dessert, Jesse," Kathryn countered sternly. "I didn't have time to make anything but the basics tonight."

Jesse snapped his fingers. "Darn. I do so love that chocolate layer cake you make."

"No cake," Kathryn insisted. "Unless you bake it yourself."

"My luck always did stink." Jesse walked toward the table, sliding onto the bench beside Dakoda and giving her an odd look. "What happened to your hair?"

Dakoda's hand rose. She fingered the choppy cut Kathryn had helped give her. "It was too damn tangled to unsnarl," she confessed about her chin-length cut. "So I decided short and simple was the way to go."

Frowning, Jesse eyed her. "It looks good," he finally announced, reaching out to trace the curve of her cheek. "Brings out your beautiful almond-shaped eyes."

Dakoda's skin heated under his simple caress. "There you go comparing me to a nut again," she laughed, trying to make light of his comment. Though she could brush off his compliment, her body couldn't toss off his touch as easily. The clutching sensation in her stomach made her breath catch. Heat began to trickle between her thighs. She pressed them together tightly, mentally willing the sensations of desire aside. It was no longer just the two of them, alone and fighting for survival. She had to think about going back to her world now, the real world outside the reservation settlement.

Jesse's hand dropped. "You know I'd think you were gorgeous even if you were bald and had no eyes."

Dakoda laughed. "If you're trying to insult the hell out of me, you're headed in the right direction. Want to try another?"

Ducking his head briefly, Jesse cleared his throat. "I think you know what I'm trying to say." He followed his words with a brief squeeze of her forearm.

Dakoda nodded. "I get it, I think," she said, watching as Joe pulled out a stack of plates and bowls and set the table for his wife. As he was handing out the utensils, Kathryn ladled heaps of her thick meaty stew into the bowls, filling them to the edge.

"Everyone eat up," Joseph urged as he sat the biscuits in the middle of the table, along with a small crock of pale, creamy butter. Two clear glass canning jars held the bounty harvested from the land; one was filled with a thick berry jam, the other with rich dark honey harvested from wild beehives.

Buttering a few biscuits, Dakoda picked up her spoon and dug into the food. The first bite was heaven. "Kathryn, this is delicious," she complimented, following the bite with another from the buttermilk biscuit. Smeared with real butter, the bread practically melted in her mouth. She'd never tasted anything so good in her entire life.

Kathryn blushed a little at the compliment. "Thanks. I'm using recipes handed down through Joe's family for ages now. I try to make as much as I can myself."

214 / Devyn Quinn

Dakoda swallowed another bite of the perfectly simmered meat. It was all she could do to eat at a normal pace instead of shoveling the stew down at top speed. There had been a point during their travels when she'd believed she'd never again get enough to eat. "That must keep you busy."

Kathryn gave a weary sigh. "It keeps my days full," she agreed. "What I can't make myself, we buy in town on our monthly trips in for supplies."

Dakoda's ears perked at the mention of civilization outside the reservation. "How long does it take to get there?" she asked.

Chief Joseph took over the conversation for his wife. "Leave in the morning and we can be in Connelly Springs by afternoon. We've actually progressed to the point where we have a few utility roads for trucks to get in and out now, so travel is a little faster."

"No more packing up and taking the horses," Kathryn added.

Dakoda didn't remember seeing any vehicles, though she hadn't seen the whole of the settlement. "Is there any way you can get me back to Connelly Springs tomorrow?" she asked.

Chief Joseph nodded. "If it's your wish to do so, then we can leave at first light."

Dakoda put down her spoon. "That would be excellent."

Jesse frowned a little at her words, but said nothing. Instead he concentrated on his food, eating slowly and methodically.

Dakoda glanced toward him. Oh, no. She'd known he was going to take this hard. Why did he have to be so freaking sensitive about it? She could feel the tension and hurt pouring off him in waves, even though he wasn't saying anything.

"I understand you are eager to pursue the men who killed your partner," Joseph continued evenly. "With that in mind, I have spoken to Ayunkini for his counsel on the matter."

Dakoda's brow rose in surprise. "And he would be?"

"Ayunkini is our shaman and spiritual advisor," Jesse answered, finally deigning to speak. "He is the one who leads you through the mind walk, helps you explore the heart and soul of the cougar inside."

Dakoda stiffened. Hunger faded, replaced with concern. She suddenly felt bloated and leaden, like a fat cow about to be slaughtered. "And he wants me to have one of these mind walks?"

Chief Joseph shook his head. "Although we would all hope you would want to, it is not necessary since you are planning to leave tomorrow."

Dakoda relaxed. "Oh, well good." She shook her head. "To tell you the truth, even though I have seen a lot with my own eyes and listened to Jesse speak about life in the mountains, it's just not something I'm sure I'm ready to pursue at this point in my life." She gave a little shrug. "In fact, I'm not sure I'll ever be ready."

The chief nodded his understanding. "Some are not ready, and we are prepared for such an eventuality, too. Just as Ayunkini can lead you through the mind walk, he can also take you down another path."

Suspicion rose all over again. "What other path?"

"The path of forgetting what you have seen and heard about the Tlvdatsi."

Dakoda stared at him in shock, her mind working double time to process everything he's said. The first thing popping into her mind was it sounded too sci-fi freaky. Then again, the whole idea of humans shifting into cougars was way past the norm. "He wants to erase my memories?" she asked incredulously.

"Ayunkini can lift away memories, easily and with no pain or trauma," the chief explained. "His plan is to take you back to the day of your partner's death, before you were taken captive and witnessed Jesse's transformation. Without those memories, you will still have all you need to pursue prosecution of the men who killed your partner, but without the knowledge of our people. The only thing you would know is that we found you wandering, dazed and a little confused, and returned you to your people."

Returned me to my people, her mind broke in, tossing the unbidden thought into the arena. *I thought you were my people...*

But no. They weren't her people. They would not—could not—accept her until she'd made a vital step toward embracing the truth simmering beneath her skin, embraced and harnessed the power of her true soul.

Dakoda struggled to sort through the implications of his proposal. She had to admit this was a turn she totally hadn't expected. And, holy cow, it was a massive one, running over her like a freight train without brakes.

If she agreed, this past week would be wiped away, as temporary as words written in chalk on a blackboard. She'd know nothing but vital facts. The rest would be gone, excised from her brain like a cancerous tumor.

A breath caught in her throat, a painful sensation working its way down into her lungs. Tightening, squeezing, then ripping and tearing as her oxygen drizzled away. Losing those days would mean losing Jesse. Everything would vanish. She wouldn't know she'd met him, shared an adventure with him. Or made love to him.

Lose Jesse, as she'd lost so much of her life already?

I can't, she thought. There had to be another way.

Using a napkin to wipe her mouth, Dakoda slowly pushed her empty bowl away. "I'm not giving up my memories," she said, keeping her words level but firm. "If there's one thing that's not negotiable, Chief, it's that one."

Jesse shot her a look, one of hopeful elation dancing across his face. "Then you'll consider staying?"

Dakoda's stomach lurched at the eagerness behind his question. Though she had no doubt about her desire for him—her body gave her away every time he touched her—she had a commitment to her duty first. There had to be a way to make the two meet and run parallel without jeopardizing either. She just wasn't ready to make a final break with either side of herself.

She laid a gentle hand on his. He knew exactly who he was and what he wanted from his life, and who he wanted in it. Her.

Dakoda knew she owed him the same consideration. Giving it should have been easy, but it wasn't. "Don't ask me to make a decision about us until after the law settles with the Barnett brothers," she said quietly. "I owe my partner a decent burial and justice from the men who put him in the ground. Anything less would dishonor his life and make me a woman who doesn't keep her word. I couldn't live with myself if I didn't do what is right."

Jesse gave her hand a soft squeeze. "As long as you'll think about coming back, Dakoda, it's good enough for me," he said, taking yet another run at the wall she'd erected around her emotions. "That's all I ask. A chance. Will you give me that? A chance?"

One brick fell, and then another.

Damn.

Dakoda nodded slowly. Every time she thought she'd made up her mind, her thoughts circled back around to Jesse. "You've got your chance." She kept her gaze level and sure, refusing to blink. "I can't say when you'll have it, but you will. I promise." It wasn't her heart, but it was a start. To what, she wasn't sure yet.

Jesse started to speak, then shrugged. "I guess I haven't got any choice." He suddenly smiled, his dark eyes twinkling with male insinuation. "They say what you wait for is the best thing to have when it finally arrives." He leaned close, pressing a soft warm kiss at the edge of her mouth. "You're worth waiting for," he whispered before slipping back into his place.

Jesse's words sent a wild, swooping sensation through Dakoda's core. It was strangely exciting, being so desired by a man, one willing to stand by in support as she did what duty required.

Chief Joseph cleared his throat. "While I am happy to see love blossom right in front of my eyes," he said in a tone not entirely laced with disapproval, "I would prefer you take your lovemaking away from my kitchen table." He cast a sly glance toward his wife. "Otherwise it may give me ideas about my own wife and that son I want her to conceive."

Kathryn blushed hot, giggling behind her hands. "We'll just have to keep trying," she said. "Until we get it right." She got up to clear away the dishes, stacking them in the sink before putting on a fresh pot of coffee to brew.

Jesse's hand slipped around Dakoda's, his grip tight and protective. "Even though I don't want to say it, this kind of leaves us at the same impasse as before." His lips quirked into a bitter smile. "Though you haven't said it, Joe, she's got two choices. To remember me—us—she has to take the mind walk. Otherwise she'll have to lose her memories."

Dakoda stared at the chief. "Let's say I took the mind walk, then decided I still didn't want to be a part of the clan at a later date."

Joseph Clawfoot's lips quirked down. "You would, of course, have to sacrifice your memories."

Dakoda swallowed tightly. "By force?"

The chief nodded. "If necessary."

Dakoda's inner mule kicked up in protest. "So what's to stop me from taking the mind walk, then going and blabbing to the media all about the wonders of the Tlvdatsi? Maybe even show a demonstration or two?" The question blasted past her lips before she'd fully considered the implications. She'd just made a threat.

The chief's gaze bore into hers from across the table. His handsome face was as blank and impassive as that of an Indian carved out of wood. "Your honor as a member of this clan," he said in a level, calm tone. "Once you take the mind walk, you *are* Tlvdatsi. To be so isn't just in your mind or your heart. It's in your soul. And I know you would no more betray your people than you would betray the man whose death you wish to avenge." His stern look gentled. "You can have both, Dakoda. You just haven't realized it yet."

Dakoda licked her lips as a multitude of feelings slithered through her mind on a chill trickle of fear and uncertainty. For a wild second she thought about getting up and walking away from the table, walking as far away as fast as she possibly could on her own two legs.

The thought brought her up short.

You're always running away, she silently chastised herself. Never making up her mind, staying in one place, or committing to one person. Hell, she'd even wanted to quit training, toss the ranger idea over her shoulder when her feet had gotten itchy and the ties to law enforcement—and to Ash Jenkins—became too binding.

It was always easier to run away.

The faster the better.

Rubbing the heels of her hands into her eyes, Dakoda sighed. It felt like the weight of the world was on her shoulders, bearing down on her with a crushing force. There were so many tugs in so many different directions she didn't know which way to turn anymore.

Her head ruled with reason, which was logical and cold. Her heart ruled with desire, which was flighty but delightful. Neither could be trusted, forcing her to burrow deeper, heading toward a side she'd always doubted existed. The spiritual—which had always been achingly empty, ignored because she had no idea how to begin satisfying it. But the waters of knowledge were pouring now, freely and openly. If only she would hold out her cup to be filled, she would be complete, a total and whole being. She would become a woman who could reconcile her three separate parts into a single, absolute entity with a past, a present, and a future.

Blinking away the sting behind her lids, Dakoda suddenly let her hands drop. This challenge would be the most difficult she'd ever faced, but she was determined not to back down. She'd flip-flopped like a fish out of water for days.

Time to make a decision and stick to it.

The fact she wouldn't be going through it alone emboldened her decision. Sitting side by side with Jesse, she could feel the heat emanating from his body. His eyes, normally so gentle and smiling, held nothing but admiration.

As if reading her mind, Jesse's hand slipped onto her upper thigh, squeezing a signal of silent encouragement and support. "You won't regret it," he murmured for her ears only. His warm palm slid higher, fingers brushing suggestively between her legs.

Dakoda automatically widened her legs, granting him all access. A silent groan slipped between her lips. Oh, man! He sure was making it hard to concentrate on the conversation at hand. She'd been hungering for his touch for days, and now when it arrived, she couldn't take advantage.

Eager to reciprocate, Dakoda slipped her hand across Jesse's back, wiggling her fingers under his T-shirt and caressing the patch of skin above the line of his jeans. An image of his body, so beautiful when naked and fully aroused, popped into her mind.

They exchanged a brief glance. Jesse's gaze heated, smoldering with arousal.

Dakoda caught her breath as a ribbon of desire snaked through her, tying dozens of little knots around her senses. Her nipples peaked with immediate response, brushing against the soft flannel of the shirt Kathryn had loaned her. Her clit pulsed softly across against the crotch of her jeans, aching for another brush of his fingers. No doubt about it. She was wet and ready for anything he wanted to do.

Dakoda knew then she'd made the right decision. "I'll do it," she said, almost surprised by the strength of assurance in her own voice. "I'll take the mind walk."

Chief Joseph nodded. "It's settled then."

Apprehension scraped her nerves. She hesitated a minute, then asked, "When will it happen?"

The Chief glanced out the window at the sky darkened by the night. "Ayunkini is waiting for you now."

Dakoda psychologically released the breath she'd been holding. "Okay," she gasped, nodding. "Let's do this."

24

Dakoda held on tightly to Jesse's hand as he led her toward the clearing prepared for her mind walk ceremony. Hand in hand with his wife, Chief Joseph led their small procession. Everyone had changed their clothing, discarding modern styles for something Dakoda believed to be their traditional garb; knee-length shirts sewn from a vividly patterned calico material tied with a beaded leather belt and worn with loose-fitting trousers and moccasins. Everyone wore their hair long and straight, their only adornment a simple headband.

Kathryn had loaned Dakoda a shirtdress similar to the one she presently wore. Tied with a beaded sash, the length of it brushed just below her knees. Along with a headband, a pair of borrowed moccasins completed her outfit.

As they approached the waiting members of the clan, Dakoda saw a portion of the clearing in front of the waterfall had been carefully prepared for the ceremony. Four torches were placed at the corners of a brightly colored blanket spread out on the grass. A fire burned nearby, heating a clay pot positioned on a three-footed iron brazier a few feet above the flames. Steam rose from the pot, scenting the evening's gentle breeze with the aroma of burned strawberries.

As Joseph and Kathryn joined the onlookers, Jesse leaned toward Dakoda. "You and I will sit on the blanket with Ayunkini. I will be beside you though the ceremony, as I am the one wishing to bring you into the clan."

Stomach doing a quick backflip, Dakoda swallowed hard and nodded. If she intended to back out, now would be the time. Despite the urge sitting at the edge of her tongue, she kept her reservations in check. "What am I supposed to do?" she asked as she slipped off her moccasins and stepped onto the blanket. The people gathered around offered no clue, murmuring among themselves.

"Ayunkini will guide you," Jesse said, leading her across the sacred space and instructing her to kneel before the old man. He settled beside her, giving the old man a brief nod.

Dakoda tried not to stare at the shaman. That, of course, was impossible. Folding her hands in front of her body, she sneaked a look toward the old man positioned between two of the torches. He was sitting cross-legged and perfectly straight. His eyes were closed and his hands rested on his knees. A cascade of long gray hair fell down his shoulders and his face was deeply etched with the strain of a long and dangerous life in the mountains. His tiny frame was whipcord thin. Even in rest his features were stern, his lips drawn down in a slight frown. There was no way to determine his age. He might have been in his eighties, or closer to a hundred. The fire's dim light cast shadows that hid the truth from prying eyes.

As if on cue, the people gathered outside the sacred perimeter fell silent.

After a moment the old man opened his eyes. His penetrating gaze brushed over Jesse. "Who is this you bring before me?"

Jesse's hand slipped back into hers. He gave her fingers a

gentle squeeze of reassurance. "This is Dakoda Jenkins. She has recently been found to be one of our own."

Ayunkini nodded his approval. "Your scent is very strong," he told Dakoda.

Not sure how to respond to such a statement, Dakoda nodded politely. "Thank you." *I think.*

The odor thing seemed to be very important to these people. Though she thought she caught traces of the deep musky odor emanating from the others, she couldn't be sure her olfactory senses were leading her correctly. To her they smelled perfectly normal, hardly offensive. *Just another thing to get used to, I suppose,* she thought.

The old man lifted a hand and reached out, leaning forward and stroking a single finger between Dakoda's brows. "Of the many who have come before me in preparation to take the mind walk, you are one I see much confusion in. You want to embrace your inner self, but you are afraid."

His words were an understatement.

Feeling very uncertain of herself, Dakoda clung to Jesse's hand. "I-I can't say I'm sure what I'm feeling," she admitted slowly. "What I have come to learn about the Tlvdatsi is amazing, but also very frightening for me. I'm told I belong among you, but I've never belonged anywhere in my life. It's hard, very hard, to start believing such a thing now."

Gaze softening, the shaman lowered his hand. "That is why you are here tonight, child. To learn the truth. Once your eyes are opened, you will see the world as you should, and not as one blind and shackled by ignorance about your race."

Dakoda followed all this sketchily; there were parts of the old man's English that she only partially understood, for he would lapse into his own language, then catch himself and resume in hers.

She nodded. "I think I understand, and I'm willing to do as you say."

Ayunkini shook his head. "You must be sure you wish to make the quest of vision," he said slowly. "To send you into a union of the spirit afraid and uncertain would do great damage. Only if you are sure may you take the mind walk."

Dakoda looked to Jesse. She couldn't imagine losing her memories of him or the time they'd shared together. As harrowing as the experience had been, it had inextricably bound them together on a level neither could ever truly break. Even if Ayunkini were to erase everything, she had a feeling some things would still linger on an unconscious level. And not knowing or being able to recognize that would be a torture she doubted she could ever live through.

A shiver clawed its way down her spine. *I'd go insane. No doubt about it.*

Forcibly calming an irrational surge of fear, Dakoda swallowed thickly. "I'm ready," she said firmly, looking outside the sacred space toward all the people watching. They had all come before Ayunkini and made the decision to proceed. She would, too. "Please tell me what I must do."

The old man made a gesture with his hand. A ladle was dipped into the brew simmering over the nearby fire, filling a small clay bowl decorated with ceremonial symbols. A silent man presented the bowl to Ayunkini before bowing and backing away.

Ayunkini offered the bowl to Dakoda. "First, you must drink of the Asi."

Hands shaking more than a little, Dakoda accepted his offering. The scent of boiled sweet berries assailed her nostrils. "What is it?"

Jesse gently put a hand on her arm. He leaned over, whispering in her ear. "It's berry wine mixed with a little peyote. It's used to open neural pathways so all parts of the brain are open and functioning at top capacity. It doesn't taste really great, but it will help you relax and take the mind walk."

Dakoda regarded the brew with suspicion. "In other words, I'm going to be tuning in, turning on, and dropping out," she grated back.

"Pretty much," Jesse whispered back.

She stiffened. "I don't use drugs," she hissed back. "Not any kind."

He laid a hand on her arm. "It's just a sip. Maybe two. The effects are minimal and you won't feel hungover. You have to drink it, though. The ceremony requires it. You will offend Ayunkini if you don't. You have to trust what Ayunkini does, and believe what you see once you are delivered."

Sounded like a bunch of hocus-pocus.

"I'm beginning to wonder if I want to meet any of these spirits," Dakoda muttered under her breath.

Jesse's gaze searched hers. "It won't be easy," he said softly. "But I'll be beside you the entire time."

"Promise?"

He nodded. "I do."

Dakoda regarded the steamy drink. Just a sip was all she needed to take. Just one teeny sip. Surely she could force a bit down. "Okay," she said aloud to acknowledge her agreement. "Let's do this."

Closing her eyes, Dakoda lifted the bowl to her lips. Pressing her mouth to the edge, she tipped back her head and opened her mouth, letting the warm liquid trickle into her mouth. She consciously fought not to taste it as the Asi rolled over her tongue. A bitter aftertaste lingered as she lowered the bowl and handed it back to the shaman.

Even as dizziness set in from the potent effects of the drink she'd consumed, Dakoda had the strange impression her skin and bones were commencing to melt away. She hadn't expected such a quick and immediate reaction to the drink, but it was clearly taking effect. When she looked into the old man's eyes, she saw enigmatic little ribbons of flame crawling in the depths of his gaze.

Pulse slowing, a quiet sense of euphoria crept in on silent, light feet. *The spirit is reaching out to touch me . . .*

She felt herself pitching forward, falling straight toward the old man. At the last possible second strong hands caught her, guiding her down onto her back. A moment later her head rested on Ayunkini's lap. His hands settled on her head, strong fingers rubbing slow circles at her temples. She looked upward into a night sky lit only by the light of far-flung stars. To her eyes they glittered like diamonds atop black velvet.

"The truth is yours to find, if only you will seek it," Ayunkini murmured, leaving words behind as he slipped into a chant to guide her journey.

Tingling from head to toe, Dakoda felt as though someone had taken a syringe and injected a pure shot of liquid energy into her veins. The force spread through her like wildfire across dry prairie grass, tearing apart and reshaping her perception of the world around her. Her mental barriers went down. Everything around her went blurry, receding into the far distance. She had reached that particular stage of relaxation when perception blurred, coherence and control ebbing away faster than she'd believed possible.

"That's some powerful shit," she mumbled, lulled by the old shaman's gentle touch. Ayunkini's bony fingers skimmed her brow, cheeks, and jawline, ushering in a strange sense of well-being.

The scene around her rippled like waves from a stone thrown into a pond. Her surroundings gradually faded away, receding into the distance.

All of a sudden Dakoda was all alone, her blood pulsing with unconscious rhythm as it followed the current of her nerve endings. She moved, gliding, unconscious of taking any physical steps. Her heart slowed beneath her rib cage, fluttering as her pulse slowed, then briefly stilled. Her fading vision focused on one star, sharper and brighter than any surrounding it. She sensed rather than physically felt the relaxing of her muscles as her spirit slipped outside the surly bonds of her physical shell.

Dakoda reached upward, lifting one phantom hand toward the pearlescent illumination beckoning her to bask in its glow. For an instant nothing existed except the pure white light, beaming down on her, embracing her in its warm pulse of welcome and acceptance. Endless space surrounded her.

Dakoda blinked, perceiving the glow of a blurry face, neither male nor female, yet bearing the demeanor of a wholly celestial being. She wasn't really seeing, but perceiving in some strange way contact with a realm—an intelligence—far greater than her own. Her mind, in comparison, was no larger than the common pissant. The invisible force reached out, caressing her consciousness. That first signaling touch of communication delivered a shock.

Drawn into the nucleus of a single perception, Dakoda felt the weight of eternity pour into her mind. She understood and comprehended that life, down to the last and smallest molecule, was powered by the same nucleus of energy. The spark of creation itself inhabited every being—plant, animal, and human. It was an energy meant to be taken, shaped, and molded. All life was really just tiny particles of energy, billions upon billions of atoms strung together to form coherent shapes for specific purposes.

With practice, a cognizant person could tap into the energies flowing through the electric netting of supersensory nerves, reshaping the body. Even upon death the energy never ceased to exist, simply returning to its natural, shapeless state within the universe. The beginning and the end all linked together, a circle always flowing and never to be broken.

The fusion complete, the pressure invading her mind slipped away. The intense radiance around her flared, shifting her focus in another direction.

With a brief tingling shock, Dakoda suddenly realized she was looking down from space, staring at her own unconscious body. A dim flare emanated around her abandoned shell, the slight glimmering the only indication of her cling to life. All she had to do was turn away, and life on earth as she knew it would end.

She would be one with the creator of all life.

An eerily toneless voice caressed her consciousness. *You are not ready to join me, my child.*

Dakoda felt deeply disquieted. A flicker of dismay crossed her mind. *I wish to stay,* she cried, though her protest slipped from no physical lips. *This is where I belong.*

The voice came again, gentle and persuasive. *There is much left to do on earth among your people.*

The brilliance surrounding her flickered, darkening alarmingly to a dull shade of gray. Suddenly the force holding her aloft let go, sending her plunging back toward earth at a terrifying speed. Terrible and twisted shapes rushed at her through the fading light, menacing half-seen faces she recognized as those whom she'd encountered in her life: her mother, Ash Jenkins, Gregory Zerbe, even the countenances of the hated poachers. They were all there, swirling around her as she made her final descent back into . . .

Dakoda felt a spasm of fear, an almost anguished longing for time to turn itself back before she'd drank down the poison infecting her mind and body. Her mind was losing its grip on sanity even as her ears were filled with a terrible piercing scream she vaguely recognized as her own.

Crying aloud at the impact of terror and agony, she reconnected with her body like a boulder tossed from a ten-story building. At the same instant she felt an enormous thrust of energy, a great electrical shock that made her senses reel. Darkness boiled across her vision, assaulting her with nightmarish stabs of pain. Spreading through her like a disease, some faceless beast ravaged her insides, shredding her down to the last tiny molecule.

Dakoda's body stiffened, going rigid, arching up against the ground until it seemed her spine would snap in half. For several long seconds a twitching, shuddering tremor shook all her limbs. Her bones unlatched, reshaping themselves into foreign contours, even as a pelt of coarse tawny fur sped across her bare skin. The black void was briefly illuminated by a dazzling crimson glare reflecting back at her like a mirror. In that light Dakoda temporarily beheld herself, wearing a savage cat's head and baring great sharp teeth.

That's not me! she cried out at the image.

The reply poured through her skull, molten and searing. A wild roar ripped through her brain space, smashing through her thoughts like a stone thrown through a plate glass window.

I am you, said the great feline. *And you are me. We are one.*

Dakoda's struggles grew fainter and fainter. She collapsed into a lifeless heap. A sense of total defeat, almost hopelessness, washed over her. It seemed like she'd been floundering in this nightmare trip for centuries.

Just as she was sure she could take no more of the terrible mind-shredding, gut-twisting convulsions, the glittering darkness retreated, draining away into nothingness. The maelstrom retreated and her senses were, again, her own.

She was complete, and she was whole.

Dakoda rolled off her back, standing stiff legged and trembling all over. She shook her head, trying to orient herself. *I'm back,* she thought dizzily, not realizing yet the physical change she'd undergone.

Gasps of wonder and cries of delight escaped from the crowd of onlookers gathered around her.

"She's shifted!" Kathryn Clawfoot cried out joyously, clapping her hands with delight. Other voices joined in, adding to the general melee of euphoria.

Still only half able to comprehend their words, Dakoda took one shaky step forward, and then another. Fighting to draw air into lungs that felt tight and small, she gasped painfully. A bizarre half-growl rolled over her rubbery lips. She was only vaguely aware the center of her balance had changed. Her two legs had become four.

Still a little confused, Dakoda plopped down on her rear. Somehow her shirtdress had slipped, lying in a heap on the blanket. She wasn't sure how it could have come off. Her head felt as if she were swaying in a sickening up-and-down rhythm. Her head and heart were pounding as hard as a jackhammer on asphalt. Pain lanced through her. Icy fingers squeezed her brain. Her thoughts felt like they no longer fit into the confines of her skull. Her skin seemed to crawl as she lifted a hand and looked down at the soft pinkish pads of a paw. She flexed her fingers. A sharp set of claws popped out.

Struggling to maintain self-control, she fought to pull her thoughts into something coherent. *Holy shit! I'm definitely not myself.* She stared, stunned and more than a little bit frightened. It vaguely occurred to her that she didn't know how to get back.

A familiar presence knelt beside her, wrapping his arms around her thick furry neck. Her fear lessened, for she knew this man, had enjoyed his touch.

Dakoda sagged against him, enjoying his embrace. *Jesse.* Her attempts to say his name rolled out of her mouth as a weak moan. A cougar's vocal cords just couldn't handle human speech.

"Don't be afraid," Jesse whispered. "Ayunkini will help you explore your new body." He stroked her head, giving her a deep scratch behind one ear. "Later, I'll explore the old one."

25

Dakoda lay on the blanket beside Jesse, enjoying the light caress of his fingers across her cheek. The night was warm, warmer than she could remember for any of the nights she'd spent in the mountains. Perhaps that was because her metabolism had recently undergone such a strange shock. Night birds and other predators of shadows rustled quietly in the nearby woods, and a few owls swooped down from overhead. Around her with her sharpened senses she smelled the clean, sharp scent carried on the breeze.

Still suffering the intense aftereffects of her first shift, Dakoda felt drowsy. Time had gone completely out of focus, slipping away unnoticed. At the moment she was completely content to lay here on the blanket beside Jesse, only dimly conscious of the shifting rainbow of images behind her eyes. Her senses felt sharper, every color brighter and more vibrant than she remembered, every smell more individual and intense.

She was tired, but in a good way. Once she'd become accustomed to her new form she'd even taken a lope around the Tlvdatsi settlement, accompanied by other members of the tribe.

All had rejoiced in the incredible success of her mind walk, welcoming her into the clan with open arms. She was truly one of them, and belonged. The recognition and outpouring of acceptance had stunned her. Nobody cared where she came from or what kind of life she'd lived. The future was wide open. All she had to do was embrace it.

Jesse traced her lips with the tips of his fingers. "I still can't believe you shifted," he whispered. "Hardly anyone does the first time. Most of us have to go through the mind walk with Ayunkini and learn how to keep our mind energies flowing."

Feeling relaxed and utterly content, Dakoda closed her eyes. Behind her eyelids she could still see the face of the great being that had drawn her away from her body, showing her a truth she never would have dreamed of. When she'd come down from the trip, she'd at first suspected she'd dreamed the entire incident. It would have been entirely reasonable to believe the hallucinogenic properties of the peyote-laced wine had caused her to imagine the entire experience.

It was only when Ayunkini explained again how she could tune into the psi-forces she'd encountered, channeling the energies she'd need for shifting, that she began to understand the experience as wholly real. Led by the old shaman, she'd shifted several times, to the amazement of many who had taken months to learn. She seemed to have a knack for the shift, was catching on with amazing ease.

"I'm still a little stunned," she admitted. "At first it felt like someone had chopped my body to pieces and tried to reassemble it into an unnatural shape. But once I did it a few times, it felt completely natural. Even the pain wasn't as bad as it was the first time."

Jesse propped himself up on an elbow. "Amazing, isn't it? To find such a power exists inside you, one you can manipulate at will. It's like being handed the keys to a magical realm."

Slipping an arm beneath her head, Dakoda nodded. "I'm

234 / Devyn Quinn

still waiting for the moment when I pinch myself and find out it was all a dream." She still felt little glimmering ripples of energy beneath her skin. That, she knew now, was the power of the cougar waiting to emerge. Once the beast had been unleashed, it would never be happy in captivity. Ayunkini had explained there would be times when she must allow the big cat freedom to roam, to live as nature intended.

Dakoda already knew going back to her old life wasn't an option. But neither was she entirely ready to embrace life with the clan. She still had obligations to fulfill. The first and foremost was to gain justice for her slain partner. And until Greg's killers were safely behind bars, there was no way she could consider relocating. The cougar inside would have to stay caged for a little while longer.

But that was something she'd think about later. Tomorrow. For the moment she was completely content to lie on the blanket and enjoy Jesse's company. Once the excitement of the night had ended, the others had drifted away to give them the privacy both desired. The other men had accepted the fact she was already spoken for.

Jesse's presence beside her was like wearing a warm, comfortable cloak. Their vibrations felt perfectly in sync. "Did you shift the first time you went through the ceremony?" she asked, suddenly curious as to how his first experience had gone.

His face more than half concealed in shadows, Jesse shook his head. "No, I didn't," he confessed. "It took me a long time to master the shift. I had to work with Ayunkini for months to gain the first change." A grating little laugh escaped him. "For a while there, it looked like I'd be one who just couldn't get it."

Her brows rose. "Oh? Why do you think that was?"

Jesse sighed, rolling over onto his back and spreading out his arms. "I think I had such a hard time simply because I didn't want to believe," he confessed quietly, his mouth a grim, set line.

Caught off guard by his admission, Dakoda sat up. "I don't know what you saw during your trip, but how could you not? I mean, what I saw was amazing, just totally awesome. And when all that knowledge came flooding into my mind, I knew it was all true."

Jesse shook his head. "Oh, I guess in the back of my mind I knew the truth. Trouble was, I wasn't ready to accept it, you know?"

"No," Dakoda admitted, more than a little puzzled by his words. In the entire time she'd known him he seemed fiercely possessive of his heritage, embracing it fully. It was a shocker to find out he hadn't accepted it as easily as she had. After all, she'd been the one dragging her feet!

Suppressing a sigh, Jesse scrubbed his face with both hands. "To tell you the truth, I wasn't really eager to try to embrace my heritage," he finally admitted. "I mean, who the hell wants to give up life—a real life—to come live on a patch of land in the mountains and run around on four paws?"

"You didn't?"

He shook his head. "Not really. I know I'm an Indian and we're supposed to have this spiritual connection with our ancestors, but I've never felt it was carved in stone. I just wanted to be average, have the same things every other guy has; the job, the house, the pretty wife, and a couple of kids. Getting off the reservation and making it in the white man's world was something I really wanted to do."

Dakoda tensed, realizing the implications behind his words. She'd always imagined it was easy for Jesse to adjust to the life he'd been drawn into. Not so. He'd apparently had to make some adjustments and concessions, too. "So you tried to pretend the shift wasn't in you?"

He nodded. "Right. I figured if I just ignored it, it would go away."

Dakoda laid a hand on his chest. The strength of his heartbeat pulsed beneath her palm. "But once you know, it doesn't go away," she murmured.

Jesse laughed shortly. "No, it doesn't. I even asked Ayunkini to lift the memories so I could go on and not know." Breath hitching in his throat, a sigh slipped between his lips. "But Ayunkini's a crafty old man. He knew I was fighting the shift, and made me keep the memories. It got to the point where it was shift or go insane. I just couldn't fight it anymore. It wasn't easy and I didn't like it, but I didn't have a choice."

Hand still in place, Dakoda eyed him for a moment. The beat of his heart was steady, reassuring. He'd had his struggle and made his peace with himself. Just as she would have to soon. "Sounds like you really fought it," she said softly.

Jesse snorted at the understatement behind her words. "I did. A lot. But there's no denying the nature of the cat inside. As much as I don't like it sometimes, this is where I belonged." His gaze searched for hers through the shadows. "I think you see now it's where you fit in, too."

Dakoda hesitated. "I won't say I don't, but I can say it's just not the right time."

He sat up. "So you're still planning to leave in the morning?"

She hesitated, deciding the best way to answer. "Yes."

Jesse pursed his lips. "I guess I understand."

She grunted. "I've got no choice. I've got to get into town and let the authorities know about Greg's death. He has a family, a wife and kids waiting at home. Living through this last week must have been hell for them. They know nothing, where he's gone, what happened. At least I can tell them, give them the details and do my best to finish what he started."

Jesse nodded thoughtfully. "I guess if I were in your shoes, I'd want to do the same thing." He reached out, settling a possessive hand on her shoulder. "Just make sure while you're gone you don't forget about me. There are a lot of Tlvdatsi males who would like to get their hands on your beautiful body."

At the touch of his hand, Dakoda's clit twitched with immediate interest. One aftereffect that definitely lingered was the desire to have sex. She could smell Jesse's need. His hot male scent perfumed the air with a rich, musky odor that was close to driving her wild with desire.

Inside her, the need of a female in heat strained against the collar she'd managed to put on. It took only seconds for Dakoda to decide to let desire have its way.

Catching the hem of her shirtdress, she lifted it over her head, revealing the hard straining tips of her nipples. She let her garment slip from her fingers, pooling on the blanket beside them. Having made the shift several times, she wore nothing else beneath.

Giving Jesse a seductive wink, Dakoda ran her hands up her flat abdomen, cupping her breasts as an offering to him. The energies flowing through her veins had sharpened her need, giving it a brutal edge. Lust was a hot, tight coil deep in her belly.

Slowly, seductively, she smiled. "You're the only one I want," she confessed, her tone husky with a combination of arousal and anticipation

Rising up on his knees, Jesse's hands trembled as he slid them around her slender hips. His lips brushed hers. "I want you tonight, and every night after that," he whispered against her mouth.

Dakoda slipped her fingers through his silky black hair, sifting the long strands away from his face. Her tongue snaked out, seductively tracing his top lip. "I wish I didn't have to go back," she murmured. There was no way she'd be able to survive the heat cycle of the mating season all by herself. "I'm going to miss you."

Jesse slid a hand toward the full mound of one breast,

stroking the tip of her cherry-ripe nipple. "I'll come as often as I can." He pulled her toward his lean torso, letting her feel the press of his cock beneath his loose fitting trousers. The throbbing heat of his need burned through the material. "If the Barnett brothers are arrested, I have decided I want to testify to their abuses."

Heart thudding heavily, Dakoda's senses began to spin from the erotic ferocity behind his need. "Really?" she gasped, trying to keep her mind on one thing when her body would rather concentrate on other, more sensual pursuits. "I thought your people didn't want to get involved."

Jesse nibbled her lower lip. "We're already involved," he breathed, guiding her down until she lay on the blanket. He came down on top of her, settling his hips between her spread thighs. Supporting his weight on outstretched arms, he looked down at her. "I'm going to go before the council tomorrow, convince them it's time for us to cooperate with outside law enforcement. Our fear of exposure has allowed these men to turn us into victims. We say we fight back by destroying their traps and camps, but in reality we're not making any headway. It's come down to murder now, and that's something I can't live with on my conscience."

Hands slipping around his neck, Dakoda looked up at him with a combination of desire and elation. "They can be stopped, without having to jeopardize the clan," she said. "If someone told me a man could turn into a cougar, I'd think they were crazy."

Jesse grinned. "It would make a great insanity plea," he countered, making a sound between a growl and a moan. "Kind of like having you wet and willing beneath me is making me crazy."

A warm flush stole across Dakoda's cheeks. "Who says I'm wet or willing?" she argued back with a mock pout. It was the truth, though. She felt the balmy moisture of stimulation between her thighs.

Jesse cocked a wicked brow. "Oh, I think I can make you very wet, and very willing." He lowered his head, mouth descending over one rosy nub, skillfully circling and flicking the tender tip with his tongue. Feasting on her breast, he ground his hips into hers, rubbing the length of his shaft against her clit. The soft doeskin trousers he wore created a heavenly friction against her most sensitive spot.

Straining against euphoria, Dakoda pressed up against him. A moan slipped from her throat. Circling both hands around his body, she tugged at his shirt. In the past, he'd maintained control, manipulating her body at his ease and leisure. Now it was time to turn the tables on him. She wanted to drive him wild, taken him to the edge, and let him dangle a little. "I think you're a little too overdressed," she panted.

Cursing beneath his breath, Jesse reared up on his knees. "Got used to going without these damn things," he muttered, tossing his shirt aside. He reached for the waistband of his trousers.

Dakoda sat up and caught his hands. "My turn," she said, staring up at him. Lust burned a white-hot path through her veins. "Tonight I'm the one delivering the goods."

Jesse looked down at her, a spill of ink-black hair curtaining his face and shoulders. He cupped one of her cheeks. "Oh, you've delivered in more ways than one," he murmured.

Breath catching in her throat, Dakoda slipped her fingers into the waistband of his trousers. "Sit back." She tugged the soft doeskin down his narrow hips, gliding it over the sensual curve of his ass. His cock rose against his abdomen, free and unrestrained. She tugged with more insistence. "I want these off."

"Yes, ma'am." Jesse sat down, allowing her to slip his

trousers off his legs. Freed of any impediment, he stretched out on top of the blanket, a splendid specimen of the fully aroused male. Hand circling his erect penis, he slowly jacked up and down its length. "Like what you see?"

Dakoda's mouth watered. "Yes, I do." Shifting onto her hands and knees, she crawled over to him. She paused for a moment, looking over his sleek body with satisfaction. Though the nearby torches and fire had burned out hours ago, the ability to shift had enhanced her human vision tenfold. Her gaze swept over him, taking in the ridges and planes of his sinewy frame.

She crawled toward him, stopping only when she'd reached the center of his body. Her legs were between his and her arms bracketed his slender hips. Lowering her head, she flicked her tongue over the broad crown of his cock. He tasted of the salty tang of pre-cum.

Jesse caught his breath. "Oh, God. Fantastic."

Dakoda's hand replaced his. Her fingers closed around a shaft thick and laced with veins. She closed her mouth around the plum-dark head, savoring the satiny feel of his skin. Exploring with her tongue, she discovered the ridge between the glans and shaft, plying the area with firm strokes.

Fingers digging into the blanket beneath his body, Jesse gasped. "That feels terrific," he gasped, his words filled with great gaps and pauses.

Dakoda raised her head, flicking at the tip. "Feel good?" she asked through a grin. His penis pulsed against her palm.

"Too damn good." He lifted his hips, attempting to drive his cock back into her mouth. "I want some more."

Dakoda resisted his silent plea. Instead of taking him into her mouth again, she instead delivered a series of sharp little nips down the length of his erection. At the same time, she used her free hand to fondle his tight, hot balls.

Jesse's body shuddered with delight. "Witch," he cursed. "Keep doing that and I'll come."

Closing her fingers around his shaft, Dakoda delivered another tiny bite to the tip. "You won't come until I want you to." She cupped and squeezed his balls, letting the suggestion of roughness salt his obvious pleasure. His ragged intake of breath told her she was hitting all the right spots.

Trembling with the need for control, Jesse slipped his hands around her head, pressing his cock against the seam of her lips. The hot pressure of his pending climax throbbed throughout his entire length. "I can't wait much longer," he warned through a rough groan. "Better get on while the getting is good."

Dakoda certainly wasn't willing to waste a good hard-on. She lifted herself up over his body, straddling his hips with her knees. Angling his erection at her core, she impaled herself to the hilt. "I think I've got it," she breathed, acutely aware of her inner muscles giving way to accommodate his length. A shudder of pure enjoyment shimmied up her spine.

Jesse gasped as she rocked her hips against his, driving his cock into her sex with long strokes. In a move to slow her down, he caught her waist, attempting to guide her. "Take it easy," he warned. "We're just getting started."

Dakoda gave in at the last moment, allowing him to set the pace. As their twofold rapport began to weave itself between them, she relaxed, bracing her weight on her knees, keeping her hips still as Jesse thrust his upward, entering her deeply before pulling out again. The erotic glide of his hard flesh into her creamy center mesmerized. Enjoyment flowed through her like liquid silver.

It was then her focus began to blur, going from physical contact into something much deeper, something more profound. As Jesse stroked into her again and again, Dakoda became aware of a new set of sensations coursing through her body, sensations not originating inside her own body, but in his. The strange feelings deepened, building into a stronger awareness that was new and strange but not frightening.

Vaguely, at the edge of her mind, Dakoda wondered if the impressions were a lingering aftereffect of the potent drug Ayunkini had administered. Or was it her unconscious desire for a closer connection with Jesse, a deeper communication than even sex could deliver?

Aware of her own body in a way she'd never been before, Dakoda stared down at his handsome face as he penetrated her. She'd never experienced a moment so powerful, so profound. "I never knew it could be this way between two people," she whispered through a long shuddery sigh.

Jesse's gaze locked with hers, electric with urgency. "It's about to get better," he grated, rolling his hips in an upward motion even as he dragged hers back into another downward arc.

"I don't think it could," she started to say.

She was wrong.

Without warning, Jesse toppled her onto the blanket. The hunger behind his move was more than need. As the male his instinct to have power over his mate was stronger, more predatory.

Flat on her back, Dakoda was no longer in the superior position. Jesse loomed over her, locking her wrists against the ground even as he aimed his shaft toward her dewy sex. Thrusting in, he slammed her with one jarring stroke after another. His imposing weight pressed down on her, each rigid stab striking just the right note with her insatiable clit.

Orgasm bubbled up from Dakoda's core like molten lava. She threw her head back, struggling to get a breath through the impulsive, overwhelming assault Jesse laid upon her like a medieval lord determined to conquer enemy lands. He stroked her deeply, knowing instinctively she craved his rough domination.

Dakoda cried out against the tide of climactic sensation. "I'm coming," she gasped, letting go of control and giving in to the rogue waves crashing through her. The fierce power tumbled her end over end, pulling her in a thousand different directions all at once. A wild shout of glee rippled across every nerve ending in her body.

Even as her heart raced inside her chest, Jesse slammed into her a final time. His cock surged, spitting a stream of liquid fire into the depths of her womb. A half-growl, half-groan simultaneously rolled past his lips.

Bodies locked together they floated, blended together from the sharing of intense physical gratification. At some point Jesse brushed his lips against her forehead. "That was too good," he mumbled in a hazy, faraway voice. Grabbing the edge of the woolen blanket, he pulled it over their sweat-soaked bodies.

Dakoda muttered back her own reply, incoherent but enough to satisfy him. She gratefully snuggled into his warm embrace. Right now she wanted nothing more than to lay motionless and just rest. But although she was half asleep, her senses were still on edge.

Frowning, she shook her head to clear away the night's phantoms, but it was no use. All too soon the sunrise would come, dragging her back toward a challenge she wasn't sure she was ready to face. Avenging Greg's death was turning into an obsession and she knew it, but somehow she couldn't break the spell. In the back of her mind she didn't really want to.

It's time to prepare, she thought through the silken cobwebs descending on her mind. *I must be ready.*

Exhausted by the past week, she finally relented long enough to let weariness have its way, reluctantly slipping into the welcome void of merciful oblivion.

26

Dakoda awoke in a strange bed.

Frowning, she lifted her head, looking around the small room. As the remnants of sleep filtered away, her vision adjusted, allowing her to see she was inside a cabin. Slivers of morning sunlight were beginning to creep in through the slats in the shutters covering two small windows.

Unlike Joe and Kathryn's larger home, this one appeared to consist of no more than a single room. On one side there was a wood-burning stove and a small table and benches. Across the room was the living space, consisting of a small hearth, a rocking chair, and a small chest of drawers. The bed she occupied was shoved up against the wall in the last empty corner. A couple of hunting rifles, clothes, and a few other miscellaneous items were scattered around in no particular order. Only the owner knew what was what.

A wry smile crept across Dakoda's lips. *A bachelor's pad.*

The bachelor in question lay pressed against her, his rangy body relaxed in sleep. Sprawled on top of the covers, one hand rested across his abdomen. His broad chest rose and fell with gentle rhythm.

Gazing at Jesse's lax features, Dakoda reached out to move a stray lock of hair away from his face. Long dark lashes any woman would kill to have fanned across his cheekbones. He was astonishingly handsome, and every time she looked at him her heart clenched.

Jesse stirred against her, muscles flexing all through his powerful body.

Dakoda smiled. She'd gotten used to waking up next to him. It felt familiar. Good. Her itchy feet, the urge to get up and go home after sex, seemed to have fled. For the first time she realized what it meant to be part of a couple. There was commitment, not just of bodies, but a meeting of minds and souls on a common level, joined toward a common cause. When they'd first met, the need to survive had joined them. After their escape, the need to stay alive had kept them together. Walking away was going to be a lot harder than she'd first imagined.

Oh, no, she realized suddenly. *I'm in love with Jesse.* It had just happened, as smoothly and naturally as her lungs drew oxygen. She'd spent most of her twenty-six years running away from emotional entanglements, and now here she was up to her ass, head over heels in love. In the space of a week, her entire life had been turned upside down. It didn't even seem strange that she thought of these mountains as her home now.

They were. They always would be.

Leaning closer to him, Dakoda inhaled the air around him. His warm skin radiated musk, the scent of the sex they'd shared the night before. Sometime during the night he'd scooped her off the cold ground outside, carrying her to his bed. They'd had sex again, not fast or hurried, but the slow gentle sweet kind that was more about their two bodies being joined together in perfect harmony rather than seeking climax.

Dakoda's gaze skimmed toward his flaccid penis. Nestled in a thick thatch of black curls, it waited for a female's touch to awaken it. She was just about to slide down and give him a nice morning surprise when a loud banging on the door disturbed the morning's silence.

"Hey, Jesse, you in there?" Robin Huskey's voice called. "Get up, man." More heavy knocks followed.

Jarred out of a sound sleep, Jesse sat up. He yawned and stretched, scratching a smooth patch of belly. "What the fuck do you want, man?" he called back, rolling over Dakoda and reaching toward a pile of clothes at the foot of the bed.

Dakoda's mouth went dry as she caught a glimpse of his firm ass sliding into a tight pair of jeans. She could feel her clit twisting as she watched him slip a T-shirt over his head. Damn. Watching him get dressed was just as sexy as watching him shuck his clothes.

"Something's happened, Jess. Something bad," Robin answered. "Come on, open the door, man."

"Shit." Rubbing his hands across his face, Jesse headed to let the impatient man inside. Dakoda had just enough time to cover herself with the blanket before Robin Huskey blew into the room.

Wild-eyed, he looked around. "We've got trouble," he breathed, panting as though he'd run a hard, long distance in a short amount of time. "Big fucking trouble, with a capital T."

Finding a pair of socks in the mess of clothing, Jesse sat down on the bed to pull them on. His long black hair tumbled around his face when he bent over. "When don't we have fucking trouble?" he muttered sourly.

Robin stiffened. "Ayunkini has been taken by the Barnett brothers," he said, his words arriving in a rush.

Dakoda's heart skidded to a halt in her chest. Icy dread congealed in her gut. "No," she murmured, shocked by the news.

Jesse immediately jumped up, rage roaring to life. "Those

rotten bastards," he shouted, reaching across the table for his rifle. He swore viciously and stomped toward the door. "This means war."

Robin caught his arm. "Slow down, Jess. It isn't going to be that easy..." His gaze turned toward Dakoda. "They've threatened to kill him unless we turn over the ranger."

Jesse's grip tightened on his gun. "You're kidding."

Robin shook his head. "No, that's their demand. They want Dakoda."

Jesse's face went grim. "That isn't going to happen."

Robin stared at him. "Joe wants to see you both, right away."

Jesse set his rifle down and threw Dakoda a wide-eyed look. "Tell him we'll be right over."

Dakoda listened in disbelief as Robin described how Ayunkini had been taken hostage by the Barnett brothers. She felt as if she'd taken a hard blow to the gut as the young Indian described the ambush. Having trailed her and Jesse back onto reservation lands, they'd boldly snatched one of the most valued members of the tribe.

It had taken a second, and then a third telling for the story to sink in. It didn't matter how many times she heard the story, though. The ending was the same.

The Barnett brothers wanted her back.

When she'd heard their demands, Dakoda had no hesitation. Not a single one. "You have to turn me over to them," she told Chief Joseph.

Jesse looked at her like she'd lost every marble in her head. "You can't be serious?"

Dakoda frowned. "Of course I am. Ayunkini is your shaman, your holy man." Her grip tightened around the mug of strong hot coffee Kathryn had provided for the meeting. "They've made it clear they'll kill him if they don't get me."

Chief Joseph broke in. "You two can argue it out all morning, but my say in the matter remains the same," he said quietly. "Ayunkini is an old man, and close to death. He would not want us to sacrifice one of our young females just to save his life."

"How can you say that?" Jesse demanded angrily. "It sounds like you're willing to throw away his life for nothing."

The chief sighed deeply. "I'm never willing to sacrifice any man's life," he said slowly. "But in this case we have to be logical. Ayunkini is an old man. Of the many things they can do to him, death is the least of his worries. Think of Dakoda, Jesse. You know the humiliations they put you both through. Would you have her suffer those again?"

Jesse slumped back in his chair, picking listlessly at the plate of food Kathryn had slid in front of him. Despite the delicious aroma of freshly made buttermilk pancakes, no one felt the least bit hungry. "You know I don't want Dakoda in their hands again," he finally said.

The Chief sipped his coffee. "They're banking on us turning her over because she's an outsider. No matter the many battles we've had with these men, the unwritten rule of these mountains is we allow no outsiders. That has always been the rule that kept us safe."

"But we're not safe," Robin Huskey said quietly. "Because we've always been afraid of exposure, we've put up with having to stay confined to our own land. But you know that's just not possible. We can't find mates by prowling the same tract of land day after day. Our women come from the outside. Jesse got snared because he scented a female and went after her. It's in our natures to do so, and you can't fight nature."

Jesse pushed his plate aside. "Robin's right. It's in our natures to roam, and we have to go off the reservation if we hope to find females. We know there's danger, and we're willing to accept it. But they've broken the rule, Joe. They've come onto our land and maliciously taken one of our people. Being hunted and caged like animals is no longer acceptable. We've got to fight back, and this time it's more than an eye for an eye or a tooth for a tooth. This time we need to strike harder." He reinforced his statement with a rippling snarl. "This time we need to kill."

The inflection of icy fury in his tone caused Dakoda's guts to tighten. She reached out, covering one of his hands with her own. "It doesn't have to come down to murder," she said. "There are other ways to deal with these men. Legal ways."

Giving a snort of disgust, Jesse pulled his hand away. Simple words weren't going to mollify him much longer. His frustration was swiftly coming to a boil, close to reaching a dangerous point. Young and hotheaded, he was apt to do something stupid, without considering the consequences. "The white man's law doesn't exist out here," he snarled. "It never has."

Kathryn looked at Jesse and frowned. "Dakoda's an outsider," she countered quietly. "And she's dangerous to them because she can bring the law into this land. As they see it, we should consider her a danger, too."

Jesse shot his sister-in-law a disgusted look. "She's not a danger, Kathryn, she's one of us. Just like you were, when Joe found you. Those men almost raped you."

Kathryn's eyes flashed. "That's right, and it's something I'll never forget. And they attacked me because they could—because they don't fear any rules in these mountains except the ones they make for themselves. It's all well and fine for you boys to fight your stupid battles with these men, but why should you have to do it in secret when you have the law on your side?"

Chief Joseph's eyes studied his wife with a too-perceptive gaze. "What are you saying, Kathryn?"

Kathryn Clawfoot turned on her husband. "I'm saying it's time to let the outsiders in, Joe. We need to have the law—the real law—at work out here. Dakoda's a ranger. She's also about to be a member of this tribe, if she wants to become one. I can think of no better person to begin putting together our own fledgling police force, someone who can work with the authorities in town to help curb problems like the Barnett clan." To emphasize her words, she put her hands on her hips and stomped one foot. "And until I get my way, there'll be no sons or daughters out of this marriage. I'm not raising my children to be afraid and hide."

By the look on his face, Chief Joseph had heard his wife's arguments many times before. After a long pause, he finally nodded. "That makes sense." Catching his mate's hand, he pressed a kiss on her knuckles. "As usual, my good wife thinks with her head as well as her heart."

Shyly tugging her hand away, Kathryn smiled. "I can't claim all the credit. It's something my good husband has been considering for a long while, too."

The chief looked toward Dakoda. "Would this be something you'd be willing to do? Take a job with the reservation as one of our law enforcement officers? The pay wouldn't be much to start, but we could provide the essentials."

Jesse snorted. "We haven't got anyone else. You'd be the first."

Dakoda found herself imagining what it would be like if she were to agree to the chief's proposal. She glanced toward Jesse, remembering how his body had felt pressed against hers. Though she'd had her share of lovers, she'd never had a man take her the way he did. Every time they'd made love, he was the aggressor, seemingly determined to claim her, to possess her, designating her as his mate in every sense of the word.

And he'd succeeded.

He'd burned his essence into her so thoroughly that her body seemed to vibrate every time he got within touching distance.

And, oh, heavens, she loved it.

She'd often imagined what it would be like to stay with him, join his life in these mountains. After last night's magical experience of discovering the untamed power of the cougar roiling beneath her skin, she'd known there would be only one answer.

Yes.

Yes, she would give herself up not only to Jesse but also to the stunning, dizzying passion of the shift. She belonged to these mountains, wanted to become a part of them forever.

Now she could do so without guilt or hesitation. Chief Joseph had just offered her a way to serve her calling and her conscience equally. She could still do the work she loved, while serving the people she wanted to call family.

The Tlvdatsi had embraced her. Now she would return the honor, and give them what they wished.

Dakoda nodded her assent. "Yes," she said. "Once I'm finished with the matters I need to pursue against the Barnetts in town, I will accept your offer. Thank you." Apprehension prickled her skin. "And the first thing I intend to do is take those bastards down."

Jesse shook his head in protest. "Don't even think we're going to give them what they want, Dakoda."

Heart giving a compulsive thump, Dakoda felt her guts knot. "The way for us to get to these men is to give them what they think they want," she pointed out. "That's me."

"It's too dangerous," Chief Joseph said tightly.

She insisted. "I can't let you sacrifice your shaman when there may be a way to save him without having to do exactly as these men demand." Her mind spun in frantic circles like a top set loose at high speed. There had to be a satisfactory solution to the mess she'd unwittingly placed these people in. There was no way she'd let an old man sacrifice his life to save hers.

That's just not acceptable, on any level.

Piqued with interest, the chief's brows rose. "And how do you propose we do that?"

Dakoda licked her lips as boldness crept through her mind on sneaky kitty feet. Cougar feet, in fact. She leaned closer to the table. Her challenging gaze met that of every onlooker. "They don't know I can shift," she pointed out. "Once Ayunkini is safe, all I would need is a moment to surprise them and break away. With you guys backing my tail, I just might make it."

27

Twelve noon. The sun hung high in the sky, its single wide, bright eye glaring down on the mountains.

The Barnett brothers waited on the edge of a clearing that gave them a clear view onto reservation land. Cannily, they'd chosen a location offering them the best advantage.

Their demand was simple. They wanted Dakoda. She was an outsider, a threat to their way of life in these mountains.

It would be a fair trade.

Or so they said.

No one trusted the Barnett brothers, but there were no other choices. The plan they'd come up with wasn't the most desirable to put into play, but it was the only game in town. With the odds against them and an old man's life hanging in the balance, they wouldn't have but one chance to make a clean getaway. Predicting the outcome of such a risky venture was impossible; the human elements involved were too unstable to be trusted. The single saving grace stood in Dakoda's ability to shift. Catching the outlaws unawares would be the key to her escape.

At the prearranged time, Dakoda stepped out into the clearing. Jesse walked beside her, levering a round into the chamber of his rifle. He lifted it at the approach of the outlaws, training the sights on Willie Barnett.

Ayunkini stood between the two men. His hands were bound behind his back, and a piece of gray duct tape covered the shaman's mouth. More than half his clothing was gone. Shirtless and barefoot, he wore only a pair of loose-fitting trousers. His long white hair hung disheveled around a face bloodied and bruised by heavy hands. He hadn't been treated gently or easily. To make sure he wouldn't cause any trouble, Waylon Barnett held a pistol to the old man's head.

Seeing them, Ayunkini began struggling against his captors. Dakoda clearly caught the desperation behind his movements. *No!* his desperate fight said. *Don't risk your life for mine.*

She briefly closed her eyes, sending him a silent message. *It will be all right,* she signaled back. Even though she knew Ayunkini couldn't read her mind, she somehow felt the shaman would be able to understand her. Last night he'd had his hand not only on the pulse of her heart but also on her soul.

Willie Barnett raised his hands to show he wasn't carrying a weapon. "Now hold on, Jesse," he said in a voice as close to amicable as he could manage. "You already know we got Rusty out there with his shotgun. No more than you've got a gun on me, he's got his on you."

Jesse kept he rifle steady. "We've got a few watching you, too. And we're just as willing to spill a little blood."

Spitting a wad of tobacco, Willie Barnett pointed toward his brother. "You know he's got an itchy trigger finger, Jesse."

Jesse refused to back down. "Maybe mine's itching, too."

Dakoda glanced toward her lover. She wished she felt as brave as he sounded. He seemed determined to push every button, doing his best to prod them toward violence. It dimly occurred to her the young brave was absolutely ready to fight—and to die—this very day.

Dying wasn't at the top of Dakoda's list of things to do today.

Easing a hand onto Jesse's arm, she leaned in. "Take it easy," she whispered.

He shot her a glance of annoyance. Frustration with the entire situation was making him reckless. "I'm not into this plan," he mouthed back. His expression tightened. "I don't trust them."

She eased closer, giving him a seriously hard look. "Just trust me." No one was convinced the plan was viable. She'd had to demonstrate to everyone more than once her ability to shift still held true.

A breathless moment passed.

Jesse wavered, flashing a quick rueful smile. "Be careful," he mouthed, then added, "I love you too much to lose you now." His black eyes, endlessly deep, were filled with her reflection.

Dakoda's heart squeezed as if it were stopping. Those were words she hadn't been expecting to hear today. Not by a long shot.

Breathing hard, she rested her forehead against his shoulder. For a long minute she stood like that, her body next to his, soaking in the strength and warmth of his brawny frame. "I love you, too," she murmured, offering a light squeeze of reassurance. *I don't want to lose you, either.*

Willie Barnett's voice broke into their private conversation, dragging them both back to the unpleasant reality at hand. "There's no need to talk that way when we can settle things right." He sucked some more on the nasty wad shoved in his lower lip. "We all got our places out here, and can get along just fine as long as we keep the outsiders away."

"Seems to me like you boys have forgotten some of the

rules, Barnett," Jesse countered, refusing to back down. "There will be a time for getting even. You can mark my words on that."

Willie Barnett spread his hands and laughed. "You just take care where you're steppin' in future times."

"I'll consider myself warned," Jesse grated back.

Waylon Barnett eyed Dakoda, his gaze slipping over her like oily slime. She couldn't help shivering. He'd seen her naked and probably thought he'd be doing so again. "Looks like you're of a mind to do some business," he said, smashing the barrel of his pistol into Ayunkini's side.

Jesse's face went stone hard. "Blackmail isn't the way men do business," he answered tautly. "Just cowards like you."

Dakoda couldn't help wincing. The plan was to cooperate as much as possible, lead the Barnett brothers to believe the Indians wanted nothing more than a clean trade. She was to appear to be nothing more than the barter.

Barnett chuckled. "Didn't think you were gonna give her up so easy, seein' as you've been fuckin' her and all."

Jesse shot a sharp glance at Dakoda, one akin to disgust. "As hard as you were trying to convince your buyer of the fact, you know she isn't one of us," he answered tightly, segueing neatly into the lie with little effort.

Willie Barnett chuckled. "Well, you can't blame a man for trying, now can you?"

The smug asshole.

Dakoda knew why they were so desperate to get her back. Once she made it back into town, she had the capability to bring the wrath of the law into these mountains. Poaching a few animals illegally was one thing for the authorities to turn a blind eye to. Murdering a ranger was another thing entirely. This time the hunt wouldn't stop until justice was satisfied.

They're afraid, she warned herself. *Jesse and I are living witnesses to Greg's murder.* Desperation made men unpredictable.

Every move she made would have to be with the greatest caution.

One false step could be fatal.

Continuing the pretense, Jesse nodded slowly. "We're willing to make the trade." Lowering the rifle, he gave Dakoda a little shove out in front of him. She stumbled forward a few steps. "You know we don't take to outsiders."

"Nope, not at all," Barnett agreed. "And you don't gotta worry 'bout her sayin' a word. Her buyer's still interested in having her for—" A lewd grin split his lips. "Other things. As long as she'll suck cock, she'll have a nice home. Ain't none of us got to worry about the law comin' in."

Dakoda shivered with disgust at his words. Did he actually think she'd willingly be a sex slave to save her own life? *Hell will freeze over first,* she fumed.

"That sounds acceptable," Jesse said in agreement. "Send Ayunkini over."

Waylon Barnett shook his head. Levering back the hammer on his revolver, he made a counter demand. "You send her first," he demanded, snorting a laugh. "Kind of a show of good faith."

Jesse prodded Dakoda with his rifle. "You heard him," he said in a voice oddly flat and emotionless. "Get over there."

"But," she started to say. It wasn't a part of the script they'd agreed on earlier, just something that slipped out. For a moment it actually felt like he was willingly sending her back into the outlaws' hands—and with no intention of getting her back.

Jesse's face might have been carved of stone for all the expression he wore. "I have to look out for my people," he said roughly. "You're not one of us."

Had she not known better, Dakoda might have believed him.

Somehow she managed to pick up her feet, forcing herself to walk toward the waiting outlaws. Her feet felt like lead blocks.

She didn't want to go, but knew she must. Somewhere her partner lay in an unmarked grave, a grave that would never be found unless she had the courage to take these men in.

Willie Barnett smiled as he reached out to grab her arm. "See?" he grunted. "Those Indians always stick with their own first. You may have a nice tight pussy, but you ain't nothin' if you ain't one of their own."

Dakoda didn't believe him for a second. "Fuck you and the horse you rode in on," she snapped, feeling it to be a perfectly appropriate response.

Barnett didn't agree. His hand shot out, and his aim was unerring. "You'll be suckin' me yet, bitch," he snarled.

Dakoda's head reeled with the unexpected blow. Her cheek went numb and she thought she heard bells. She certainly saw more than a few stars. She staggered a little, but managed to stay upright.

The hair rose on Dakoda's nape. She pulled in an unsteady breath. *Hold tight,* she warned herself. She needed to remain focused, alert. Her mind cleared a little as she mentally swept away the pain and centered on the anger. That would help her shift faster. Beneath her skin the anger of the cougar inside boiled, aching to get out. *But not until the time is right.*

"Send Ayunkini over," Jesse demanded.

Cutting the ties holding the old man's hands behind his back, Waylon Barnett gave the old man a shove between the shoulder blades. Caught unaware, Ayunkini stumbled, hitting the ground hard.

Dakoda's heart rate bumped up a notch. A new chill took the air from her throat. *Oh shit.* This wasn't good.

"You ain't movin' fast enough, ol' man," the outlaw cackled. He raised his pistol and fired without hesitation. The bullet caught the old shaman directly in the head. Ayunkini slumped to the ground. Blood oozed from the hole in his temple.

Dakoda flinched. The shot was like a blow penetrating her

breastbone. Images of Gregory Zerbe's death flashed in front of Dakoda's eyes. Her mouth dropped open and it was all she could do not to scream. A strangled sob died in her throat. Oh, God! It was happening all over again.

Skeeter Barnett had killed Ayunkini.

Shot him down like a dog.

Pure panic struck. For ten, maybe twenty seconds, Dakoda couldn't move, not even to breathe. Her gaze zeroed in on the blood pooling around the old man's shattered skull. "You didn't have to kill him," she yelled, struggling to get the words out. "He was just an old man."

Witnessing the old man's murder, fury boiled up inside Jesse. He lifted his rifle, prepared to take the outlaw down. "You'll die for that, you son of a bitch." His words were no threat, but a promise.

Waylon took instant action to cover himself. Dakoda felt a strong arm encircle her neck and the cold press of a pistol against her head. "Back off or she's dead," he warned.

Acutely aware of the gun pressed at her temple, Dakoda realized the outlaws hadn't meant to let any of them walk away alive today. Not Ayunkini, Jesse, or herself. It was an ambush, a setup to get rid of all the witnesses.

Inside, the cougar roared.

Enough was enough.

Concealing the ability to shift meant keeping it locked up, letting the wildness of the animal inside sear her mind. Somehow she'd managed to hold the beast inside after seeing the old shaman gunned down. But the idea of possibly losing Jesse, too, was more than she could handle.

Now!

Nerve endings sparking with fire, Dakoda deliberately let her own consciousness ebb away. She felt the hum of power ripple through her veins. The sensation was like standing in a Jacuzzi on jet power, electric shafts of energy bursting under her skin. The sensation throbbed through her skull, the pressure building behind her eyes.

Every ounce of hate exploded outward. Her skin prickled, white-hot needles clawing upward through her flesh. Adrenaline seared through her veins. A series of bright lights flashed behind her eyes. The final shreds of control slipped through her fingers. Like hundred-proof whiskey taken straight from the bottle, the shift was delivering a shot of undiluted power and it was strong stuff.

Come on, cat, she called, opening the cage door on the irate feline. Every instinct she had screamed: REVENGE!

The cougar inside her came blasting outward, breaking the hold the outlaw had on her body. Twisting in midair, Dakoda felt the remnants of her clothing slip away. A screech of outrage tore from her throat as she sent the entire force of her weight crashing down on the hapless man.

Waylon Barnett cried out as he realized what was happening. Screaming mightily, he threw his weight against her, trying to wrestle himself out from under her hold even as he scrambled for the weapon she'd knocked from his hand. Dakoda felt his desperation, his fear. She knew he'd kill her if he got the chance.

He wasn't getting it.

The instinct driving the cougar inside shoved her human side away. Far away. She was all animal.

Gathering every bit of anger she had, Dakoda lowered her head. She clamped her massive jaws around the outlaw's neck, felt her sharp teeth dig into fragile human skin. She heard his scream of agony reverberating off her eardrums, but the sound of human fear meant nothing to her. Nothing at all. He had an instant to realize he was about to die. That was all the mercy she would grant him.

Dakoda knew what it felt like to be the one afraid. Now it was his turn, and she reveled in the power of the cat that had granted her the strength to kill. His skin tasted hot and salty beneath her fangs.

Perfect.

She was about to rip the man's throat out when a savage blow came out of nowhere, knocking her senseless.

"Get off him, you bitch!"

From the corner of her eye, Dakoda saw Willie Barnett raise his pistol, aiming it right for the center of her skull. The bastard had kicked her and when his attack didn't back her off, he'd had resorted to a more permanent solution.

The fucker.

Barnett thumbed back the hammer on his pistol. "You're gonna buy it!" he snarled. "Them claws and paws will still sell."

Dakoda bit down harder, refusing to let go of her prey. A low growl rumbled up from her chest. The man was a swine, rabid and extremely dangerous. Rotten to the core. He needed to be put down, out of everyone's misery.

But she never made the final, fatal bite.

A faraway thwacking sound cut through the air.

Gun slipping from his grasp, Willie Barnett staggered, falling down into the ground. Screaming with pain, he clutched at his shoulder. A long arrow protruded from the affected area. He was writhing like a bug impaled on a pin. An unintelligible series of curses slipped over his lips. So did his chewing tobacco. Choking on the mass, he gagged himself into silence.

Chief Joseph Clawfoot slithered out of the overgrowth. Instead of a gun, he held the traditional weapons of his people, the bow and arrow. He was wearing the customary clothing of a hunter, and had a knife strapped at one hip.

The chief curled a lip over his fallen prey. "Guess this one forgot to look over his shoulder."

Approaching the downed men, Jesse kept his rifle level. "There's another," he warned his brother.

The chief nodded. "Robin's got their lookout trussed up tighter than a Thanksgiving turkey," he said, grinning.

Jesse prodded Willie Barnett with one booted foot. "I was just about to shoot that fucker dead," he grunted. "Man, that arrow has to hurt ten times worse, though."

"Serrated." The chief flashed a predatory grin. "It won't be coming out easily or painlessly."

Jesse Clawfoot eyed the outlaws. "Killing was too easy of an out for these two, anyway," he said. "I want them to stay alive and pay for what they've done. For a long time. A very long time."

Dakoda's ears perked up as Joseph's words filtered through the mind of the predatory cat. The words made sense. She understood them. A glimmer of human thought burst through the irrational anger driving the furious cougar she'd become.

Sudden dizziness overtook Dakoda. An itching, creeping sensation drizzled over her, as if her skin was ripping in a thousand places. Everything around her began to waver. The blood in her veins felt like slivers of pure ice.

Still crouched over her prey, she shifted. For a moment she was immobile. Crawling away seemed like a good idea, but her limbs just wouldn't obey the commands of her brain. Her clothes lay a few feet away, little more than a tattered pile. She'd shifted so fast and so hard the material had come apart at the seams. Her body still pulsed from the raw surge of sheer force she'd pressed into her shift; every muscle and nerve felt shredded. Her captive convulsed under her, trying to push her weight off his chest.

"Get off me, bitch," he shouted, swatting at her.

Turning his rifle around, Jesse cracked the outlaw across the forehead with the stock. "I'd shut the fuck up and talk nice to the lady, since she's got some pretty sharp teeth." Handing his rifle to his brother, he slipped off his shirt. He draped it over Dakoda's shoulders, covering her nudity. "It's over," he murmured. "We did it." His encouraging smile held a tinge of pain.

Eyes narrowing on the hated outlaw, Dakoda shook her head. A growl rose in her chest. Bitter regret sifted into her mind. *I should have killed him.* One chomp and that bastard would have been toast.

"No, it's not." Pushing her arms into the sleeves, she pulled Jesse's shirt tighter around her body. His smell, so familiar and welcome, sifted into her nostrils.

Walking over to Ayunkini's body, she knelt beside the old man. The sight of him turned the tide on her ebbing energy. The sun wreathed his body in rays of bright, warm light. The day was going to be clear, beautiful, and full of promise. For a brief moment she was able to imagine the shaman as the lithe cougar he'd once been, perhaps young and headstrong like the man she now loved. It was a perfect day for running through the forest, unhampered by human limbs or limitations.

Tears instantly brimmed, blurring her vision. She felt numb, absolutely exhausted. A raw deep wound had been torn into her, going past mere flesh to penetrate all the way to the bone. She'd only known the old man a few hours, yet he'd changed her life immensely. The gift he'd given her was invaluable, and one she could neither deny nor turn away from. In following this wise spirit guide and learning the truth, she'd finally discovered that piece of herself she'd always been missing.

"I'm sorry," Dakoda murmured, her voice shaken, almost inaudible. "But I swear your killers won't go unpunished. I promise you here and now I will always help watch out for my people." She reached out, shutting the old man's sightless eyes. Though his life on earth had ended this day, she knew without doubt his spirit lived on, roaming free and far on another plane. Her mind walk had showed her the beginning and the end all came together on the spirit plane.

Jesse knelt beside her, wrapping her in his strong embrace. He stared gravely down at her. "I think your words would please Ayunkini very much."

Snuggling next to him for warmth, Dakoda trembled. "Do you think so?" she asked, feeling slow, familiar warmth spread through her. "It hardly seems enough."

Jesse slid a hand down to hers, twining their fingers together. His gaze bore into hers, looking straight into her soul. A slow smile spread across his fine mouth. "I know it comes from your soul," he said softly.

Dakoda pursed her lips against a faint quiver of emotion. "It does." She tightened her grip on her lover's hand, enjoying the simple awareness that she had no desire to pull away. "It always will." She closed her eyes, no longer feeling emotionally hollow and unsatisfied.

Her heart was so full of love for him it felt ready to burst right out of her chest. It was time to stop running and time to start facing herself and her true feelings. Destiny had finally showed her where she belonged. And whatever challenges the future might hold, she could face them all—as long as she had Jesse by her side.

Turn the page for a preview of "Heart of the Wildcat,"
Devyn Quinn's novella from SEXY BEAST VIII,
available from Aphrodisia in April 2010!

1

Kathryn Dayton didn't like the looks of the men walking into her camp. Sometimes you could tell with a glance that certain people in this world were bad news. She had no doubts about these two.

They definitely weren't up to any good.

Gaze steady and unflinching, Kathryn stayed down in a crouch, leaning in closer to her campfire, establishing her territory. She didn't say a word or reach toward the hunting knife strapped to her hip. She just watched as the men casually ambled into the perimeter she'd staked out as a place to roost after sundown. Other than members of her own crew, she hadn't expected company this far into the backcountry.

One of the men stepped boldly up to the fire. "Howdy." The second man lingered a few steps behind, as if watching his partner's back. One hand wrapped tightly around the strap of the rifle slung over his back.

Kathryn's gaze narrowed. "Howdy." Both wore backpacks and bedrolls and walked with the gait of men who spent a lot of time on foot in treacherous terrain. Hardcore mountain men, right down to the ruddy skin, shaggy beards, faded jeans, flannel shirts, jackets, and heavy hiking boots.

But that wasn't what disturbed her.

The guns did.

Both carried hunting rifles. Both had dangerous-looking knives strapped on for ease of access. More horribly, each man carried a set of claw-tooth traps commonly used for large game such as bear. *Illegal* traps.

A chill scurried down her spine. *Shit.* She was all too familiar with those vicious creations. Once an animal got a limb in, it didn't get loose. Men carrying weapons and traps meant only one thing.

Poachers.

They were fairly safe from prosecution because of the remote location. No towns existed in the immediate region, and it had taken a helicopter to get her and four crewmates into the remote area. An isolated remnant branching off the Appalachians and carved out of the Blue Ridge by erosion, much of the South Mountains of North Carolina were almost as pure as the day God created them. Even the rush of gold fever in the eighteenth century hadn't inflicted much of an impact on the old-growth forests.

Still, snakes lingered in paradise.

Kathryn ran a quick mental check of her own supplies. Aside from basic food and water, she carried a few hunting knives, a walkie-talkie, a small tent, and a sleeping bag. She'd deliberately turned her radio off, detouring away from the rest of the crew to spend the night alone. She'd needed some time to herself. The recent news her team had received hadn't been encouraging.

Her mouth quirked down. *So much for time alone.* The knot of automatic distrust settled deep in her guts.

Kathryn had no respect for men who committed brutal

crimes against nature. There were plenty of other places to hunt throughout the state. Legal places. Not that she condoned killing wildlife for pleasure. She found nothing sporting in shooting down beautiful animals through the sights of a high-powered scope.

The stranger held out his hands, palms down, soaking in the welcome heat. A cheery glow radiated from the flames consuming the wood. High summer in the mountains didn't necessarily mean the nights were warm or dry.

"Got cold," he said by the way of starting conversation. The wind kicked up, tugging at the wide brim of his hat. "Feels like a front's about to come through." His words were laced with the slow, down-home cornpone accent so familiar in the South.

Gaze lifting to the brewing sky, Kathryn felt as if the coming storm warned her something wicked had arrived. Lightning scratched the sky's leaden underbelly the way a predator would rip open prey. Thunder crashed through the night's uneasy silence. "Yep. Sure does." Another ten or twenty minutes and they'd all be driven out of the clearing by the rain.

The stranger eyed the blackened tin pot she'd positioned at the edge of the fire. "You mind if we sit a spell and drink a cup?" He inhaled, drawing in the smell. The enticing scent of pure dark Colombian coffee mingled with the pungent smoke. The chilly night air was doubly fragrant with the aroma.

Since she couldn't very well tell these two big boys to fuck off and find their own place to sit a spell, Kathryn shrugged. "Take a load off."

The stranger grinned. "Much obliged, Ma'am." He slid the heavy backpack off his shoulders and set it down. His hunting rifle followed, barrel propped at an angle pointing away from the camp. His silent companion followed suit, nodding in agreement before stepping up and relieving himself of his own load.

The first man reached over, offering a brief handshake. The odor of stale tobacco, whiskey, and sour male sweat assailed her nostrils. "My name's Willie. Willie Barnett."

Kathryn warily accepted his offer. Her hand practically disappeared in the maw of his callused grip. She gave as good as she got. "Kathryn." She didn't offer a last name.

The slight wasn't noticed.

Withdrawing his hand, Willie's elbow jerked toward his companion. "This here's my little brother, Skeeter."

"Howdy, Ma'am." Scrawnier and scruffier than his brother, Skeeter also offered his hand. His fingernails were caked with what must have been a lifetime of grime. He looked like he was many years shy of a good hot shower and hard scrub. No telling what kind of vermin might be living inside his less-than-clean clothes.

After a week of hard hiking and camping, Kathryn didn't exactly smell like a daisy herself.

She shook his hand, keeping her lips in that rictal smile of friendly acceptance she'd perfected through the lifetime trial of being a congresswoman's daughter. "Skeeter's an, uh, interesting name."

Skeeter grinned, more snaggles than actual teeth. "That ain't my real name," he confessed. "It's, uh, Waylon."

Kathryn resisted rolling her eyes. Oh, God. Willie and Waylon. The parents of these two were probably first cousins, and country music fans to boot.

Broad face breaking into a grin, Willie explained. "We call him 'Skeeter' 'cause when he was born, he weren't no bigger than a 'skeeter bug."

Skeeter cackled as though hearing the story for the first time. "But I sure growed up big," he filled in, hammering in the impression that he wasn't the brightest of the two. He smiled at Kathryn again. "You sure are purdy."

Kathryn refused to be baited. "Thanks."

Willie gave her a head to toe eye-fuck. "Don't see many women up here."

She gritted her teeth and glowered back. Terrific. Just what she needed. Two horny mountain men. "Wasn't like I expected to see any men, either."

Willie shrugged and smiled. "I know what ya mean. Been months since we laid eyes on 'nother human face." His attention moved back to what had lured them to her camp. "I sure could use a cup of that coffee, Ma'am."

Kathryn forced herself to relax. At least they were polite. Not that she was accustomed to hearing that word applied to her. She was only thirty-three, many years away from that moniker best suited to half-deaf old ladies with walkers.

She nodded amicably. "Sure." Maybe if she gave them each a cup, they'd drink it and move on.

The small old-fashioned percolator wasn't exactly the newest or most modern piece of camping equipment, but it made a drinkable cup of coffee. Dinged and more than a little battered, it had traveled the world with her. That it had been a gift from her late father made it that much more valuable. Unlike her career-oriented mother, he hadn't been too damn tied up with work to spend some time with his kid. He'd patiently fostered her love of wide-open spaces and the freedom of the wild, untamed lands.

The two men dug cups out of their packs.

Kathryn filled, careful not to spill one drop of the precious black gold. After walking for hours without a break, she'd been looking forward to a good, hot cup of the mud-thick brew to restore her flagging energy.

Her supplies were limited to what she could comfortably carry in her own backpack. Before leaving base camp, she'd pared down to the bare essentials in preparation for the rigorous hike. Survival in hostile and remote regions was a part of her profession as an ecologist and wildlife conservationist.

Willie lifted the cup to his nose, inhaling deeply. "Christ, that smells better than anything Skeeter ever made. His fuckin' coffee's like drinkin' pure horse piss, and just as unhealthy." He gulped, smacking his lips after he swallowed. A moment later every last drop was drunk.

Kathryn sipped her coffee, relishing the soothing warmth settling into her bones. It was hot and strong, but this was hardly the way she liked drinking it. She'd already decided to keep the sugar and few precious cans of condensed milk out of sight.

Skeeter wasn't as quick to drink. He apparently had his own stash of luxury items. He fumbled inside his coat, fishing out a small bottle of Wild Turkey. "Coffee'd taste better if you'd add to it." He poured a liberal dose into his cup, then tipped the bottle toward Willie's cup.

Willie held his not-so-empty cup out. "I'd be much obliged if you'd fill'er up again, Ma'am."

Resigned, Kathryn refilled. "Glad you're enjoying it." *Yeah, just what these two need to mix,* she thought acidly. *Guns and alcohol.*

Skeeter offered her a tip from his bottle. "Have a bit," he offered with all the amicability of a true Southern gentleman. "It does keep the chills away."

The icy wind whipping up the fire hastened her acceptance. "Thanks."

"Welcome, Ma'am."

Kathryn sipped again, tasting the strong Kentucky bourbon mixing with the tar-black brew. It went down smoothly, leaving a comforting glow in its wake. The temperature was definitely dropping, and would go lower before the night ended.

For a few minutes everyone concentrated on their drinks. The coffee went fast, leaving the two men sharing the bottle between them. The lower the whiskey went, the more they grinned like fools.

Willie scooted closer to Kathryn. By the fire's glow she saw his thick brown hair and bushy beard were heavily tinged with gray. "So what's a nice lady doin' out here all alone?" A big hand settled on her knee. "You lost?"

Kathryn caught a whiff. God! He smelled worse than a pig living in shit. No telling when soap and water had last touched his skin.

Brushing off his hand, she quickly resettled herself a few inches away. "I don't like things easy. Parking an RV, that's not real camping." Probably better not to reveal that she worked for the Wildlife Resources Commission. They were natural enemies.

Skeeter snorted his agreement. "I hear you there."

Kathryn eyed the traps on their packs. "You catch anything with those?"

Willie scooted in and patted her leg again. "Not a goddamned thang," he said. "Haven't been able to bring one of those fuckin' cats down for weeks."

Nervous about the way he kept invading her personal space, Kathryn scooted over again. "Cats?" The region was home to most common wildlife. Bobcats were plentiful, and not endangered.

A smile played around one corner of his tobacco stained mouth. "The *anitsasgili wesa*," he breathed.

"The what?"

"What the Cherokees call the ghost cat. Cougars."

Kathryn didn't believe him. "Impossible." The Eastern cougar was extinct. "There are no cougars here."

Taking a shot straight from the bottle, Willie solemnly disagreed. "You're dead wrong, little girl." As if expecting to see one that minute, he cast a quick glance over one shoulder. "There's cougar in these mountains, as sure as we're sittin' here now."

Swallowing more whiskey, Skeeter backed him up. "There's

274 / Devyn Quinn

good money in 'em. Asians want 'em, from the pelt to the teeth. Hell, even the goddamn paws and claws." He carelessly tossed the empty bottle. "Catchin' the damn thangs is the hard part."

Eager to tell more tales, Willie cut back in. "Those cats . . ." He visibly shivered. "They're smart, like men. They're mean as Satan, too."

Kathryn doubted she'd be very nice if these assholes were hunting her. "I can imagine."

Leaning closer, Willie pushed up the heavy sleeve covering his right arm. The firelight easily revealed the long scars marring his entire forearm and part of his hand. "See that?"

She momentarily held her breath. "Yes."

Willie pulled his sleeve back into place over his mutilated arm. "There's the proof. Fuckin' cat nearly took my arm off once." His heavy gaze drilled into hers. "I'm gonna get that bastard someday, too. I ain't the only one that took some scarrin'. I got him a few times with my knife. Ol' Scar 'n me, we're gonna tangle up a'gin. When we do, I swear I'll have that cat's balls." Exacerbated by the alcohol he'd consumed, his words were almost unintelligible.

The thunder boomed at that exact moment, hammering in his vow of vengeance.

Heart racing, Kathryn's mind worked furiously. Could it really be true the *Puma concolor couguar* had somehow returned to the area? Herds of white-tailed deer, a primary food source for the cougar, had recently increased in number. Given the almost pristine preservation of the old-growth forest, it was also possible that a few hardy cougar holdouts had survived undetected— perhaps breeding themselves back into significant numbers. If that were true, efforts to conserve the region would be more vital than ever.

Then Skeeter belched and farted. "'Scuse me," he mumbled.

Kathryn reconsidered her sources, both rude and socially unacceptable. The cougar tales might be Wild Turkey combined with a couple of good ol' boys telling some tall tales to impress her. She regarded her now drunken companions and sighed. *Until an actual cougar sighting is confirmed, hearsay is all I have.*

The storm kicked up again. More fat drops fell, sizzling when the water contacted the crackling flames. Seconds later the rain pelted a little harder.

Tugging the wide brim of her hat lower to shield her face, Kathryn reached for her coffeepot, removing its lid and dumping the grounds into the fire.

"Well, fellas, it's been nice visiting," she said, tucking her cup and coffeepot into her backpack. "But I really want to get out of the storm." Earlier she'd made plans to head for a nearby ravine. The low cliffside would provide a good windbreak and place to spend the night. Come morning she'd head back to base.

Willie's big hand closed around her wrist. "Hang on there," he slurred. "Where ya goin' all the sudden, sweet thang?"

Jerked out of private concerns, Kathryn shot him a glare. She tugged, but couldn't break his iron grip. An unbidden surge of anger obliterated sense. "Let go of me."

Grinning like a monkey eating shit, Willie held tight. "Just enjoyin' the pleasure of your company," he said softly, ominously.

Kathryn planted her weight and yanked harder. "I'm not enjoying the pleasure of yours!" Heart thumping hard in her chest, panic clawed her throat. "Let me go, asshole!"

Willie grinned. "Yes, Ma'am." He let her go.

Driven by her own velocity, Kathryn stumbled backward. Tripping over an unseen stone protruding from the ground, she landed on her back. Her head struck the ground, and a smattering of white stars sped in front of her rapidly blurring vision. A mass of thick hair tumbled out from under her cap. Arms and legs akimbo, she lay stunned.

Both brothers got to their feet, casually inspecting the damage.

Pulse pounding in her ears, Kathryn made a quick grab for the knife sheathed on her hip.

Willie guffawed and expertly knocked it out of her grip.

Skeeter stepped between her open legs, settling a heavy boot at each of her ankles, effectively pinning her legs in place. Swaying, his gaze never strayed from her crotch. "We could have a l'il fun here now."

Willie knelt beside her. He reached out, fingers skimming the inch-wide expanse of bare skin between her jeans and coat. "Been a long time since we had a taste of pussy fine as this," he leered.

Their words reverberated through Kathryn's mind. Suddenly her body quaked, their intent setting off a chain reaction deep inside her. If they raped her, they would probably kill her. Concealing a body in these dense woods would be a piece of cake. Every second she squandered put her that much closer to dead.

Fighting to clear the haze in her pounding head, she swallowed hard and struggled to sit up, move away from the range of danger. Unable to find her footing, she scrabbled backward like a hermit crab. She got a foot, maybe two, away.

A grin hitched up one corner of Willie's mouth. "You ain't goin' nowhere, honey."

Hands like manacles captured and pinned her wrists to the ground above her head. Dazed and confused, she hadn't even been aware of Skeeter coming around to cut off her retreat. He'd moved a hell of a lot faster than she had.

Grinning and straddling her body, Willie's big hands worked the zipper of her coat. He fumbled her shirt, ripping it open when he couldn't undo the buttons fast enough. Pushing up her sports bra, his big callused palms settled on her breasts. "Nice tits." He squeezed. "Bet it makes you wet when they're sucked."

Fear jetting through her veins, she kicked, scratched, but nothing would break the men's dominance. "Get off me, you big apes!"

Skeeter snarled, twisting her arms. "Be still. We're just gonna have a little fun."

Kathryn spat toward the ugly face looming over her. "Fun, my ass!"

"Fun with your ass," Willie cheerfully unbuttoned and unzipped her jeans.

Kathryn moaned, but didn't stop fighting. "Don't, please." Her plea went unheard.

Fingers hooking in the waistband, Willie slid her jeans down her thighs. Her panties went down, too, leaving her totally exposed. "Nothin' I like better than stickin' my dick up a nice, tight asshole."

Kathryn clenched her eyes against the chill rush of fear spiraling through her. She considered her options and realized there were none. Zero. No way she'd get out of this one. Maybe if she just gave in and gave them what they obviously intended to take, she'd have a better chance of getting out alive. Damn. She should have trusted her gut, not let her guard down.

I don't have to remember this . . .

Hard to forget as thick fingers probed between her naked thighs. "An' this sweet piece o' poontang . . . Hot damn, it's nice an' slick."

The stroke of his fingers against her clit sent tiny little tremors of disgust through her. "No—ah . . . hell . . ." The ability to speak all of a sudden eluded her.

Goosebumps tripping over her exposed skin, Kathryn gasped. Her stomach clenched into tight knots and a wave of mortified disgust washed over her. She felt absolutely paralyzed. Nothing

in a woman's life could adequately prepare her for such a brutal
assault. She swallowed hard, fighting to keep her wits about her
and stay calm. Staying alive meant getting a grip on her emotions. Lose control and she would most likely lose her life.

Willie stroked deeper. A smile curved the corner of his
mouth. "Goddamn, my cock's rock hard jes' feelin' her cunt."
He grinned up at his brother and winked. "Hold this li'l wildcat still."

Skeeter's grip tightened on her wrists, his steely fingers digging in painfully. "Don't use it all up," he chuckled.

"Plenty here," Willie breathed. "Enough for both o' us."

She started to pray. *Please, God, this isn't happening . . .*

But it wasn't stopping. Not until the men were done with
her.

Lungs burning with the need to drag in air, Kathryn opened
her mouth. A horrifying wail ensued, turning the blood in her
veins to icy water. Yet the oh-so-terrible scream tearing against
her ears hadn't come from her throat.

Something else screeched a high wild howl of vengeance.

Some*thing* fierce and terrible.

Both men immediately let her go. "Shit! Cougar!" they bellowed simultaneously. "Get the guns."

Eyes immediately snapping open, Kathryn lifted her body
off the ground, pawing stupidly at the remnants of her clothing. Between flashes of lightning and fire, she saw at least half a
dozen big cats circling around them with dizzying speed.

Taken aback by the sight, air filtered out of her lungs. "My
God." To her utter shock she felt strangely calmed by their unexpected arrival. Even the drenching rain couldn't stay the
thrill of sexual awareness, sending a hot tremor all the way to
the tips of her toes. "They're beautiful."

The cougars were magnificent, sheer poetry in motion. In
addition, they were huge; all fur, sinew, and muscle. Cold brutality simmered in glowing amber eyes.

With a subtle display of intelligence, the big felines were canny enough to cut the men off from the campfire and their guns. If they wanted to fight, it'd be claw to hard steel, and no guarantee the humans would win.

Knives drawn, both men watched the cougars weaving around them, stalking closer to their prey.

Willie swiped his blade at the closest animal. "Ya ain't gettin' a taste o' me!" he bellowed.

Wrong.

Sharp claws tore across his hand.

Willie screeched in pain. "Oweee!" Blood dripped from the gaping wound.

Drawn by the scent, the big cats turned loose and waged an all-out attack.

Kathryn jumped, violently startled by the detonation of motion surrounding her. Right in front of her eyes, she saw one of the big cats leap on Willie, bellowing in displeasure as the frantic slash of a knife penetrated vulnerable fur. Shocked by the violence of the attack, her mind vaguely processed two more of the cougars pouncing on Skeeter. He screamed and ran, unwilling to try to fight.

But there were more cats, and not all were occupied with the hunters.

Kathryn vaguely registered one of the cougars breaking off from the fight. Its unblinking gaze settled on her. A wild cougar stared her in the eyes with the intent to kill. The hair on the back of its trunk-thick neck rippled.

She started to pray. "Oh, Lordamightygetmeoutofthisnow . . ."

Bounding into motion, the cougar sped at her with lethal precision. It leapt into the air, all four paws sailing off the ground in defiance of gravity.

Scrambling madly to her feet, Kathryn looked around frantically for a way to escape. All she could do was run.

She wasn't fast enough and couldn't get far enough. In that

instant everything around her took on a surreal quality, as if she now viewed events in slow motion through a distant lens.

Two huge paws made contact with her shoulders, the mass of the cougar's weight forcing her back to the ground.

Hardly able to think through the thudding echo of her heart, Kathryn automatically rolled over onto her back to find herself pinned under the gargantuan beast. Shards of pain radiated through her head and neck. The cougar's huge head simultaneously came down over her face. Hot, moist breath misted her face.

Her mind struggled to compute the fact the cougar was about to eat her for dinner. Tears of pure shock stung her eyes. *I'm toast.*

The cougar's head dipped lower. Broad pink nostrils flared, drawing in her human scent. Fangs beared, an intense hiss rippled over the cougar's tongue. Ears pinning down, perilously sharp fangs were bared.

That was all it took for her to lose control.

Kathryn frantically beat at the big cat, twisting and struggling to free herself from its domination.

Her struggle failed.

The beast would not be deterred from claiming its prize.

Stray bolts of lightning struck the ground nearby, instantly electrifying the atmosphere around them, creating a corona of crackling, spluttering sparks all around them. Shimmering distortions of crimson and orange glimmered, dizzying and swift, wrapping like grasping fingers around their downed bodies. Thunder snapped the air asunder in a tremendous bashing, and the ground beneath them quaked.

Disoriented by the blistering power the lightning had unleashed, Kathryn vaguely heard the creature bellow, felt the weight of its big furry body envelop hers. Terror consumed her as her body unwillingly arched into the muscular feline frame, joining and merging. For a moment the impression that she was becoming a being of sinew and fur bewildered her. In the same instant the cougar's face blurred, momentarily appearing to metamorphose into distinct and recognizable human features. Behind the mask of the cougar, a sentient soul lived and breathed.

The strange effect lasted only seconds, no more than the time it took her heart to beat a single time.

Moaning in delirious agony, Kathryn felt herself slipping into the grasp of unconsciousness, tumbling downward as if the earth beneath her had mysteriously crumbled. Mind short-circuiting from too many impressions force-fed into her brain at quantum speed, she willingly sacrificed herself to the overwhelming grip of absolute shock and terror.

Time and space ceased to exist and her world went entirely black.